THE PRICE OF JADE

a suspense novel

LIZ HASTINGS

Covenant Communications, Inc.

Cover images: *Rainforest and Mayan Temples* © Diegograndi, *Young Woman* © CoffeeAndMilk, *Mineral Jadeite* © Real444. Courtesy of istockphoto.com

Cover design by Diego Santos
Cover design copyright © 2018 by Covenant Communications, Inc.

Published by Covenant Communications, Inc.
American Fork, Utah

Copyright © 2018 by Liz Hastings
All rights reserved. No part of this book may be reproduced in any format or in any medium without the written permission of the publisher, Covenant Communications, Inc., P.O. Box 416, American Fork, UT 84003. The views expressed within this work are the sole responsibility of the author and do not necessarily reflect the position of Covenant Communications, Inc., or any other entity.

This is a work of fiction. The characters, names, incidents, places, and dialogue are either products of the author's imagination, and are not to be construed as real, or are used fictitiously.

Printed in the United States of America
First Printing: July 2018

24 23 22 21 20 19 18   10 9 8 7 6 5 4 3 2 1

ISBN 978-1-52440-523-6

Dedicated to my children:
Jenny, Christy, Eric,
Amy, Daniel, Julie, and Andrew.
And to my mom, who always believed in me.

ACKNOWLEDGMENTS

I AM MOST GRATEFUL TO my family, who encouraged me, believed in me, and tolerated dinner conversations that began with questions like, "What would you do if you woke up and discovered that you were tied up in the bottom of a pit in the middle of the rainforest? How would you feel? What would you think? What physiological responses would you have?"

I owe a special thanks to Alan Hoffman for helping me brainstorm the original plot and to my son Danny, who not only provided the title but also spent some of his first post-mission days lying on the living room floor, patiently walking through every storyline with me, and who has continued to ask questions and encourage me through the subsequent years!

Thanks to all those who read earlier versions of the book and gave invaluable feedback. Thank you to the Spanish-speaking members of my family, who provided me with Spanish words, and to Iliana Gutierrez, who corrected and improved upon those words.

And last, thanks to Covenant Communications for taking a chance on me!

PROLOGUE

July 1982—Plan de Sánchez, Guatemala

SHE HEARD THE POUNDING, THE voices—loud, demanding. Sofía knew they would not go away. Not this time. She grabbed her sister's hand and pushed her beneath the bed. The smell of dirt filled her nostrils as she and her sister clung together, their faces pressed against the hard ground.

Outside, screams pierced the calm of that Sunday afternoon. Soldiers pummeling doors, barking commands. Feet running, running, running.

A spray of gunfire.

Sofía felt Gabriela shudder against her.

If only Raul were here—Raul, the man she planned to marry, the man she imagined as the father of her future children. He'd said he would come today, but it would be too late. What could he do anyway—one against so many?

She was too young to die.

A boot smashed against the door. Her arm tightened around Gabriela as the younger girl whimpered. Her mother screamed again and again; her father begged for mercy. A scuffle, shouting, footsteps. She buried her face in Gabriela's hair and whispered, "Be brave, little sister. I won't let them hurt you."

Her parents' protests were lost in the chaos as they were dragged from the house.

One soldier remained. He moved around the room. From under the bed, Sofía could see his tall black boots stop a few feet from the bed. Her heart hammered in her chest. The soldier backed away, turned toward the door, and then stopped again. Sofía placed her hand over Gabriela's mouth, willing her sister to be silent. The soldier hesitated. Then he crossed the room and yanked down the covers of their carefully made bed with the butt of his gun, knocking Gabriela's hand-stitched doll onto the hard-packed dirt floor. He bent to pick up the doll.

Sofía could see his profile. He was young, hardly older than she was. She held her breath and waited. Finally he turned his head, and their eyes met.

Sofía gasped; she recognized him. He was a friend of Raul's. Surely, when he realized—

"*¡Sálgase de ahi!*" he commanded.

Sofía crawled from beneath the bed, straightened, and faced him. The soldier stepped back. Surprise crossed his face, then horror. His expression hardened; he lifted his gun and motioned for the girls to go with him.

CHAPTER 1

Thirty years later—Day 1

CATHY MILLER HAD IMAGINED THIS day at least a hundred times over the past three months, but not once like this. As many times as she'd flown, she'd never become completely comfortable with it. She slipped her boarding pass into her purse, double-checked her seatbelt, and adjusted the overhead air flow.

It was spring break at the junior high where Cathy taught, and not a moment too soon. The entire school seemed to have cabin fever. Last Wednesday, two girls had glared at each other during her entire fourth-period English class.

"Let's be honest: when two eighth-grade girls are mad at each other, everybody else in class knows about it—whether they want to or not," she'd said to the other teachers seated at the table in the faculty room. "The tension in the room was so thick you could have cut it with a knife."

"Maddie and Kayla—I thought they were best friends."

"Oh, that was so last week," Cathy said. "These are eighth graders, remember? And I am so ready to be out of here. Two weeks away from the little felines and all their hormones is just what the doctor ordered."

The others had laughed. "I wish *we* were going on a second honeymoon," another teacher said. "My big plans for spring break include cleaning out the garage. How'd you get Matt to take off work?"

"I wouldn't exactly call it a second honeymoon. Let's not forget we're taking our daughter with us. As for Matt, would you believe this was his idea?" she'd said.

Cathy liked her job. She even liked eighth graders. Underneath all the turmoil, they were just a bunch of scared kids trying to act big. The junior high was the one place Cathy felt like she really excelled. At home it was different. No matter how hard she tried, it never seemed to be enough.

The cool air blowing on her face felt good.

The seat next to her—Matt's seat—was empty.

She glanced at the young woman seated to her right, staring out the window. *Just give her space; she'll come around.* At least, that's what Matt always said. "This is going to be the best thing for her. A couple weeks exploring the jungles of Guatemala. Give her time to clear her head, figure out what she wants." *You mean figure out what you want, don't you, Matt?*

Passengers moved around the cabin, slamming overhead baggage compartment doors. A flight attendant made her way down the aisle, pausing to check for fastened seatbelts and properly stowed carry-ons.

Cathy watched out the window as they taxied toward the runway, turned, and paused. The engines revved as the thrust built; the plane moved again, accelerating as it raced toward the end of the runway. Then it tilted and lifted off the ground.

"We're off," Cathy said. She reached over and touched her daughter's long red hair. Melissa flinched. "Everything is going to be okay, 'Lissa. We're going to have a great time."

"Sure, Mom. Whatever you say."

Cathy opened her mouth and then pressed her lips together again.

A child in the back of the plane started to cry.

When did everything get so hard?

The moment Cathy's mind formed the question, she knew the answer. She could pinpoint the day, the very hour, she had lost Melissa. Of course, she didn't realize it then, didn't see it coming, but looking back she knew, and it hurt to know there was absolutely nothing she could do about it—nothing then, nothing now. And that's something Matt just didn't get. He'd gotten too old to remember how intoxicating young love can be. And now, after shattering whatever relationship they had left with Melissa by forcing her to take this trip, he wasn't there to pick up the pieces and put them together again.

Cathy leaned her seat back and closed her eyes. She was tired—tired of walking on eggshells with Melissa, tired of cleaning up Matt's messes, tired of being disappointed.

Just yesterday, she'd been standing at the kitchen sink rinsing the dinner dishes. Matt had come over and kissed her on the back of the neck.

"Let me do those," he'd said.

"What's up?"

"What do you mean, 'What's up?' Do I need a reason to help my wife?"

But of course, he did, and it came out a few minutes later.

"I have some bad news." He'd turned off the water, dried his hands, and turned to face her. "I'm really sorry, but something's come up at work and I'm

not going to be able to leave with you tomorrow. I'll take care of things here and then meet up with you as quickly as I can, hopefully within a day or two."

"Something's come up? Doesn't your boss know how long we've been planning this trip?"

"Nick doesn't know anything about it. He's out of town, remember? This is my decision. It's something that needs to be taken care of, and there's nobody else to do it. If you have a problem with that, you can blame me."

She did blame him, of course, but that didn't change anything. Being frustrated wouldn't help at this point. It was what it was.

Cathy pulled a book from her bag. Since Melissa wasn't in the mood to talk, Cathy might as well read. She opened the book to the first page, but her mind wouldn't stop going in circles. Finally she put the book away, leaned her seat back, and closed her eyes.

Some time later, Cathy felt Melissa shift in the seat next to her. She opened her eyes and turned to face her daughter. "Comfortable?"

"Why don't you and Dad like Josh?"

Here goes. "What do you mean, Honey? We do like Josh."

"Oh, come on. The least you can do is be honest."

"I am being honest. I think Josh is a charming young man. I'm just not sure he's good for you."

"How isn't he good for me?"

"Look, Honey, I know you really like him, and I know he's fun to be with. I'm just not sure he helps you be your best self."

"So you don't like him because he doesn't have a missionary haircut?"

"That's not what I said."

"Well, that's what Dad thinks. He thinks if a guy's hair is a millimeter past his ears he's going to—"

"Melissa!"

"What? That's what you guys think. You don't know anything about Josh. But guess what? He loves me, and I love him, and you're just going to have to deal with it. You think I don't know what you're trying to do? Why you forced me to come on this stupid trip? You're trying to keep me away from Josh, and you think if I go on this stupid tour, I'm going to find my testimony and then everything will be okay." She paused before adding, "I'll see the error of my ways. Go ahead and tell me I'm wrong, Mother."

"You're not being fair." Cathy took a deep breath and tried again. "'Lissa, you're only seventeen. It's not that Josh is a bad kid. It's just that you're so young."

The captain's voice interrupted their conversation. "In a few minutes, we'll be leaving the United States of America. We're due to arrive in Guatemala

City in approximately two and a half hours. The temperature there is a balmy seventy-five degrees. The flight attendant will bring around your customs declaration in the next few minutes, which you'll need to have filled out and together with your passport when we exit the plane."

It was a welcome interruption. After filling out the paperwork, Melissa put in her earbuds and stared out the window for the remainder of the flight. *She wouldn't have listened to anything I had to say anyway,* Cathy thought.

When the plane landed in Guatemala City, Cathy and Melissa followed the other passengers through the long corridor into the airport. Half a dozen uniformed guards carrying assault rifles lined each side of the exit. Neon signs flashed in Spanish. The balcony was jammed with locals gaping at the tourists.

They followed the line through customs and across the airport to retrieve their luggage. Cathy scanned the crowd of people. "Keep your eyes open for our group."

"And how exactly am I supposed to do that?" Melissa said. "Is everyone going to be wearing matchy-matchy T-shirts? Oh no, did we miss the memo?"

"There they are." Cathy motioned to a group congregating around a man carrying a clipboard.

"Oh great, we're joining the Cane and Walker Club," Melissa said.

"Hey, be nice; I don't see a single cane or walker in the group. Oxygen tank, maybe—I think I see one now. There; see that guy? Oh wait. I guess it's just his suitcase."

Melissa's lips twisted into a reluctant smile. "Very funny."

"I thought so. Anyway, so what if we're the youngest people on the tour? We'll hang out together."

"That makes me feel a whole lot better, Mom—you and me, hanging around with a bunch of old people."

"That's right, and you can carry all the oxygen tanks when we go to Tikal."

"Yeah, too bad I don't know CPR."

"True, but everyone knows how to give mouth-to-mouth—"

"Don't even go there!"

Cathy laughed. "I'm glad you're with me."

"Just because you don't know any *español* and I do," Melissa said.

"I hate to burst your bubble, but I'm not sure how much help a year of high school Spanish is going to be."

A broad-shouldered man with a ruddy complexion stuck out his hand as they reached the group. "Are you young'uns joining us?"

"I think we are," Cathy said, clasping his hand. "I'm Cathy Miller, and this is my daughter, Melissa."

"Well, I'm Vernon Taylor, and this here's my wife, Blanche," he said, motioning to the woman beside him. She looked spunky and petite, with tanned skin and brown, spiky hair; only the wrinkles on her neck betrayed her age. "We're farmers from Wayne County, Utah."

The man with the clipboard approached them. "You must be the Millers," he said. "I see you've already met Vernon and Blanche."

"And you must be—"

"Scott Stevens. And since I'm going to be your tour guide, I get to officially welcome you to Guatemala, the land of the Book of Mormon."

"Then you're the one I need to thank for changing Matt's ticket on such short notice."

"Not a problem. It's great to meet you both finally." He raised his voice to address the group. "I think everyone's here now. I've counted thirty-two of us, and that's what I'm looking for. Two couples flew in earlier today, and they're already at the hotel, so my math brings our total to thirty-six. And we're still hoping Cathy's husband will be able to join us." He looked at Cathy. "Any word on that yet?" She shook her head. "Okay, we'll keep our fingers crossed. And now, if you'll follow me."

Once everyone was settled on the bus, Scott picked up a microphone.

"We're excited to have all of you on this Book of Mormon tour. I've been doing tours to Guatemala for seventeen years, and I love it here. The people are great, the weather's just about perfect, and it's got some of the most beautiful scenery you'll ever find. In fact, Lake Atitlán has been described as the most beautiful place on earth. But more importantly, and probably the reason most of you are here with us, is the historical and spiritual significance we find as we consider Guatemala as the proposed site for many of the events which took place in the Book of Mormon.

"We'll be talking a lot about the Book of Mormon over the next two weeks, but before we get into that, we need to get some business out of the way. First, I want to introduce you to some people who will be traveling with us.

"Julio, nod your head," he said to the man driving the bus. "I don't know about the rest of you, but I want him to keep both hands solidly planted on the wheel. Julio's our bus driver, and I want you to know he's never been in an accident with one of our buses." He squeezed Julio's shoulder before adding, "You might appreciate knowing that later on."

Scott then motioned to a man seated in the back of the bus across from Cathy and Melissa. "And that's Raul Silva. Raul, wave your arm. Raul's been with us for nearly—what? Ten years?"

The man nodded.

Scott laughed. "In fact, Raul liked our discussions about the Book of Mormon so much we finally convinced him to get baptized a couple of years ago. We bring him along to entertain us mostly, but just in case there is ever any kind of problem, he's the guy who'll keep us safe and tell us what to do."

"Keep us safe from what?" Melissa whispered. "Man-eating rabbits?"

Cathy glanced at the Maya man seated across the aisle and smiled. He didn't look much taller than she was, and she wasn't particularly tall. But there was a calm steadiness in his eyes. "I'm sure we'll all be just fine."

As the bus lumbered down narrow cobblestone streets, Scott answered questions about drinking the water and exchanging money.

"We're going to give you some time to settle in and relax. Then we'll meet in the hotel lobby at six o'clock for dinner. We don't want to keep you up late tonight, because we've got a big day planned tomorrow."

Scott looked around the bus and grinned. "So let me ask you something: If you were going to hike through a jungle inhabited by crocodiles and jaguars and monkeys to see one of the largest archaeological sites in the world, wouldn't that be worth getting up early for? If you were going to see a place that was occupied more than 2,000 years ago, with pyramids more than a hundred feet tall, wouldn't that be worth getting up *really* early for? Wouldn't that be worth getting up at, say, four o'clock in the morning for breakfast before you catch a flight at six? That would be worth it, wouldn't it, to see a place like that?"

Melissa leaned over to Cathy. "Please tell me he's not serious."

Scott chuckled and looked straight at Melissa. "I heard that, and you'd better believe I'm serious. Tomorrow we're going to see things that'll make your hair stand on end."

"My hair will be standing on end, all right," Melissa muttered as the bus slowed to a stop. "I can hardly wait."

They exited the bus, found their room, and freshened up before heading down to the dining room. As soon as they finished eating, Cathy excused herself. "I'm going to find a quiet place and try to call your dad," she said. "I'll see you in a few minutes."

Matt picked up on the first ring. "I've been waiting to hear from you. Everything go okay with the flight?"

"Everything's fine. Except that the seat next to mine was empty."

"I know, Hon. It's not the way we planned it."

"No, it's not," Cathy said. "So how was the meeting today?"

"The usual. We're making some progress, but it's going to take time. Hopefully we'll have finished negotiations within a couple of days, and I'll be on my way to join you."

"That would be wonderful," Cathy said. "We're going to Tikal tomorrow. I'm sorry you're going to miss it."

"Me too. I was looking forward to showing it to you. So how's Melissa doing?"

"Well, she's been texting Josh nonstop." Cathy sighed. "I think she'll be okay. I hope she will. It's not a snap-your-fingers kind of thing."

"I know. Maybe it's good I'm not there right now. It'll give you some mother-daughter time to work your magic. You're a lot better with her than I am."

"That's because I listen to her, Matt."

"That's what I pay you for."

"But you don't pay me, remember?" Cathy glanced at her watch. "I should go now. Melissa's probably wondering what I'm doing."

"Okay. Tell her I love her. And have fun in Tikal, okay?" His voice grew soft. "You know I miss you, don't you?"

"I miss you too, Matt."

"We'll talk tomorrow. And uh—keep Melissa on the marked paths at Tikal, okay? I don't want a crocodile to have her for lunch."

"I'll tell her you said that." Cathy turned to see Melissa walking up. "Better yet, you can tell her yourself."

She held the phone out to Melissa, but Melissa stepped back and shook her head. Cathy spoke into the phone again. "Maybe next time."

"Doesn't want to talk to me, huh? Well, tell her I love her anyway."

"I'll do that."

They said goodbye, and then Cathy turned to face Melissa. "So, how's Josh?"

"Okay, but—I just got the creepiest feeling, like I was being watched or something."

"You probably were being watched! Have you looked in a mirror lately?"

"Maybe . . . but it really spooked me. This guy—I could swear I saw him at the airport. Remember those people up in the balcony? I think I saw him up there."

"I'm sure there's nothing to worry about. Besides, if anything should happen, we've got our bodyguard on the bus to take care of us."

"Yeah, right. He'll need me to take care of him."

"Before I forget, Dad wanted me to tell you to stay on the paths tomorrow. He doesn't want a crocodile to eat you. And he said to tell you he loves you."

"He has a funny way of showing it."

"Melissa—"

"What?"

"Nothing. Let's just go back to our room. It sounds like we're going to want all the sleep we can get."

"Now that's what I call service," Cathy said when she opened the door to their room and saw their luggage sitting on the floor just inside. She glanced down the hall before stepping into the room. A man stood nearly hidden behind a plant at the end of the hall. He turned toward her; their eyes met briefly. He smiled and moved back into the shadows. A shiver ran down Cathy's spine; she backed into the room and closed the door.

* * *

The phone rang twice before it was answered.

"I trust everything went as planned?" the man said. He swiveled his chair to face the window, his freshly trimmed blond hair touching the collar of his starched white shirt. On his right hand, a gold ring with a large flawless ruby sparkled in the light.

"There's been a complication. He was not on the plane."

"You must be mistaken. We verified the passenger list."

"It listed an M. Miller. An assumption was made. His seat was empty. M. Miller is the daughter."

The blond man cursed.

Eduardo Guerrero spoke again. "There's another plan which may work even better." He paused. "She *is* Daddy's little girl."

The man stood and walked to the window. He was tall, well over six feet, and well-built. He pulled back the curtains and studied the rooftops below. "She's not to be hurt."

"Of course not. She's just very attractive bait."

He nodded slowly. "That could work."

CHAPTER 2

Day 2

THE ALARM RANG TOO EARLY, waking Cathy from a deep sleep. She leaned over to shut off the incessant beeping and turned on the lamp. Melissa was still asleep in the bed next to her, her long, thick hair spread across the pillow, her porcelain face relaxed. A wave of nostalgia hit Cathy as she watched Melissa. She'd desperately wanted to have at least one more child, but when it hadn't happened, Cathy had thrown everything she had into her daughter.

Cathy reached over and touched Melissa's arm. "It's time, Sweetie."

Melissa groaned and pulled the blanket over her head.

"I know; I feel the same way. But Dad tells me it's really worth getting up for."

"It better be."

Melissa waited until Cathy was nearly ready before she rolled out of bed and pulled on some clothes. *Oh, to look that good with so little effort,* Cathy thought as they made their way down to the dining room.

"It's too early to eat," Melissa said as she picked up a yogurt and some frosted flakes at the hotel's breakfast buffet.

Vernon snorted from behind her. "You're in Guatemala, and you're eating cereal? You should eat some of this hot sauce; put some hair on your chest."

"Now, Vernon, she doesn't want any hair on her chest," Blanche said, poking his arm and smiling at Melissa. "Don't let him bother you; he's just an old coot."

Cathy and Melissa joined a group from the tour at a large round table. A tall, thin man with smiling eyes and a shock of white hair stood and held out his hand to introduce himself. "I'm Lyle Goodman, and this is my wife, Lila," he said, motioning to the woman seated next to him.

Lila smiled and tucked a strand of hair behind her ear as Cathy slid into the chair next to her. "You must be the lady who's waiting for her husband to join her."

"That's right."

"I do hope everything's okay with your husband."

"Oh, you know; it's work. Something came up at the last minute and, as luck would have it, his boss was out of town, so Matt felt he had to stay behind and handle it."

Lyle shook his head. "I had a boss like that once. Every time things got busy at work, it seemed like he was out vacationing and I was stuck in the office fixing the problem. 'Jump,' he'd say, and I'd jump. Drove Lila crazy. She always said I should stand up to him—tell him I had a life too." He glanced at Lila and winked. "And, looking back now, after seventy-two years of life, I think she was probably right. Life's too short to be stuck in an office when your family needs you. But, of course, I was always afraid I'd lose my job if I told him that, and even though Lila got mad at me sometimes, at least I didn't think she'd fire me."

Lila raised her eyebrows. "Sounds like you were taking me for granted."

"Don't pay any attention to her," Lyle said. "She loves me, even if she doesn't sound like it."

Melissa broke in from the other side of Cathy. "The thing is, my dad doesn't feel like you did."

Cathy turned to face her daughter. "What are you talking about, Melissa?"

"He chose not to be here with us. His boss didn't have anything to do with it."

"Why do you say that?"

"Because it's true. I have ears, you know. I heard you and Dad fighting about it."

"We weren't fighting."

"Oh, I forgot—you were discussing."

Cathy flushed. She stared at her plate and took a deep breath before she raised her eyes and looked around at the others seated at their table. "I'm terribly sorry."

Lila reached out and patted her hand. "Don't be. We all understand."

A man seated across the table cleared his throat. "What line of business did you say your husband is in?"

"Jade," Cathy said. "He imports jade."

"Jade? Now that's something different."

Cathy nodded. "He imports jade from Guatemala, actually."

"Have you been here before then?" Lila asked.

Cathy shook her head. "Matt comes down on buying trips a couple of times a year and has talked about bringing me along, but—well, you know how it is." She sipped her cantaloupe juice and grimaced. "This is awful," she said. "Matt said I should try it." She set her glass down and leaned back in her chair. "Anyway, when he saw the Book of Mormon tour ad, we decided it was time. So here we are."

Melissa snickered. "Oh, is that how that happened? Good to know."

Ignoring Melissa, Lyle smiled at Cathy. "So you're here and your husband isn't. Isn't that just the way life is? I'll bet he's been hankering to show you this place for years. Probably driving him crazy that he's not here with you right now."

"Matt served his mission in Guatemala, so I've been hearing about what a wonderful place this is since before we got married. But this isn't exactly how we planned it."

"Well, hopefully that'll change soon," Lila said.

Just then Scott walked over to the group and tapped his watch. "The bus pulls out in half an hour. If you're going to Tikal, you need to be on it."

The group finished their breakfast and headed for the bus. Cathy gazed out the window as the bus moved down the narrow cobblestone streets of Guatemala City toward the airport. The city was alive with color—blue, orange, purple, and green houses lined the streets, their lower-level windows striped with bars. Spiral barbed-wire fences and walls topped with shards of broken glass separated the sidewalk from the buildings. Modern, ornate architecture had been erected next to broken-down, crumbling structures. Political graffiti covered the buildings. On too many corners stood a uniformed police officer carrying a shotgun. It was all as Matt had described but even more vivid than she had imagined.

The bus stopped in front of the airport, and Scott led the group through two sets of double doors to a waiting area. An hour later they boarded the plane and found their seats. Cathy braced herself as she felt the plane begin to move and heard the shrill whine that signaled takeoff. The plane bumped as it sped down the runway, and then they were in the air again. After a few minutes, the plane settled into a smooth flight.

Melissa was already asleep. *Good.*

It hadn't always been like this. Melissa used to bounce into the house, eager to share every thought that came into her head. The day Josh moved into town, Melissa came home and hopped onto the kitchen counter like she did every day.

"There was a new boy in school today," she'd said.

"Oh yeah? Is he cute?"

"Mmmm. You could say that."

"What's his name?"

"I don't know, but I'm going to find out."

It didn't take long. Melissa was the kind of girl boys noticed, and Josh was no exception.

It was easy to see why Melissa was so enamored. Josh had that ability to make a girl feel like she was the only girl in the world. And he was bright and funny.

You liked him too, you know. Defended him to Matt.

Matt had disliked him from the beginning. *Gut instinct,* he'd said. That night when Melissa had come home an hour late just pounded a nail into Josh's coffin.

Melissa had breezed into their bedroom. "Sorry I'm late, but it wasn't our fault."

"I'll be the judge of that. You want to tell your mom and me what happened?"

"It was hilarious, Dad. Even you would've laughed. Even *you.*" Her eyes had widened then, and she'd punched Matt's arm and giggled. "So this cop pulls us over, and when he comes up to the window, Josh says, 'I'd like a burger and an order of fries, and can I get a chocolate shake to go with that?'"

"Really? And what did the police officer think about that?"

"You should've seen the look on his face. Don't you think that's hilarious?" When Matt didn't laugh, she'd said, "Oh, come on, Dad, lighten up; have a good time."

"What did the officer do?"

"He gave him a ticket. But it was totally worth it."

"Money must grow on trees at his house. So why did you say he got pulled over?"

"Oh, who knows? The cops have it out for Josh."

"Police officers don't give people tickets because they 'have it out for them.' What did he get a ticket for?"

"I don't know—"

"What do you mean, you don't know? How could you not know? Weren't you in the car?"

"I wasn't really listening, okay? I was laughing. Anyway, it doesn't matter, because Josh didn't do anything wrong. The cop just made something up."

Later that night, when they were alone in the dark, Cathy had approached the subject. "You have to admit Josh has a sense of humor."

"The kid's got no respect for authority. And our daughter's hanging out with him."

The captain's voice on the intercom brought Cathy back to the present. She leaned over to wake Melissa. In spite of everything, she couldn't help feeling excited; after all these years, she was finally going to see Tikal!

* * *

César led two men with a mule through several miles of jungle growth to a small clearing east of Tikal National Park. The others waited while he surveyed the area. He lowered a ladder into a deep cenote and climbed down into the dark hole. A perfect place. Returning to the surface, he directed the others to unload the supplies from the mule and set up camp.

"When do I get my money?" asked the youngest man in the group.

"When the job's done, that's when." César spoke sharply. "That's the way it always works."

"I just need—"

"You'll get your money, but first you get the girl."

The third man spoke for the first time. "What's the matter, Carlitos? You scared? Maybe I should get the girl." He laughed raucously and licked his lips.

"*¡Cállense!*" César scowled at the two younger men.

They finished setting up camp and retraced their steps back through the jungle.

* * *

"Remember, we're headed into the jungle," Scott said as he gathered everyone around him in the Flores airport. "Not only is it hot but it's also humid, and we don't want to carry anybody out with heatstroke. So if you forgot to bring water, buy some. The bus will be here in about an hour."

Cathy and Melissa wandered around the airport shop, looking at miniature stone temple replicas and necklace souvenirs. Melissa bargained for a pair of colorful quetzal bird earrings and slipped them into her ears as the bus arrived.

Once everyone was settled on the bus, Scott picked up the microphone.

"Some of you may be wondering if we've identified Tikal as a site in the Book of Mormon, and the answer is we're not sure. Many scholars consider this area to be the east wilderness, where the Nephites, under the direction of Moroni, built and fortified many cities. But anything the Nephites built then would have been underneath the structures you're going to see today and were probably a lot less elaborate. Still, Tikal is Tikal, and a trip to Guatemala wouldn't be complete if

you didn't see it. Now, as is our custom, anytime we have some time on the bus, we like to work on getting to know each other. So I'm going to invite these folks next to me to take the microphone and tell us a little about themselves."

A man wearing a navy polo shirt stood, steadying himself against the seat in front of him, and grasped the microphone. "My name's Gary Clark, and this lovely lady sitting next to me is Ella, my blushing bride of more than forty years. We have eight children, all of them married, and a whole bunch of grandkids— you'll have to get the up-to-the-minute count from my wife since it seems to change from day to day." Gary chuckled. "Well, anyway, I retired from teaching at BYU last year, and we moved back to Southern Utah, where Ella and I grew up. Now we can stomp around in the red rocks and see the stars at night, and as far as I'm concerned, that's just about as good as life gets. Sure beats sitting in a rocking chair all day."

Cathy felt her eyes droop as Gary's voice droned on. She blinked several times and stifled a yawn.

Finally, the bus pulled into a parking lot and stopped.

The fragrant combination of dirt, water, and vegetation greeted Cathy as she stepped off the air-conditioned bus into a muggy furnace. Everything smelled green.

Scott led them down the narrowing road from the parking lot past the visitor's center, a museum, and several hotels. A vibrantly colored ocellated turkey strutted past, his bronze and green feathers iridescent in the sunlight. The tour group followed the road around a swampy pond. Scott pointed out a toucan along the water's edge and then a dark line in the water. A crocodile was swimming just below the surface.

Past the pond, they came to an open-air snack bar. Two teenage boys in khaki shirts balanced on the roof of the white concrete-and-stucco building, systematically removing the old thatching from the wooden framework, replacing it with new bundles of palm leaves. An older man stood below, directing the boys in their work.

Scott motioned toward the project. "Done right, those roofs can last twenty or thirty years."

As they moved into the rainforest leading to Tikal, the road narrowed to a path lined with palm trees; branches stretched across the top to form a dense canopy. Everything was lush green, the heat stifling, the air thick with moisture. The jungle resonated with the drone of insects and the chorus of frogs. The tangle of trees, vines, saplings, and bushes made leaving the path a near impossibility.

"Someone could be standing just a few feet away from us and we wouldn't even be able to see them," Melissa said.

Scott nodded. "Remember all those places in the Book of Mormon where it talks about people getting lost or escaping? I always wondered how they could disappear so fast. But when I see places like this, it makes a lot more sense. If you left this path right now, how long do you think it would take before you were out of sight?"

"And eaten by a crocodile," Melissa said. "Not long."

Scott laughed. "You stick with me; I'll make sure the crocs don't get you."

A few moments later, the group came to a massive tree. It loomed over the landscape; its trunk was as wide as four men standing shoulder to shoulder, the roots extending outward in all directions. Cathy tilted her head back to see the top of the tree. Its gnarled branches were covered with reddish-brown moss, tipped with green foliage and yellowish cotton-filled pods.

"The branches look like enormous fuzzy caterpillars," Melissa said.

A nearby park ranger chuckled. "Caterpillars, you say? These trees were sacred to the Maya," he said in amazingly clear English as he waited for the group to circle around him. "Welcome to Tikal National Park! My name is Roberto, and I will be your guide as we enter this magnificent place." He pointed toward the massive tree. "To your right, you see a mighty ceiba tree. The ceiba is our national tree. To the Maya, it was a sacred tree. Even today, Maya often leave the ceiba tree standing when they are harvesting forest timber. The Maya believed it provided a link to heaven. You see, the ceiba stands at the earth's center, and the vines"—he pointed at the thick draping vines—"provide a foothold so that souls can rise into the spirit world. The Maya call it the *tree of life*." He glanced around the group. "You are Mormons, no? I think this *tree of life* may mean something sacred to you too." Several members of the group nodded, and they continued down the path.

The trail widened, allowing more sunlight to penetrate the rainforest. They walked on as the path curved, and then, through the trees, they caught their first breathtaking glimpse of the ancient city of Tikal. A towering pyramid stood before them like a sentinel guarding forgotten mysteries. Nothing Cathy had seen in the travel brochures or Matt's pictures had prepared her for that moment.

"There are between three and four thousand structures in Tikal," Roberto explained. "The Maya began building Tikal around 600 BC, and it remained an important city for the next 1500 years. It is estimated that nearly 100,000 people lived here at one time during the classical period, around 250 AD. Then, more than a thousand years ago, Tikal was abandoned. In time, it was completely overgrown and hidden by the relentless jungle. Tikal remained a mystery for centuries."

Roberto looked around the group. "A legend about a lost city was passed down among the native people, but it wasn't until 1848 that Tikal was discovered by a gum collector by the name of Ambrosio Tut who first saw the temple's roof combs in the distance. He ran to tell the governor of the Petén, Modesto Méndez. Can you imagine how the two of them must have felt when they saw these majestic temples for the first time? Ever since that day, people have been coming here to discover Tikal for themselves. And today, I invite each of you to make your own discovery."

Roberto knelt on the ground, picked up a stick, and drew a map in the dirt, showing the location of the courtyard and each of the six temples. "You can see Temple I from here." He motioned behind him. "It is more than 150 feet tall and is called the *Temple of the Great Jaguar*. It was erected in about 700 AD by order of Ah Cacao, whose tomb was discovered inside." He then described the remaining temples, mentioning the unique characteristics of each. Finally, he pointed out the stone stelae standing before each temple and explained how the Maya built over existing structures so that the oldest architecture was buried under layers of newer construction.

"And now, go and discover Tikal," Roberto said.

Cathy and Melissa followed the others as they moved toward the Great Plaza. Stepping into the maze of buildings, they peeked through the windows and climbed around inside the tall gray ruins. Cathy looked at the fire-blackened walls and thought of another time when those stone walls were filled with the sounds and smells of women cooking dinner and children laughing.

"Can you imagine what it must have been like?" Cathy said as she and Melissa crossed the grassy plaza to an area between two temples where there were dozens of stelae and altars. They wandered along the twin rows, studying the elaborate glyphs on each stone stela. Finally they headed west toward Temple IV, the tallest of Tikal's structures.

Cathy eyed the moss-covered steps extending to the top. A steep wooden ladder was built in the middle of a massive root system against the side of the structure. "Dad says this is the one to climb," she said.

A line of tourists were slowly making their way to the top of the pyramid. Straight ahead they saw Vernon and Blanche headed up the steps of Temple IV.

"I'm not going to be beat by them," Melissa said.

"Then, what are we waiting for? Somebody's got to save them when they have heart attacks, right?"

Just as they reached the bottom of the ladder, Vernon looked down from his halfway vantage point and waved. "Just don't look down, and you'll be fine."

"He says as he looks down," Melissa said.

Cathy smiled. "Okay, see you at the top." She grasped the handrail and tested the first step. "So far so good."

"Great, Mom." Melissa reached for the railing and began the two-hundred-foot climb to the top. "With my luck, I'll trip and fall."

A male voice chuckled behind her. "I won't let you fall," he said.

CHAPTER 3

MELISSA GLANCED DOWN AND SAW brown muscular arms right behind her own. Her stomach flip-flopped, but she climbed steadily without responding.

"You okay?" the voice asked as she reached the top. Melissa looked over her shoulder and saw a young man about her own age with deeply tanned skin, black curly hair, and brown eyes. He smiled broadly, his teeth white against his dark skin.

"My *inglés* is not so good," he said. "Are you visiting from *Los Estados Unidos*?"

"Uh, yes—I mean, *sí*," Melissa said.

"I am Carlos, and—how do you say—I am happy to meet you? What do you call yourself?"

"I'm Melissa, and this is my mom, Cathy Miller," Melissa said, motioning toward her mother.

Carlos smiled. "It is good to meet you both. This is your first time to visit Tikal, no?"

"Yes, it is," Cathy said. "My husband has been here several times, but it's the first time for Melissa and me."

"Your husband—he is here?"

"No. He's not with us."

Carlos turned to Melissa and grinned. "Come with me. I will show the best view of Tikal."

Melissa looked back at her mother, her eyes pleading. Cathy raised her eyebrows and shrugged.

They followed Carlos around on the top of the pyramid and took several pictures. Finally they found a shady spot to sit and gaze out over the maze of Maya structures. From where they sat, they could see the tops of three temples rising from the dense rainforest; beyond that, there was nothing but green trees and blue cloudless sky stretching as far as they could see.

"Hey, this is like that scene out of *Star Wars*," Melissa said.

"*Star Wars?*" Carlos grinned again. "Yes, I think I have seen this film. Luke Skywalker."

Melissa laughed. "That's right!"

"Do you come to Tikal a lot?" Cathy asked.

"No, not so much. But I come when I can—to think, you know. It is a good place for thinking."

"I can see that," Cathy said. "I think I could sit here for a very long time and ponder the mysteries of the universe."

"Wow, Mom, way to go deep," Melissa said.

Cathy laughed. "I guess I have a lot on my mind." Then she turned to Carlos and added, "I'm glad you decided to come to Tikal today."

"I am too," he said, looking at Melissa. "Because today I meet the *chica linda*."

A smile played at the corners of Melissa's mouth. "So you're one of those *latinos guapos* my dad warned me about."

Carlos raised his hands in defense. "What are you saying to me?"

"*Yo hablo un poquito español*, and you know exactly what I'm saying to you."

He laughed and shook his head. "You have caught me, I am afraid."

Melissa glanced at her mom. Her head was ducked as she scrolled through pictures on her phone and pretended she wasn't listening to their conversation, but Melissa could tell she was smiling. At least she wasn't saying anything.

Melissa returned her attention to Carlos. "So, Carlos, what things do you think about when you come to Tikal?" she asked.

Another flash of perfect teeth.

"Well, I think about many things, and now I will think about you."

"Flattery will get you nowhere." Melissa dropped her voice to make it harder for her mom to hear. "I wonder what secrets you have—do you have a secret girlfriend you meet here? Or maybe you're married."

Carlos laughed hard. "No, no, I am not married! I have no secrets. I will tell you anything you want to know."

"Then tell me about your family."

"I have a brother and two sisters. And my mother."

"What about your father?"

"My father is gone. He died when I was a small boy."

Melissa felt her mother stiffen beside her. She was listening. Of course she was. And Melissa knew if she turned even slightly she'd see that look of

sympathy on her mother's face she'd seen every time she came home from school feeling sorry for herself. She liked it then, but right now it annoyed her. She pulled herself back to Carlos.

"I'm sorry," she said. "That must have been hard for you."

"Yes, very hard." Carlos looked off into the distance. Neither spoke for a while. Melissa glanced at her mom and saw that she was still looking at her phone.

"So how did you learn to speak English?"

"Everyone who goes to school in Guatemala learns inglés. It is—what do you say?"

"Required?"

"Sí. It is required."

"That's cool. I took a year of Spanish in school, but it's not required."

Her mom looked up from her phone. "Can you believe it? I've got a signal! I'm going to call your dad and tell him where we are."

"What about you?" Carlos asked. "Do you have brothers or sisters?"

"No, I'm the only one."

Melissa could hear her mother talking. "Hey!" she said. "You'll never guess where I am." A pause and then, "It's amazing! Absolutely amazing! I just wish you were here with us."

Turning back to Carlos, Melissa continued. "I always wanted a sister, but my parents couldn't have any more kids. At least I don't have to worry about someone getting into all my stuff."

Melissa saw an expression she didn't recognize cross Carlos's face. Then he smiled again.

"Maybe it is time for us to go," he said. "There are more temples to climb."

"More climbing? Are you kidding? I'm still out of breath from this one!"

"Ah, but there is much more. You have traveled far and must see what you came to see."

"Okay, you talked me into it." Melissa turned toward her mom. "Are you ready to go, Mom?"

Cathy shook her head and raised a finger. "I'll be finished in just a minute," she mouthed.

Melissa rolled her eyes at Carlos.

"I miss you too, Matt," Melissa heard her mother say. "How much longer do you think you're going to be?"

Melissa stood. "I don't want to just sit here while you talk to Dad, so we're going to go. You can catch up with us after you're finished. And if you don't

find us, I'll meet you back at the plaza at five o'clock when we're supposed to meet the rest of our group."

Cathy shook her head at Melissa. "No, I want you to wait for me. It'll just be a couple of minutes."

"It's okay, we can be patient," Carlos said. He patted the step beside him and Melissa sat back down.

"Sorry, Matt," Cathy said, "I needed to say something to Melissa."

Melissa looked at Carlos and made a face.

"Mothers are all the same," he said. "They worry too much."

"She treats me like I'm five years old instead of almost eighteen," Melissa said.

Cathy had moved a few steps away and turned her back to them. She was speaking in a low voice. Melissa strained to hear what she was saying. "She's doing okay," she heard. "Not making things easy for me, but she's definitely enjoying Tikal."

Melissa flushed and wondered if Carlos had heard what her mother said. She stood and motioned for Carlos to follow. "Let's go."

Melissa felt almost giddy as she walked along the path with Carlos. This was an unexpected bonus. Not that she really minded hanging out with her mother, but being with an attractive boy definitely had its perks.

"So how old are you, Carlos?"

"Old enough." He flashed another smile at her, his eyes flirting. He reached over and took her hand. "May I?"

Her hand burned at his touch, and she felt her face flush.

"I want to show you the Tikal nobody else sees." He paused and looked around at the masses of people. "It is the place where I go when I want to be by myself. I call it my secret place." He grinned at her again. "You think I am silly, no?"

"No, not at all. I have a place near my home where I like to go to be alone. It isn't nearly this beautiful, though."

Carlos squeezed her hand. "If we are very quiet, we might see a monkey in the trees."

He led her along the narrowing path, pushing branches out of the way as they walked. She grasped his hand, oblivious to anything else but the pounding in her chest and the butterflies in her stomach. Not until they were deep in the jungle did she realize there was no one else around.

He stopped and turned her toward him. "You are so beautiful," he said softly, reaching out to touch her hair.

Melissa felt a sharp blow from behind, and then everything was black.

CHAPTER 4

ELLA CLARK PULLED A HANDKERCHIEF from her purse and wiped the back of her neck. Good thing she'd pulled her hair up into a clip today. Her husband, Gary, looked as drenched as she felt.

"Hot enough for you?" Gary asked.

Ella laughed. "Aren't you glad we came?"

"Yes, I am glad. I like having you all to myself for a couple of weeks."

"What are you saying?"

"You know what I'm saying. If you're not babysitting the grandkids, you're organizing a funeral or taking dinner to a neighbor or grocery shopping for your mother."

"I don't organize funerals, Dear. The bishop does that."

Gary covered her lips with his palm. "Now don't you start arguing with me, because you and I both know it's true. And I wouldn't have it any other way." Then he smiled that smile that still made her melt, even after forty-two years. "All I'm saying is it's nice to have you to myself for a while."

A voice boomed behind them. "Are you two having a good time?"

Ella turned as Scott walked up to them. "This is a marvelous place," she said.

"It is, isn't it? I never get tired of coming here." Scott motioned to a nearby pyramid. That's Temple III. Come with me, and I'll show you something." As they walked toward the pyramid, Scott said, "Temple III's claim to fame is that its lintel is still in Tikal. The only one in Tikal."

"Lintel?"

"Threshold. The Maya used a hard wood, sapodilla, to carve beautiful thresholds on their temple doors. Unfortunately, I believe all the other lintels were removed in the 1800s and taken to museums in Europe. They're considered to be quite the treasure, as you can imagine, since they were carved more than a thousand years ago."

He walked over to a stela and pointed out the altar in front of it. "This is interesting. If you look closely, you'll notice a long-nosed god. Beside him, there's a mat, like those that would have covered a king's throne. They think it's depicting some kind of ancient ceremony, and apparently the mat was a symbol of power among the Maya."

Scott raised his eyes to the top of the pyramid and made a sweeping gesture. "It's called the Temple of the Jaguar Priest."

"They had a thing for jaguars, didn't they?" Ella said.

"There were a lot of superstitions surrounding jaguars among the Maya, and I suppose having little children disappear when they wandered too far from home probably fueled that."

"So, are there still jaguars around here?"

"Oh yes. Not that you'll see any. They keep pretty hidden, but they're out there. You're a lot more likely to see an ocelot or a puma than a jaguar. But either way, it's a good idea to stay on the beaten path."

Ella noticed a woman with red hair hurrying in their direction, her eyes scanning the park. "I recognize that woman. Isn't she on the tour?"

Scott looked to where Ella was pointing. "Yes, that's Cathy Miller."

Scott jogged toward where Cathy had paused on the side of the path to catch her breath; the others followed.

"Where's Melissa?" Scott said.

"That's a good question," Cathy said. "She took off with a boy."

"She took off?"

Cathy sighed. "We met this boy when we were on Temple IV. He showed us around a little, and then Melissa and he decided they wanted to hike to the top of another temple. I was talking on the phone to Matt and told them to wait for me, but I turned my back for two minutes and they were gone."

"I can see why you're upset."

"Well, let's just say that Melissa isn't exactly going out of her way to make this trip pleasant for me."

"How long has she been gone?"

Cathy glanced at her watch. "It's been at least an hour. She said she'd meet us at five in the Great Plaza. I guess I'm being paranoid."

"I haven't formally met you yet," Ella said. "I'm Ella Clark. And for the record, I'd be paranoid too. It comes with being a mother. But I'm sure she's fine."

"We'll help you look for her," Gary said.

"No, I don't want to ruin everyone else's day. I'm sure she's okay. He seemed like a nice boy, and let's face it, Mom's just not as much fun as a cute boy when

you're seventeen." She wiped her brow with the back of her hand. "I've been searching for them, but this place is huge. I think I'm going to have to wait until she shows up."

"Oh look, there are Lyle and Lila," Gary said as the Goodmans approached them.

"Fancy meeting you guys here," Lyle said to the Clarks before turning to Cathy. "And I remember you, but where's that daughter of yours?"

"I'm afraid Melissa found somebody better-looking than me and left me in the dust."

Scott reached over and squeezed Cathy's arm. "I'd better get going, but I'll keep my eyes open for Melissa. The plaza is straight ahead when you're ready. I need to get there a little early to set up for our group photo."

"You didn't say anything about a group photo," Lila said.

"That's because I wanted you to come back on time," Scott called over his shoulder.

Ella linked arms with Cathy. "Why don't we head back to the plaza now. I'm guessing you're not in the mood for more sightseeing, and by the time we get there, it'll be almost five anyway."

"Don't you want to stay with your husband?"

"Oh, he'll be fine without me for a few minutes. The Goodmans will keep him company." She winked at Gary, and he nodded.

They walked along the path until they came to the plaza and found a quiet spot to sit on the amphitheater steps.

"I keep thinking about the people who lived here—what it must have been like," Ella said.

"I know what you mean." Cathy leaned back against the steps and tilted her face toward the sky. "Do you have a daughter?"

"Four of them. They're all married now, but we had our moments when they were growing up. How about you—do you have other children?"

"No," Cathy said. "I wanted more, but it didn't happen. I'm grateful we were able to have Melissa." Her voice caught.

Ella put her arm around Cathy's shoulders. "Hey, she's fine, and she's going to get here any minute so you can ground her for the rest of her life."

It was five to five, and the others were starting to arrive. Gary waved from across the plaza, and Vernon and Blanche approached from the opposite direction.

"You haven't seen Cathy's daughter, Melissa, have you?" Ella asked Blanche. "She made a friend, and they left to do some exploring. She told her mom she'd meet us here."

"Wait a minute," Vernon said. "I think I did see her. Was she with a local boy?"

"Yes. When did you see her?"

"It's been a couple of hours, I'd say. Don't you remember, Blanche? "

Blanche shrugged.

"I was wondering why she wasn't with her mother and who that boy was. I think I said something to you, or maybe I just thought it. Pretty sure it was her, though."

"Do you remember where you were when you saw her?" Cathy said.

Vernon shook his head. "I'll have to think about that; I'll let you know if I remember."

"I'd appreciate that," Cathy said. "Now she's officially late."

Word spread that Melissa was missing, but no one else remembered seeing her after she left Cathy. Scott invited everyone to join him for the group photo.

"We do need to move along, so we'll just have to photoshop Melissa in," he said. "Our plane leaves at eight-thirty, and we've got to hike out of here and catch the bus into Flores before that. It's a little tight, but I wanted you to have all the time you could in Tikal."

After the picture was taken, Scott pulled Gary aside and spoke to him. Then he returned to where Cathy and Ella sat on the amphitheater steps. "Here's what I'm thinking. Some of these people are going to need to take their time hiking out, so I'm going to go ahead and send them on. I'll wait here with you until Melissa comes, and then we'll book it. Does that sound okay to you?"

Cathy nodded.

"I'm going to ask the park rangers to watch for her," Scott said, "and if they see her, to tell her to check the time and make haste—after they contact us, of course."

Scott gathered everyone around him. "I'm going to wait here with Cathy until we find Melissa. I've given instructions to Gary—Gary, come on up here so everyone knows who you are—and he's going to take my place until we meet up with you. If for any reason we don't make it by the time the bus pulls out, you go on ahead and take the bus into Flores. Gary has your plane tickets back to Guatemala City, so you just keep going, and we'll get there as quickly as we can."

Murmurs circulated through the group as a number of people expressed a desire to stay behind and search. Scott raised his hand to get their attention. "I appreciate your willingness to help. But, really, the best thing all of you can do is go back with Gary. If we have to, the two of us plus Melissa can stow away on a plane later tonight, but I don't think I can fit the whole group in the baggage

compartment! Now, before it gets any later, let's pray together for Melissa's safe and immediate return and then have you take off."

As soon as the group was gone, Scott sat next to Cathy on the steps. "It's easy to get turned around in Tikal, Cathy. She's going to be okay."

"This is so typical," Cathy said. "Melissa is always unaware of the time; she's late everywhere she goes—especially when she's with a boy. She forgets about everything but herself. I'm really sorry about all this, Scott. You have a tour to run and—"

"Don't worry about the tour. Gary has kept track of college freshmen for years; I'm sure he can handle a group of senior citizens. And if I need to, I can call the tour company first thing in the morning, and they'll have a replacement here in no time. Believe me, I'm easy to replace."

"Melissa never wears a watch. I don't know how many times we've bought her a watch, and she refuses to wear it. She says she doesn't need one because she has her cell phone, but then she doesn't check the time on it, either. How can you function without knowing what time it is?" She answered her own question. "By being late everywhere, I guess."

"I don't think anybody in her generation wears a watch."

"No, they don't." She glanced away from Scott at the vast expanse of green jungle. "I tried to text her, but I couldn't get a signal."

Just then Roberto, the park ranger who had welcomed their group to Tikal, approached them. "I heard about the girl who is missing." He turned his eyes toward Cathy. "You are her mother?"

Cathy nodded.

"*Señora,* do not worry. We will find her. Many times people get turned around in the ruins. I am leaving to join the search for her now." He studied Cathy's face. "I remember your daughter. She said the ceiba branches looked like caterpillars."

Cathy attempted a smile. "I'm coming with you," she said, jumping to her feet.

Scott stood. "Cathy—"

"Please. I need to look for my daughter."

"Cathy, you're exhausted—"

"Scott"—Cathy's eyes brimmed with tears—"Scott, I didn't even know him."

CHAPTER 5

THE HOSTESS LED MATT TO a table in the corner of the restaurant. He turned his phone on vibrate and stuck it in his jacket pocket. Matt greeted the other men at the table, removed his jacket, and hung it on the back of his chair. They'd been in negotiations all afternoon; now it was time for some schmoozing. It was the part of his job he liked least. *During the day, show them you know your stuff, and then, at night, show them you're a person.* He sat down, loosened his tie, and leaned back in the chair.

"So how's the wife and kid?" one of the men asked.

"They're doing great. Cathy called this afternoon from Tikal." Matt smiled at their surprised expressions. "I'll be joining them as soon as I finish up with you guys."

"They're in Guatemala? Are they looking for jade also?"

"No, they leave the jade to me. All they're hunting for are souvenirs." He forced a laugh.

The waitress appeared and took their order.

"So, Matt, tell us how you got into the jade business. We hear it's an interesting story."

"Oh, I don't know how interesting it is," Matt said. He swirled the water in his glass. "Here's the short version. I served as a missionary in Guatemala for The Church of Jesus Christ of Latter-day Saints when I was nineteen. While I was there, I met this family who sold jade on the street to the tourists. Necklaces, key chains, that sort of thing—nothing big. They were dirt poor. Everybody was. Anyway, I bought some necklaces from them to send home for Christmas. I wanted to get a necklace for my little sister, but, of course, they wanted to sell more. So we bartered. I offered less money; they offered more necklaces. By the time they were finished with me, I had enough for my sister, my mother, my ex-girlfriend, my grandmothers, and I don't remember who else. And then I

asked them if they'd like to learn how families can be together forever. They said they would, so my companion and I taught them and eventually baptized their family." He paused to sip his water.

"After I got home, I tried to stay in touch with them. They were such a good family. And they kept going to church, which, frankly, a lot of people didn't do. I especially connected with the oldest son, Santiago. He was probably fifteen, sixteen then, and we used to joke about how I was going to bring jade to the United States and turn it into big business. Then in 1998, Guatemala was hit by Hurricane Mitch. It was devastating—practically destroyed their home. But, in the aftermath of the hurricane, they found jade. And not just green jade. Pink, lavender, yellow, white. And of course the Olmec blue, which created quite a stir in the archaeological community. Apparently the hurricane cleared out a lot of vegetation that had been hiding the jade. Almost overnight, Asian jade had real competition." He paused to take another sip. "Burma's black jade can't even come close to Guatemalan galactic gold. It's the richest, creamiest black jade in the world, to say nothing of the fact that it's laced with gold, silver, and platinum. Our only challenge is getting it off the mountain and into the stores." He leaned back in his chair and laughed. "I guess I've gotten a little carried away. Sorry about that. To finish the story, after the hurricane, Santiago called me, and this time he was serious. He convinced me to come and see what he had. And the rest, as they say, is history."

"So where is this cache of jade?"

"Ah—if I told you that, I'd be out a job, wouldn't I? Let's just say they found the remnants of an ancient stone road that led them through the jungles of Guatemala. It takes several days hiking on foot to get there."

"So you're a real Indiana Jones. Excuse me if I'm missing something here, but the question that begs to be asked is why don't you put in a road and go in with trucks and mine the jade?"

"You're not the first person to ask that question. Could we go in, build a road, take in heavy equipment, and excavate until we've removed every last piece of jade all at once? That would be the American way, wouldn't it?"

"And the problem with that would be . . . ?"

"Well, it's not our land, to start with." Matt glanced around the table before continuing. "But it's more than that. To do that would be to ravage their land. Santiago, the friend I told you about—he makes a good living bringing the jade out a little at a time. Maybe not by American standards, but by Guatemalan standards. He makes enough to take care of his family, his aging parents, and help his extended family. That's what's important to him." He paused to consider his

words. "The Guatemalan people are simple; they don't have to have everything. It's something I'm trying to learn from them." Matt shook his head. "I'm sorry; I'm afraid I've climbed onto my soapbox again. Please understand that this is an issue I've tried to explain over and over again to the powers that be. The concept of enough just isn't part of our culture."

The waitress reappeared with their plates of food, and the conversation turned to small talk.

An hour and a half later, Matt pushed back his chair. "It's time for me to be on my way," he said, slipping on his suit jacket. He fished in his pocket for his car keys and pulled out his cell phone instead.

"Looks like I missed some calls." Matt studied his phone.

"What's wrong, Matt?" one of the men said.

"That's what I'm wondering. Cathy's been trying to call. There must be a dozen calls. You'll excuse me?" The men nodded, and Matt stood.

He stared at the call record as he strode out to the parking lot. It'd only been a few hours since he and Cathy last talked. It was probably nothing. Still . . .

Cathy answered his call almost immediately. "Matt—" Her voice broke.

"What's going on, Cathy?"

He could hear her jagged breathing as she struggled to talk. "Melissa's gone. She took off with a boy here in Tikal. I told her not to go, but she wouldn't listen. I've been searching; everyone has been searching—the park rangers, Scott, everyone." Her voice wavered. "I'm scared."

Matt's head was spinning. He reached out to steady himself on the car. "Listen, Honey, I need you to start at the beginning and tell me exactly what happened."

Matt could tell Cathy was struggling to keep her composure as she pieced together the events of the last several hours. "Everyone keeps telling me how easy it is to get turned around in Tikal, especially when you're distracted, and I know they're right, but—"

"I'm coming, Cathy. I'll be on the next plane to Guatemala. We're going to find her. I promise you, we will find her."

"Can you do that?"

"I should have been there in the first place. I need to go so I can work on getting a ticket, but I'll call you as soon as I've made arrangements."

"I'm so scared."

"I know, but it's going to be okay. We'll find her. Now try to get some sleep." Advice he knew she wouldn't be able to follow any better than he would.

He held the phone until he heard the click on the other end then climbed in the car and drove straight home.

The house was silent. Matt missed, probably for the first time, hearing Melissa's music blaring from her bedroom. A sob caught in his throat, and he steeled himself. He had to focus, to think. Think about what he needed to take—what he needed to do. Later, there would be time to feel.

He walked over to his laptop and turned it on. While the website pulled up, he grabbed some clothes and tossed them into a suitcase. Returning to the computer, he scrolled through the list of flights to Guatemala City, clicked on the earliest one he could make, and jotted down the time and flight number. After booking the flight, he zipped his suitcase shut, glanced at his watch, and picked up the phone. He pressed the numbers and waited until he heard voice messaging.

"Hello, Nick. This is Matt. I'm calling to let you know that an emergency has come up and I need to leave for Guatemala immediately." He hesitated before adding, "Melissa is lost in Tikal. I'm flying out tonight, but you can reach me on my cell if you need me."

Matt disconnected his phone and looked around the room. *What else?* He stood still for several seconds before returning to his laptop to do a quick search. He picked up the phone again.

"I need to talk to the U.S. Embassy in Guatemala City."

The man on duty agreed to investigate the situation and advised Matt to contact the embassy as soon as he reached the country.

One more call, and then he was out of there. He thumbed through his planner, dialed a number, and spoke to the person on the other end of the line.

"Muchas gracias," he said as he finished his conversation. "I'll meet you just outside the airport at Flores."

The flight to Guatemala City was long. Matt was restless. He leaned his seat back and closed his eyes, but sleep evaded him.

Instead, he saw Cathy's face the way he imagined it now. He saw the tightening of her neck muscles and the panic in her eyes. She went from zero to sixty on the fear scale faster than anyone he knew, always sure that every sniffle was life-threatening and every late-night phone call would bring tragic news, when in truth most of them were false alarms and wrong numbers.

"Having a child does that to a woman," his mom used to say.

And losing one does it even more.

It had been nearly fifteen years, but he remembered it like it was yesterday. He remembered looking up from the stack of papers on his desk, seeing Cathy standing in his office doorway, her face streaked with tears.

"The doctor couldn't find a heartbeat," she'd said.

The doctor had ordered an ultrasound just to be sure, so they'd gone to the hospital. He'd held her hand while they waited to hear what they already knew. The technician apologized for the cold gel. As if anyone cared. The room had been completely quiet. Quiet and cold. Hospitals were always cold.

Cathy had made it to twenty-eight weeks that time. She was supposed to be out of the danger zone. But for some reason nobody ever knew, the baby's heart had just stopped beating.

It was a boy, a tiny boy who needed time to grow. He would have been a younger brother for Melissa.

The plane jolted. Matt looked out the window, but all he could see were clouds in every direction.

Where are you, Melissa?

Melissa had been pretty upset when she and Cathy left. What if she'd decided to take off? She used to do that when she was little and got really mad. They'd find her halfway around the block, trudging down the sidewalk, her backpack filled with candy, clothes, and toys. But not now, not in a foreign country. She wasn't that stupid—or cocky. She might threaten them at home, but she wouldn't take off alone in Guatemala.

He glanced at his watch.

The man seated next to him on the plane smiled. "A little anxious?"

Matt nodded. "That obvious, huh?"

His reply was interrupted by the pilot who came on the intercom and announced their final approach to Guatemala City.

As soon as the plane landed, Matt grabbed his suitcase, rushed through customs, and found the gate for his flight into Flores. The flight took less than an hour. Finally, he felt the plane bank, level, and bank again. There was a long, slow glide then a bump as the wheels touched the ground. The brakes squealed, and the plane slowed and came to a stop.

A man was waiting for him just outside the airport. He motioned for Matt to follow him around the corner to a private place.

"Gracias por venir," Matt said in a low voice. *"¿La tienes?"*

"Sí, señor."

Matt reached inside his pocket and withdrew an envelope. The man glanced around before he accepted payment and handed Matt a heavy woven bag. Then he was gone. Matt felt through the fabric: the handle, the metal cylinder. Satisfied, he slipped the bag into his suitcase. That had been easier than he'd expected.

CHAPTER 6

Slowly Melissa began to stir. *Where am I?*

Terror choked her as she gasped for breath and battled the impulse to scream. Her heart pounded; she strained against the rope binding her hands and feet. Fighting to control her breathing, she listened for any sound—any hint that she was not alone.

The underground room where Melissa lay was almost completely dark. It was a round stone room, accessible only by a hole in the ceiling through which a ladder could be lowered. Water pooled in a depression in the center of the floor. She lay near one of the walls.

Something moved against her arm. Melissa stifled a scream and twisted away, bumping her head against the wall. She whimpered as tears filled her eyes and trickled down her cheeks. Her head throbbed. She swallowed; her mouth was dry. She licked her lips and tasted blood. Rolling onto her side, she pulled her knees to her chest and buried her face in her arms. Lying in the darkness, she closed her eyes and succumbed to hopelessness.

When sleep refused to come, Melissa's mind returned to the events of the last several hours. *What happened?* She had to remember.

Carlos. He'd wanted to show her his favorite place in Tikal. He'd said it was his secret place, and he wanted to share it with her. He had smiled at her, his teeth white against his dark skin. He'd reached over to take her hand with his warm one. She remembered how she felt when his fingers had touched hers, how she had smiled at him, flirted with him. They'd walked down a path, a long path. And then—what happened?

She froze as the sound of voices reached her ears. Fresh panic flooded her body; she forced herself to lie still.

She strained to hear what they were saying but couldn't make out any words. The voices grew louder, more insistent. They were speaking Spanish. She closed

her eyes and concentrated. *Nothing.* Mom was right about her Spanish being worthless.

Mom! Melissa swallowed the moan that rose to her lips.

And then she thought of her dad, of their last conversation before she'd left. She remembered how she had refused to talk to him on the phone. Refused to hear him tell her he loved her. Her chest ached as tears formed in her eyes and spilled onto her cheeks.

CHAPTER 7

Day 3

RAUL SILVA HAD BEEN WAITING for the shuttle bus to Tikal for nearly an hour when it finally pulled into the station. He had stayed in the background where he could observe people without being questioned. Not that anyone would notice an indigenous man waiting for a bus. There was nothing unique or particularly interesting about Raul. His salt-and-pepper hair was combed flat against his head; creases brought by years of living were etched into his weathered brown skin.

The bus will be almost full today, he thought as he glanced around at the growing number of people waiting to board. As always, he studied each person as they arrived. Their chatter, casual dress, and cameras told him they were tourists—which he would expect on a shuttle from Flores to Tikal.

All except the middle-aged man who stood apart from the others. It wasn't just that the man was alone, although that in itself was unusual. It was that the man looked haggard. Instinctively, Raul knew the man was afraid.

Fear was something Raul understood. He had learned to recognize it in people's faces—and he saw it now in the way this man carried himself, the way he swung his arms as he walked. Raul saw fear in the man's eyes, in his lips, in the set of his jaw. It was that fear—that terror he'd seen in so many pairs of eyes—which had made Raul decide to turn his back on duty and honor years before.

Raul followed the man onto the bus and settled into a seat across from him. The man was not quite six feet tall and had dark hair, silver around the temples; his blue-gray eyes had gold flecks in the center. He wore a dress shirt with rolled-up sleeves. Now that Raul was closer to him, he could see that the shirt was crumpled, as if it had been slept in. And the man hadn't shaved in more than a day. All of this was highly unusual on a bus full of tourists anticipating their first glimpse of the magnificent Tikal.

Raul was bone weary. Traveling back and forth to Guatemala City with the tour group and then turning right around to come back again was tiring, of course, but it was more than that. In all the years since he'd been hired by the tour company, there had never been a serious incident—until yesterday. He had been charged with the safety of the group. He knew the girl's disappearance wasn't his fault, but his head and his heart battled.

Ten years. He remembered the first time he met Scott. Grateful to be offered a job, he could not have known then how completely their acquaintance would change his life. Raul had come to admire Scott and the people who filled his tour buses year after year. Good solid people, with one thing in common. That was the real reason he'd finally agreed to meet with the missionaries. He had sensed something in them, a calmness he hungered for in his own life.

The bus pulled into the parking lot. Raul followed the man traveling alone as he climbed off the bus and walked past several hotels and the park museum to the open-air visitors' center. A woman stood at the top of the steps; Raul recognized her as Cathy Miller, the girl's mother. Weaving his way through the other tourists, the man from the bus reached the woman and embraced her. *Of course.* He was the girl's father. Raul should have put that together.

Raul followed them into the visitor's center, where Scott stood just inside the door. Scott greeted Raul and introduced him to Matt and then ushered them into a private office, where they were joined by the park administrator and two police officers from Flores.

The park administrator explained the searchers' strategy. He finished by saying, "Mr. Miller, Tikal is a big place. It is easy to get lost. Why don't you and your wife return to Flores, and we will call you when we find your daughter."

"I'm sorry, sir, but I can't do that. I can't just sit and wait. I've got to get out into the ruins and try to retrace her steps. See if I can find something someone else might have missed."

"Mr. Miller, we understand your concern, and now we want you to understand ours. This place is dangerous for someone who does not know what they are doing. Tikal has marked paths, but once you leave those paths, you are not safe. We are trained. Our people are trained. We have one missing person to find. If you go out, we will have two or more to find. It is best for us to handle it. We will call you as soon as we find her." The park administrator stood to leave. "We are doing everything we can. I am sure your daughter will be found."

"I'm sorry, but I can't just sit here," Matt said, pushing back his chair. "I have to look for her. She can't spend another night out there—" Matt paused to gain control of his emotions. "You understand, sir. There are animals out there. She has no protection. We have to find her tonight."

"Mr. Miller, I understand how you are feeling, but I must insist you allow us to do our job. We will find her."

"Do you have a daughter, sir? I beg you as a father—"

"We will call you as soon as we have more information. I'm sure we will have good news for you tomorrow."

The park administrator and police officers left the room, leaving Raul alone with Matt, Cathy, and Scott. Matt looked exhausted. He leaned forward on his elbows and rubbed his eyes then sat up straight. "I can't just sit here," he said. "I have to look for her."

"Then let's go," Scott said.

They walked down the path and into the ruins until they reached the base of Temple IV. Sweat ran down the back of Raul's neck. He wiped his brow. Even in the evening, the humidity was overpowering.

"Remind me what Carlos said about where he wanted to take her," Matt said to Cathy. "Tell me everything you remember about your conversation with him."

Cathy rehearsed their conversation again as well as she could remember. As she finished, her voice broke. "I've been praying constantly ever since it all happened, but the answers don't come. Why doesn't He answer me?"

Matt cupped Cathy's face in his hands and looked into her eyes. "He is listening, Cathy. We've got to have faith in that. He's going to help us find her."

Raul studied the darkening jungle. *Where did Carlos and Melissa go?*

"It's getting late, Matt," Scott said.

"I know," Matt said. "And as hard as it is to admit, maybe the park administrator was right." He paused to gain control of his voice before continuing. "There's nothing more we can do except wait and pray she'll be protected through the night."

Raul looked at Cathy. Her eyes were brimming with tears. She touched Matt's arm, and he pulled her into an embrace. "I don't know what else to do," he said. "And I'm too tired to think."

"Why don't we go back to the hotel," Scott said. "Get some rest."

As they left the park together, Raul approached Scott. "If I may be released from my responsibilities on the tour, I would like to search for the girl."

"What did you have in mind, Raul?"

"The authorities will search inside the park; I am hopeful they will find her. However, I will begin my search in the villages outside the park." He paused before adding, "With your permission."

"Of course," Scott said.

Raul turned to Matt and Cathy. "I will find your daughter," he said. "I know this land and this people, and I will not give up until I have found her."

CHAPTER 8

MELISSA LAY STILL IN THE dark, exhausted from her attempts to break free of the rope that bound her hands and feet. *It's no use. I'll never get out of here.* Moving even a little was a tedious chore and offered small comfort. *If only I could reach my phone.* Twice she had heard voices, twice she had braced herself for whatever was to come, and twice they had stopped as suddenly as they'd begun. Now she almost wished for the voices. Anything was better than waiting.

She pulled her knees toward her chin and shifted position. That provided some relief, and she relaxed against the ropes. Hunger gnawed at her stomach. Her wrists and ankles were swollen and sore from the friction of the rope.

The voices came again, but unlike the last times, they didn't stop immediately. She heard scraping followed by a thud as a ladder was lowered through the hole and set into place. First one foot and then another was placed onto the ladder rungs. Her heart pounded as she listened to hands sliding down the wood, feet slowly descending. Then a crunch as the feet reached the bottom of the ladder and stepped onto the ground. She could hear someone breathing. The footsteps came closer.

A rough hand shook her shoulder and rolled her onto her back. The rope around her ankles and wrists was cut. She was jerked to her feet and blindfolded. Body odor reached her nostrils, and she almost gagged.

"*Señorita,*" a voice said. "You come."

Her captor pushed her toward the ladder. She grasped the sides and raised her foot to feel for the first rung. Her foot slid into place; she moved her hands up the ladder and felt for another rung. Step by step, she climbed until she reached the top. Hands pried her fingers from the ladder and dragged her out of the hole. A rough palm covered her mouth as its owner yanked her to her feet, forced her to walk a distance, and then pushed her to the ground and retied her feet.

"You do what I say, and you eat," the voice said. *"¿Comprendes?"*

Melissa nodded.

"No scream."

Melissa nodded again. The man withdrew his hand and then gave her something hard. She raised it to her mouth and tasted it. Bread. It was stale, but she ate it, savoring each bite until it was gone. Another piece was offered, accepted, and eaten. And then a bowl of water. Water spilled down her chin and onto her clothes. Fighting back the tears that stung at her eyelids, she tried to concentrate on the voices. How many were there? Two? Three?

As soon as she finished drinking the water, Melissa's captor forced her back into the pit, took off her blindfold, and left her untied. *"Buena suerte,"* he taunted as he climbed out of the cenote and removed the ladder.

Alone again, Melissa felt for the travel pouch she wore around her neck. She unzipped it, retrieved her phone, and pressed a button. No signal. She'd expected that. How was the battery holding out? Fifty-nine percent. She had to preserve the battery. Wait for an opportunity to use her phone. It was her only hope of being found. She stared at the screen for several moments before she held the power button and waited for the power-off screen to come up. She slid her finger across the screen and then placed the phone back in her pouch. It wasn't much, but it was something.

Sometime later, wave after wave of agonizing spasms gripped Melissa's stomach. *The water*, she thought. *I drank the water.*

CHAPTER 9

Day 4

"I CALLED THE EMBASSY BEFORE I left home and asked them to look into the situation," Matt said the next morning after an unsatisfying conversation with the authorities in Tikal. "I want to go there and talk to someone in person."

Cathy and Scott agreed that it was time to get the embassy involved. They checked out of the Jungle Lodge and headed for the airport.

They boarded a plane for Guatemala City and took a bus to the U.S. Embassy—an imposing building with a tall wrought-iron fence completely circling the property. Armed guards stood on each corner and at the entrance; otherwise, it could have been any government building in the United States. They waited for nearly an hour before being ushered into the office of the U.S. consul, a well-dressed man with sandy-blond hair.

Matt explained why they were there. The man who introduced himself as Curtis Whittaker listened to everything that was said. After Matt finished, the room was silent as Mr. Whittaker studied each person in the room. Finally he spoke.

"Have you considered the possibility that your daughter doesn't want to be found?"

The words struck Matt like a fist slamming into his stomach. "What do you mean, doesn't want to be found?"

"Mr. Miller, I've got to ask you some pretty direct questions, and I need honest answers to be able to help you." Mr. Whittaker leaned back in his chair.

"Okay."

"How are things between you and your daughter?" When Matt hesitated, the consul rephrased the question. "How is your relationship with your daughter?" Mr. Whittaker stared straight into Matt's eyes, waiting for a response.

"What are you trying to say, that she ran away?"

"All I'm saying is that she's a teenager, and heaven knows I know about teenagers. They can get their jaws bent out of shape over just about anything."

"Well, sure, we've had our moments, but—"

Mr. Whittaker continued as if he hadn't heard Matt. "So we have this teenager. Maybe she's a little bugged with Mom. She meets a good-looking boy, and they decide to spend some time together." He looked slowly from Cathy to Matt. "It wouldn't be the first time it's happened. So she turns up in a couple of days when the money runs out or she decides she's had enough of Romeo. Maybe she misses Mom and Dad, figures out you aren't so bad after all."

"Melissa wouldn't do that," Matt said.

"Are you sure? Because it might prove a little embarrassing to you if we wage an all-out search for her, bringing in the dogs and the media and all that, and it turns out she's holed up in some little hotel in Flores. If I were you, I'd just hang tight for a few days, and I'll bet she'll show up just fine. No worse for the wear. She'll have an exciting story to tell her girlfriends, and that's about it."

"Melissa wouldn't take off with some boy she doesn't know," Cathy said.

"Pardon my stating the obvious, ma'am," Mr. Whittaker said, "but isn't that exactly what she did?"

Cathy flushed.

"So what are you telling us?" Matt asked.

"I'm telling you to enjoy the sights. Sure, I wouldn't turn my phone off, but I wouldn't let this ruin your vacation either. We'll call you as soon as we hear anything. Check in with us every day if it'll make you feel better. She's going to turn up, ready to eat humble pie, and you'll be glad it wasn't all over the news."

"Are you telling me you won't help us?"

"No, I'm not saying we won't help you. I'm just trying to speak a little reason here, Mr. Miller. No need to get hot around the collar." Mr. Whittaker pursed his lips. "What line of work are you in?"

"What does that have to do with anything?"

"Well, my sources say you're involved in jade trading. And a scandal won't help business. The Guatemalan government doesn't want this thing leaked, because it's not good for tourism. People will think she's been kidnapped or some such deal—and for the record, there's absolutely no evidence of foul play. But those people who heard she was missing just might not turn on the TV the day she shows up with a smile on her face. They'll just connect Guatemala with missing daughters, and I don't have to tell you that we don't like missing daughters. So it's bad for tourism, and it's bad for business. Silly as it seems, people think if you can't keep a handle on your daughter's behavior, you probably

can't keep a handle on your business either." He paused before adding, "So let's just keep this thing under wraps, and I guarantee you'll be glad we did."

"Well, I can see we're wasting our time here," Matt said. He turned to Scott. "Do you know where the Guatemalan state department offices are located?"

Mr. Whittaker stood and walked to a file in the corner of the room. He opened the top drawer and pulled out a piece of paper.

"Here's what you're looking for, and you're welcome to go see them." He walked around the front of his desk to hand the paper to Matt. "It's been good to meet you," he said, extending his hand. Matt stood and accepted the paper but not the hand.

"You know, I hate to be the bad-news guy, but the truth is they're on the same page as the embassy. You go ahead and talk to the folks over there, but the bottom line is you're just going to have to wait for her to show up." He chuckled. "'Course, they're not going to tell you that. You know the Guatemalans—most agreeable people in the world. They don't like confrontation, I'll give them that. So if it makes you feel better, go see them, but you need to know you're beating your head against a wall. Give it a few days. She'll surface, and when she does, you're going to thank me."

"Thank you? My daughter is missing, has been missing for more than two days now, and you think I'm going to thank you because you're—what?— protecting my reputation or something? You have the audacity to suggest she's having some kind of romantic liaison with a boy she's never met before. You're the most pompous windbag I've ever met, and when this is over, I'm going to do everything in my power to see that you are removed from your position." Matt slammed his fist on the desk. "You are here to represent the United States of America. My daughter is a U.S. citizen. She has rights—the right to protection. That's your job, Mr. Whittaker, your job—to protect her! All I've heard from you are slanderous accusations and excuses. How dare you suggest—" His voice broke, and he stopped speaking as he fought to regain control. When he spoke again, his voice was steady and direct. "I'm going to find my daughter, Mr. Whittaker. And then I'm going to do whatever it takes to see that you never treat another U.S. citizen the way you have treated us. I am a U.S. citizen with rights. Melissa is a U.S. citizen. It is your job to protect her, and I demand you pull out every resource you have to find her. I demand you do your job!"

His words hung in the air for several seconds before Mr. Whittaker broke the silence, his voice no longer friendly. "Mr. Miller, you are in Guatemala, not the United States. You would do well to remember that."

Matt stared at Mr. Whittaker. "I don't know how you sleep at night," he said as he reached for the doorknob.

Matt, Cathy, and Scott headed straight for the Guatemalan state offices. The officer they spoke with was respectful as he listened to their concerns. He assured them that the government was aware of the situation and was doing all they could to find Melissa, but Matt had the sinking feeling that Mr. Whittaker had been right. In spite of his words to the contrary, the officer believed Melissa was gone of her own volition and was most anxious to keep a lid on her disappearance.

As they left the office, Scott said, "If you're okay for a few minutes, I would like to run over to the hotel and check on the tour group before they leave for Kaminaljuyu."

"Of course," Cathy said. "I'm afraid we've been so absorbed in all this that we haven't given a thought to them—or to you."

"They're fine. I called the tour company, and they sent a replacement immediately, so I'm yours as long as you need me. But I would like to touch base with them."

Matt motioned toward a nearby bench. "We'll wait for you over there," he said.

After Scott left, Cathy and Matt walked to the bench and sat down. Matt leaned back and closed his eyes. The sun on his face felt warm. The smell of raw meat wafted from a nearby open-air butcher shop. A street vendor sat on the sidewalk near them, a colorful tapestry spread in piles around her. A child, no older than eight, approached them and held out a necklace. "You buy from me? I make you good deal," she said.

"No. No, thank you," Cathy said.

"Maybe later?"

Cathy nodded. The little girl grinned and skipped down the street.

Matt felt Cathy looking at him. "Hey," she said softly. She touched his face with her finger, tracing the outline of his cheek, and then reached for his hand. He grabbed it, squeezed it, and then clamped his eyes shut, swallowing hard as a tear escaped. She reached up to wipe the tear from his face. There was another tear and another. He dropped his head, and the sobs came. She pulled him to her, cradling his head on her chest, stroking his hair as he wept, his tears mingling with hers.

"What are we going to do, Matt?" she whispered.

"I don't know. I feel so helpless."

They cried together and sat in silence until Scott returned from the hotel.

"All the people on the tour are concerned about Melissa," Scott said. "They kept asking what they could do. I think every one of them would abandon the tour if they could think of a single thing they could do to help."

Just then, Matt's phone vibrated. He pulled it from his pocket and touched the screen. His mind raced as he read the text message then read it again. He felt like he was going to vomit.

"They wanted me to tell you that," Scott said.

"What's wrong, Matt?" Cathy said.

"It's nothing." Matt returned the phone to his pocket. "I just need to make a couple of calls for work."

Cathy stared at him. "Your work is contacting you? Do they have any idea what we're going through here?"

"No, Cathy, they don't. Why would they?"

"I assumed you told them before you left. You must have given them some explanation."

Matt blew out his breath. "You're right. I'm sorry. I'm just on edge right now."

"Why don't we take a break and get something to eat," Scott said. "Food always helps me think more clearly."

Matt nodded. "That's a good idea, Scott. That'll give us a chance to regroup and decided where to go from here."

Cathy and Matt followed Scott as he made his way toward a nearby street café. They ordered a meal and found a place to sit.

"I've been thinking about what Mr. Whittaker said." Matt pushed his food around on his plate. "As much as I hate to admit it, the truth is, Melissa and I did have a falling out just before the trip. The authorities have assured us they're doing everything they can to find her. Maybe we really are going to have to wait for them to do their jobs."

"Matt, what are you saying?" Cathy said.

"Scott, you've done so much for us these last couple of days. You've been there with us every moment, helping us, supporting us, and I want you to know how much I appreciate that. But I'm not unaware that you have other responsibilities that need your attention. That phone call isn't going to come any faster because there are three of us waiting for it. And you've got an entire tour group who paid good money for you to show them the lands of the Book of Mormon. I want you to rejoin the group. Cathy and I will keep doing everything we can, and we'll let you know as soon as we find her."

"The tour is covered—"

"I know. But the guy they called in to cover for you wasn't planning on this. Who knows what he's missing to be here?"

Scott studied Matt's face. "Matt, are you sure everything is okay?"

"Everything's fine, Scott."

"But Matt—" Cathy began.

"Cathy, it's going to be okay. I know my way around this city. I speak the language. I even have a few connections. We'll be okay. Let's let Scott get back to his responsibilities." He paused. "I think it's time for us to look in a different direction. We need to get on the phone—call Melissa's friends and Josh. Maybe someone has heard from her. I should have thought of that before, but I guess I didn't want to believe she would take off like that. I think we need to explore that possibility. Check the buses and airplanes leaving Tikal. And that's going to be a lot of time in a hotel on the phone."

When neither of them spoke, Matt continued. "I've got to get this work problem off my back first anyway, so let's go back to the hotel. Scott can get back to his tour, and I'll start making calls."

"How can you even think about work right now?" Cathy's voice was strained.

"The sooner I deal with it, the sooner I can get back to finding Melissa."

"Why can't you just say no, Matt? For once in your life, why can't you just say no to work? What on earth could be going on at work that would be more important than finding Melissa?"

"Cathy, I'm sorry. Some things can't wait. It'll only take a few minutes."

They finished their lunch in silence and walked back to the hotel. Scott gave Matt his cell number and agreed to give them time to make calls. Then, he insisted, he'd be back to help them in their search. Matt nodded and thanked him.

"What's going on, Matt?" Cathy said as soon as the door closed. "What aren't you telling me?"

Matt placed his hands on Cathy's shoulders and tried to pull her into an embrace. She pushed him away. "Tell me what's going on."

"I need you to trust me, Cathy. We need to leave right now."

"I'm not going anywhere until you tell me what's going on."

"I'm trying to protect Melissa. And you."

"Protect us? You said there were problems at work."

"It's not about work." Matt shook his head. "I had to change directions, and I didn't know how else to do it."

"That message—"

"We've got to go, Cathy." Matt stuffed Melissa's scattered belongings into her suitcase and clicked it shut. "We've got to get out of here before Scott comes back. I'll explain once we're on our way."

"No. Tell me what's going on."

Matt exhaled slowly. "Okay, but—"

"Someone has her. That's what you're not telling me, isn't it?"

When Matt didn't answer, Cathy sank onto the bed. Tears filled her eyes and overflowed onto her cheeks.

Matt sat beside her and reached for her hand. "I'm sorry I lied to you."

She nodded and tried to speak, but her throat constricted and she choked on her words. "The message—"

"We're going to do exactly what we're told to do, and we're going to get her back. You've got to trust in that."

"Let me see it."

Reluctantly, Matt pulled his phone from his pocket and handed it to her.

Mr. Miller,

If you ever want to see your daughter again, you will be at the Hotel Casa Santo Domingo in Antigua by 9 tonight. They are expecting you. Do not talk to anyone, and lose the guy who is with you.

CHAPTER 10

As the first rays of light shone through the hole, Melissa sat up, listening to the sounds of the jungle coming from outside her prison walls. Eventually she heard twigs snap as her captors moved around. Their conversation was muffled. Then she heard the same sounds she had heard before as someone descended the ladder to bring her to the surface. He replaced her blindfold and pushed her toward the ladder.

Sunlight warmed her skin as she reached the top. Again she was offered stale bread to eat. The bread made her thirsty, but remembering the agony of the previous night, she refused water. When she finished eating, her hands were tied, and she was left alone.

The men spoke, but she soon grew weary of trying to decipher unfamiliar words. Then a voice caught her attention. *Carlos?* She tried to remember the events that had led to her capture, the sound of his voice. Was it the same? She concentrated, trying to hear his voice again. And finally she did.

Her fists clenched as tears formed in her eyes and trickled down her cheeks. *Stupid. So stupid! I trusted him!* She yanked against the rope, wincing as it cut into her wrists. She slumped back against a tree. It was no use.

Footsteps approached. His voice. He spoke softly. It took her a moment to realize he was speaking English.

"I am sorry, señorita." His voice was pleading.

More footsteps. And then another voice, mocking. *"Mira Carlitos."*

She felt a rough hand touch her hair, picking up a strand and kissing it. She could smell stale wine as he breathed on her neck. Then the hand touched her cheek. She winced.

"¡No! ¡Déjala!" It was Carlos's voice.

The other voice laughed as the footsteps moved away.

CHAPTER 11

CATHY STARED OUT THE BUS window as they left Guatemala City. Hillsides on the outskirts of the city were crowded with sheet metal and cinder block shacks. Scraps of corrugated metal and colorful clothing lay scattered on the ground. The slopes below the houses were terraced and planted with neat rows. Women with bundles strapped to their backs worked in the fields, gathering vegetables for market. All along the road, people walked, pulling carts or carrying bundles of sugarcane on their backs or baskets full of produce on their heads. The terraced mountains jutted up steeply on all sides and were covered in lush, green vegetation. The poverty stood in stark contrast to the beauty of the countryside.

It was early evening when the bus arrived in Antigua and stopped at the Parque Central, where Cathy and Matt exited the bus. The plaza was surrounded by beautiful colonial buildings. A fountain stood in the middle of the square, water spouting from the top and each side and pooling in the bottom. People were everywhere, eating, chatting, and selling their wares. A group of schoolgirls walked past dressed in matching red-and-blue plaid skirts with red cardigans over white button-up shirts and red knee socks. Backpacks were slung over their shoulders, their long black hair tied in ponytails or hanging past their shoulders.

"There's a tuk tuk," Matt said, motioning toward a three-wheeled red-and-white taxi cart coming toward them.

The driver stopped and waited for them to squeeze onto the bench behind him. Cathy clung to the bar in front of her as Matt gave the driver directions in Spanish. They wove through the streets of Antigua beside cars, buses, and horse-drawn carriages. Women wearing beaded blouses tucked into long coarsely woven skirts walked along the street. It was a picturesque city with brightly colored buildings; only the bars on the windows suggested that it was not safe.

The taxi slowed in front of a pink stucco building with heavy wooden doors. Matt paid the driver and held Cathy's hand as she stepped out of the cart onto the sidewalk.

"This is it," Matt said. He carried their luggage through the doors into an open-air lobby. While Matt secured their room, Cathy stared out at the adjoining courtyard. A fountain surrounded by overflowing pots of flowers and chunks of broken wall stood in the middle of the grounds.

"It was a monastery back in the 1500s before an earthquake destroyed it," Matt said. "These ruins are all that's left."

"It's beautiful," Cathy said. "I wish I could enjoy it."

They walked down the open-air corridor until they came to their room; it was unlike any Cathy had imagined she would find in Guatemala. At another time, the high beams on the ceiling, the wooden posts, and the corner fireplace would have looked romantic. She sat on the bed and watched as Matt scanned the room.

"What do we do now?"

Matt sat beside her on the bed. "We wait."

"What time is it?"

He looked at his watch. "Nearly six o'clock. We should probably try to get something to eat."

"I'm not hungry."

"I don't feel like eating either." Matt reached over and took Cathy's hand. "At least we know she didn't run away. That's something."

"Yeah." Cathy's voice was subdued.

"I want to tell you something," Matt said. "Something I've been thinking a lot about the last few days. Even before . . ." He cleared his throat. "Do you know how much I appreciate everything you do? For me? For Melissa? I don't know what I'd do without you. I've been thinking a lot about that the last couple of days. I haven't appreciated you enough. And I know I haven't helped you the way I should have. Especially with Melissa."

"You've had a lot on your plate."

"That's not an excuse. But I'm going to try to do better. I want you to know that."

"Something like this brings everything into perspective, doesn't it?"

"Sure does." His voice was husky.

Cathy felt restless. "Three more hours," she murmured. She stood and crossed to the window. It was getting dark.

"I'd like to walk around this place before it gets any later," Matt said. "Get a feel for the layout. Do you want to come with me or stay here and try to get some rest?"

"I don't want to stay alone."

Matt put his arm around Cathy and pulled her close. "We're going to get through this, with the Lord's help." He kissed her hair and cheek and held her against his chest, feeling the wetness of her face through his shirt.

"I'm okay," Cathy said after a few minutes. "Let's go."

Matt stepped out into the hallway and looked both ways before beckoning for Cathy to follow him down the dimly lit corridor. It was a labyrinth of stone columns and hand-carved wooden posts. Indentations in the walls housed statues of saints and the crucifix. Plants lined the hallways and wooden beams crossed the ceiling. Geometrically patterned tile steps led to another floor and to an open-air courtyard scattered with empty tables and chairs. It was dark, except for the tiny lights hung in the trees. In the distance, a marimba band played a haunting melody Cathy recognized as "Spanish Eyes."

They moved through the courtyard and past the dining room until they reached a conference hall filled with people listening to a lecture. As Cathy glanced over the audience, the profile of a blond man seated in the back row jarred a memory.

"I just remembered something," she said. "I don't know if it's significant."

Matt nodded and motioned for her to follow him away from the room. They walked out onto the hotel grounds and found a secluded place to sit.

"What is it?"

"Melissa said she felt like someone was watching her."

"When was this?"

"The first night, in the hotel. It was right after I talked to you. And then . . ." She hesitated. "She mentioned it a couple of other times the next day. I thought it was just the product of an overactive imagination."

"Did she say what the person looked like?"

"She tried to point him out, but I didn't get a good look. I tried to brush it off."

"But?"

"But I felt it too."

"You think you were being followed?"

"I don't know, Matt. At the time I chalked it up to the power of suggestion, but now I wonder." She stared at the shadows shaped by the uneven rubble scattered around the grounds. "What time is it?"

Matt glanced at his watch. "Eight twenty." He reached over and squeezed Cathy's hand. They sat together for a few more minutes before returning to their room to wait.

At exactly nine o'clock, there was a knock on their door. Cathy grasped the back of a chair and braced herself. Matt walked to the door and opened

it. A bellhop stood just outside, carrying a basket full of fruit. He held it out to Matt.

"Buenas noches, señor," he said then bowed and walked away.

Matt closed the door. Inside the fruit bowl, he saw a folded note. He opened the paper and read it aloud. *"Welcome to Antigua."*

It was unsigned.

CHAPTER 12

MELISSA'S MIND RACED. *CARLOS!* HE was here, a part of this. Why did he bring her here? What did the men want with her? She shuddered as she remembered the touch of a hand on her cheek. She had to get away from here. She had to escape; go back to Tikal.

Her mom must be frantic. She must have contacted Melissa's dad. He had friends in Guatemala. He'd get them to search for her. They'd find her. They had to find her. If only she could send them a text message.

She wondered if Josh knew she was gone.

It had been several hours since her captors had brought her out of the dark pit and she'd eaten bread and heard Carlos's voice. Tears stung at her eyelids. Never before had she felt so completely alone.

Again she heard footsteps.

"Señorita, you okay?" It was Carlos.

Melissa refused to answer. A tear trickled down her cheek.

"I did not mean for this to happen."

She sat still, waiting.

"You okay?"

Finally she shook her head. "I'm thirsty."

"You need water?"

"Water makes me sick."

"Oh, okay, *comprendo.*"

She heard him walk away, returning momentarily.

"Here, I have a drink for you," Carlos said, placing the bottle in her hand. She tilted her face to drink and then jerked away, gagging as she spat the liquid onto the ground. "What is that?"

"It is wine, señorita."

"Wine?" The tears began again.

"You do not like wine?"

She shook her head, her tears falling harder and faster. She turned her face away from Carlos.

"Señorita, what is wrong? I want to help you."

"I can't drink wine," she said.

"You cannot drink the wine? Why not?"

"I just can't. That's all. What are you going to do to me?"

"I will not hurt you," he said. "Please, believe me; I did not know. They said—" His words stopped as footsteps approached them.

Words were exchanged, and although Melissa couldn't understand what was said, she recognized the tone and flushed.

Again she felt rough fingers touch her cheek, and she flinched. She heard Carlos's voice, angry, followed by the other man's laughter. Then she heard the man walk away again.

"I am sorry, señorita," Carlos said. "I won't let them hurt you."

Her tears began again, spilling onto her face.

"I did not know," he said softly. "I needed money for my family. The men told me you would not be hurt."

"What do they want?"

Before he could respond, a man's voice called out, "Eh, Carlitos."

"I must go," Carlos said.

CHAPTER 13

VERNON TAYLOR WAS NOT A man to be put off easily. This trip, his wife had said, was to usher in the beginning of a new phase of their life together. A new season, she had called it. He called it being put out to pasture. Retirement was a lot harder than he had expected it to be. It wasn't that he didn't trust his son to run the farm. Heaven knows he'd been teaching him everything he knew since the tike was knee-high to a grasshopper. But still, there were things you could only know if you'd been up to your knees in manure every day for nearly fifty years. He thought he should hang around the place for a while—sort of ease out of it, in case his son had a question. But his wife disagreed and had told him so. She said their son needed to stand on his own two feet and not in his father's shadow. So she booked this trip to Guatemala. He didn't care about Guatemala. In fact, he didn't care a whole lot for travel in general. But he knew it would make Blanche happy, so he'd agreed to go.

Word got out that they were taking a trip, and next thing he knew, Lyle Goodman and Gary Clark were signed up to go too. Apparently, the wives had talked in Relief Society, and they'd decided it would be triple the fun if they all went. And that was okay. He liked the men well enough. Certainly respected them. Anybody'd tell you Lyle was a man of his word, and that said a lot. And Gary'd just been released from the stake presidency. He told the congregation it'd probably been thirty years since he'd sat by his wife in sacrament meeting and he was ready to sit on the back row and hold her hand again. But Vernon suspected that wasn't true. Suspected it was just as hard for Gary to take a backseat as it was for him. It's just plain difficult, when you're used to being in the thick of things, to suddenly find out you're not anymore.

And that's why the current state of affairs had Vernon stymied. He'd listened as Scott explained that everything possible was being done to find Melissa. He'd listened as their repeated offers of help were rejected. And he'd

listened when Scott came back from being with the Millers and told the group that the authorities and even Melissa's dad suspected she might have left with that boy of her own free will. But that didn't ring true to Vernon, and he decided it was time to act. So he called a private meeting with his two buddies.

He told them what was on his mind. "The way I see it, there's a young girl who's in trouble. No matter how she got there, and frankly, I don't buy that story that she took off on her own, but anyway, however she ended up where she is, she's in need of rescuing." What he didn't tell them was that he felt terribly guilty for not doing something when he saw her with that boy in Tikal. He should have stopped her then and there, and if he had, none of this would be happening.

The others listened thoughtfully, and then Lyle spoke up. "I'd sure rather search for Melissa than shop for trinkets with my wife."

The others chuckled.

"So what do you have in mind, Vernon?" Gary asked.

"Well, I don't exactly have a plan, Gary. But I figure we're three good men. We've got a lot of experience and a lot of horse sense. So the way I see it, if we put our heads together, we just might be able to come up with something. And at the end of the day, that's going to be the most important thing we could have done."

The others nodded.

"I've got a granddaughter her age," Lyle said. He cleared his throat and wiped his nose with a handkerchief he'd pulled out of his pocket.

"Tricia's got a girl that old? That makes you really old," Vernon said, and they all laughed.

"Well, men, let's make a plan," Gary said. "But first, what do you say we ask the good Lord for His help?"

After they prayed, the three men sat in silence for a few seconds. Then Vernon spoke. "It seems to me we're going to need to leave the group to accomplish anything. We're going to need to return to the scene of the crime." The others nodded, and he continued. "So the question is, what are we going to tell the others? Our wives, for instance?"

"After four decades of living together, my wife can smell a rat a mile away," Gary said.

"I think Lila would want me to go. She's just as worried about that little girl as I am," Lyle said.

"So's Blanche," Vernon said.

"Okay then, what about Scott?" Gary said. "He's the one who said they don't need our help."

"That's true, but on the other hand, he'd be a good resource. And if we don't tell him, how will our wives explain our sudden disappearance?"

In the end it was decided that they'd see how much information they could get out of Scott without divulging their plan to return to Tikal. If that didn't work, they'd revisit the issue, but for now, they were going to keep it between the six of them—once they talked to their wives, of course. And that seemed to be the next step. So they agreed to meet again in one hour, each with a wife in tow.

"You're certainly being mysterious, Mr. Taylor," Blanche said as he escorted her down the hall of their hotel at the appointed time. He knocked three times on the Goodmans' door and waited for it to open. "Well, my stars, you've got a regular party going on here," she said when she saw the other two couples in the room.

Vernon steered her inside and shut the door behind her. Blanche crossed the room to where Lila and Ella were standing. "Any idea what this is about?"

Ella shook her head. "Gary's been acting strangely ever since he came back to the room an hour ago."

"Yeah, well, Vernon's been acting strange for the last fifty years."

The three women laughed and then turned their attention to the men, who were standing together, facing them.

"We have something to tell you," Vernon began.

"Now there's something new," Blanche said, grinning at her husband. Ordinarily he would fire something back and then she would follow with a retort, and on it would go. That's how their relationship was—had been for half a century. But not today. Today Vernon failed to take the bait and simply waited for her smile to fade before he continued.

"We've been talking about the Miller girl, and we've decided we're tired of being told to sit tight."

"We'd like to help them find her," Gary said.

"What do you intend to do?" Ella asked.

"We're not sure, but what we don't want to do is stand around with our hands in our pockets. We've been doing that for too long already," Vernon said.

Lyle said, "We want to see what we can find out from Scott first—"

"And that's where you can help us," Vernon interrupted. "Sometimes women are . . . er . . . better at getting stuff out of people than men are."

"Getting people to divulge things without their even knowing what they're saying," Gary said.

Lyle nodded. "It's true. My wife finds out more stuff in two minutes from the women in the lady's room than I find out in a whole month of Sundays in high priests."

"Is that supposed to be a compliment?" Blanche asked the other women.

"I'm not sure. It sounds a little like one but not exactly," said Lila.

"So, what did you want us to find out with our unique and extraordinary detective skills?" Ella asked.

"Well, that's the thing. We don't exactly know," said Lyle.

"Anything might be helpful. But let's start with the basics. What the Millers know, what they suspect," said Gary.

"Who they're talking to. Phone numbers," said Vernon.

"Phone numbers! You expect us to get phone numbers without raising suspicion?" said Ella.

"Oh, Hon. You women have your ways," said Gary. "I don't pretend to understand, but I'm confident in your abilities. And now that Scott's back with us, it should be easy enough to ask a few questions."

"But, uh, let's not dillydally about it either. We've already sat around for too long. I don't know about the rest of you, but I was going crazy in Kaminaljuyu today, just thinking about what we should be doing." Vernon said.

"I looked at our schedule, and it looks to me like tomorrow will be our best time to leave," Gary said. "We're supposed to be taking a boat ride on Lake Atitlán, followed by an afternoon of shopping in Panajachel."

Vernon grunted. "Shopping!"

Gary nodded. "Bus leaves at seven for Panajachel. Three hours there, a couple of hours on Lake Atitlán, a couple of hours shopping, three hours back. Arrive just in time for dinner and our last night in this hotel. So—"

Ella broke in. "And just like that, you expect us to buy into this? The three of you taking off to who knows where?"

"We'll be fine," Vernon said. "Lyle can get us around with his Spanish—"

"His Spanish! It's been fifty years since his mission!" Lila said.

"It hasn't been fifty years, has it?" Lyle said.

"At least."

"Okay, but I still remember, and it'll come back when I start using it."

Gary had been studying the floor. Now he looked at the three women. "Ladies, we know this is a lot to ask. But these people are suffering. You know they are. You know how you'd feel if she was your daughter. We just want to help them. That's all. And we're asking you to believe in us, to believe we can be the men you thought we were when you married us."

"Gary—" Ella began.

"Do you believe the Lord can help us?"

"Of course, but—"

"But you're scared. I'm scared too. But this is something we need to do. Can you support us in that?"

When Ella didn't answer right away, Gary said, "So, as I was saying, tomorrow we wake up with a nasty case of Montezuma's revenge and say we're going to lie low for the day. By the time you get back from the day on the lake and shopping, we'll be long gone."

"You *all* wake up sick; you really think people will believe that?" Ella said.

"We all drank the same water. You can tell them we thought drinking bottled water was for wimps," Vernon said.

"And then what? You don't think anyone will notice three men are gone?" Ella said.

"You'll just have to stall as long as you can," said Gary.

In the end, the men were right: Scott never suspected a thing when the women approached him with their questions.

"What's the latest on Melissa? I'm so worried about her."

"They must be so scared. Do they have any clues at all about what happened?"

"I'd like to give Cathy a call, offer her some encouragement—you know, as one mother to another. Do you happen to have her phone number?"

The Millers, according to Scott, were back in Guatemala City. In fact, they were staying in the same hotel. They had decided it was best to leave the searching to the professionals and were spending their time making phone calls and working with the embassy.

Vernon snorted when he heard that. For all intents and purposes, it seemed to him they'd pretty much given up on finding her. "If it were me, I wouldn't have left that place without her, no matter how long it took," he said.

The women reported that Scott was concerned that he hadn't been able to contact them since he'd left them. He'd stopped by their room several times, but they weren't there, and they weren't answering their cell phones either.

"I'll bet with everything that's going on, they forgot to plug it in and the battery died," Lila said. "That's something I'd do."

After mulling over the information, the men decided against contacting the Millers directly. After all, Scott had rejected their offers of help more than once; the Millers would probably do the same.

* * *

The blond man had just gone to bed when the phone rang. He sat up, turned on the lamp, and reached for the phone lying on the nightstand next to his ruby ring.

"Contact has been made," said the voice on the other end of the line.

"And?"

"They're going to be very cooperative," Eduardo Guerrero said.

"And the girl?"

"They tell me she's pretty."

The blond man narrowed his eyes. "That's not what I asked."

"They know it's in their best interest for her to stay alive."

"Keep it that way."

CHAPTER 14

Day 5

MELISSA SPENT ANOTHER NIGHT ALONE in the pit. She slept fitfully, nightmares waking her often. Huddling in the dark, she listened to the sounds of the jungle and waited for the first rays of sunlight. She was becoming accustomed to the routine.

For the first time, her captor failed to blindfold her when he pulled her from the pit. She tried not to look at him. Instead, she stared at his feet. He wore athletic shoes, the same kind Josh might have had, except that his were stained with dirt and too much wear. Above his shoes, she could see dark-brown muscular calves.

He pushed her toward a tree and kneeled to tie her ankle to the trunk. She looked down at his head, at a baseball cap covering his black hair, and felt his hand linger on her leg. He stood and looked boldly at her, his mouth sneering, his eyes traveling slowly from her face down to her feet. Then he turned and walked away to join another man seated in a chair a few yards away smoking a cigarette. The other man was older, his hair long, his jeans ripped and dirty. He wore sandals on his calloused feet. Which one had touched her cheek? Shuddering, she looked away from the men.

Palm branches hung thickly over the makeshift campsite, blocking the sunlight. A tent stood a few yards away, across from where the men sat on camp stools. A jug of water was near the tent; beside it sat a case of bottled wine and a large duffle bag. Cigarette butts were scattered on the ground near the remains of a charcoal fire. She glanced over her shoulder and was surprised to see a mule tethered to a tree, munching on the green foliage. Carlos stood near the animal, offering him water from a bucket. *He's still here!*

* * *

Vernon, Gary, and Lyle filled their day packs with an extra change of clothes, water bottles, and first aid kits. Each stashed a compass and map into a pocket, and each gave his wife an extra-long kiss as they said goodbye and promised to call soon.

As soon as the tour bus pulled out, the three men went to the airport and on to Tikal. Once there, they walked into the visitors' center and asked a park ranger what was being done to find Melissa.

"I am sorry, *señores*, but we have no new information about the girl. For three days we have searched the park, but we have not found her. Maybe she is not here."

"If she's not here," Vernon said, turning to his companions, "then where is she? Let's just say for a minute that she did leave on her own with that boy. Where would they go?"

Lyle nodded. "I know what you're thinking. Let's go check out the hotels in Flores. An American girl with red hair would be hard to miss."

An hour and a half later, they were back on the streets in Flores, where they checked into the first hotel they saw, the Petén Esplendido. They dropped off their packs and talked to the hotel clerk who said no one fitting Melissa's description had stayed there. They spent the remainder of the afternoon walking the streets of Flores and talking to everyone they saw. They paused in every hotel, guesthouse, and restaurant along the cobblestone streets. No one had seen Melissa.

* * *

From where he stood watering the mule, Carlos could see the cenote where they were keeping Melissa. He'd watched as Javier climbed down the ladder and emerged moments later grasping Melissa's arm. Carlos didn't trust Javier. He'd seen the way Javier looked at her, the way he pushed her up against the tree, the way he moved in close—too close—to remove her blindfold.

Melissa hadn't flinched, but he knew she was afraid.

When Javier walked away, Melissa had turned toward him. He'd seen surprise in her eyes, and then relief.

"Hola, señorita," he said now.

She looked at him and then looked away. It was his fault she was here.

He walked to the duffle bag and pulled out a piece of bread and a banana then untied her hands and held them out to her. "I will bring you water."

He walked over to the water jug and filled an empty can with water. Then he knelt in the dirt and pulled out a lighter.

"What are you doing?" César said sharply.

"I'm getting the girl water."

The man narrowed his eyes and stared at Melissa. Carlos placed the can on a rock near the flame.

"Why are you doing this?" asked César, motioning to the fire.

"The water makes her sick."

"Then give her wine," said Javier. "Wine will make her friendlier."

Carlos clenched his fists. "You will not hurt her, Javier."

"Oh, I do not want to hurt her." Javier kissed his fingertips and laughed. "What's the matter, Carlitos? Are you jealous of Javier? Of his ways with *las chicas?*"

"Enough!" César said.

Carlos glared at Javier before returning his attention to the boiling water. He moved it away from the heat and brought it to Melissa.

"What were they saying?" Melissa asked.

"Oh, it is nothing."

"You sounded angry when you talked to them."

Carlos shrugged. "I told you I will not let them hurt you."

"What are they going to do with me?"

Before Carlos could answer, he heard his name. "I must go," he said.

CHAPTER 15

MATT LAY AWAKE MUCH OF the night, playing and replaying the events of the last four days. When Cathy finally stirred, he was already up and dressed.

"We're in an elaborate game of cat and mouse," he said. "They're toying with us."

Cathy nodded. "What kind of monster kidnaps our daughter and then gives us a fruit basket?" She shivered and stared at the untouched basket.

"I don't know. I hate feeling so completely out of control. I've been going over everything, every word, trying to make sense of it. And I can't. They have to want something from us. But what? Why are they playing with us? It doesn't make sense."

"Do you think Melissa is okay?"

"I'm sure she is," he said too quickly. "There's no reason for them to hurt her." Matt walked to the window and pulled back the curtain. He could see mountains in the distance. He turned back from the window to face Cathy. "I can't sit in this room all day waiting."

"What do you want to do?"

"I want to go outside and walk around." When she didn't answer, he sat on the bed next to her. "This person, whoever it is, has gone to a lot of trouble. He wants something, although I can't for the life of me think of what it could be. He knows we're here, cowering in this room, willing to do absolutely anything. I guess I want to take back some little bit of control. He's not going to give up until he has what he wants. But sitting here, waiting for his next bizarre move—I can't do that. I've got to get out of this room, just for a little while. Can you understand that?"

Half an hour later, Cathy and Matt left their hotel room and walked down the open-air corridors to the outer courtyard. It was beautiful by daylight. Green vines covered the crumbling walls that were the remains of the majestic

monastery. Stone steps led to a fountain surrounded by purple and blue flowers. In the middle of the courtyard, a pair of brightly colored macaws sat on a perch.

A group of women selling souvenirs greeted them as they stepped off the hotel grounds. They offered necklaces, key chains, pens. Several women had babies slung on their backs as they reached out to Cathy. "You buy from me? Help me feed my baby?"

"No. Muchas gracias," Matt said as he put his arm around Cathy and led her away.

"Maybe later? You come back and buy from me later?"

"Sí. Maybe later."

As they walked, they saw uniformed school children and street vendors pushing carts. A truck filled with cola bottles drove past, and a woman balancing a woven purse on top of her head walked just ahead of them. Straight ahead and several blocks away, a yellow-and-white arch with a clock tower bridged the road. A bell hung at the top of the tower.

"The Arch of Santa Catalina," Matt said, pointing. He took Cathy's hand as they crossed onto the Calle del Arco. "Before the earthquake destroyed it, there was a convent over there," he said, pointing. "The arch was built to provide a way for the nuns to cross the street without being seen."

Cathy stopped. "What are you doing? How can you talk about this, like you're some kind of tour guide?"

"There's nothing I can do about Melissa right now," Matt said. "If I thought there was anything else I could do, I would do it. But right now someone else is holding all the cards. All we can do is wait. If I just sit in the hotel room and wring my hands, I'll go crazy. I thought maybe if we had a little fresh air, a little distraction, it would clear our minds so we'll be able to think better when the time comes. Kind of like Lamaze. It doesn't really take away the pain, but it makes it bearable."

"Like you know anything about Lamaze."

"Do you think that was easy, watching you give birth?"

Cathy raised her eyebrows and started walking again. "I feel really sorry for you, sitting there in the hospital room all those hours, watching TV and joking with the nurses, waiting for Melissa—" Her voice broke, and she looked away.

They passed under the arch and came to a cathedral. Matching the color and baroque style of the arch, La Merced was covered in a yellow-and-white stucco façade, with arched windows and intricate floral patterns. Statues of saints stood on ornately decorated platforms in alcoves around the door. Columns framed the entrance to the church.

Matt and Cathy stepped inside the cathedral. Wooden benches lined both sides of the center aisle. An altar near the front was draped with a white cloth and covered with flowers and lighted candles. Above it stood a statue of the Virgin Mary; on either side, statues of saints held crucifixes.

A couple entered the cathedral and walked to the altar in the front. As they lit a candle and knelt to pray, Matt and Cathy slid into a pew.

Matt didn't know how long they'd been sitting there before he felt rather than heard someone slip onto the bench directly behind them. The hair on the back of his neck stood on end, and his palms grew moist. He bowed his head and closed his eyes as though to pray. Moments passed without a sound, without a movement. He straightened up in the pew. Cathy leaned against him and reached for his hand.

Did I imagine someone?

He listened. Then he heard it, an almost imperceptible shift in movement right behind him. He felt Cathy stiffen and tighten her grip on his hand. She must have heard it too. He waited for what seemed like an hour. He could hear his heart pounding in his ears, could feel Cathy trembling beside him. He tried to concentrate, make a plan, but his mind wouldn't focus. Then he heard another sound. The sound of someone clearing his throat.

CHAPTER 16

THE COUPLE AT THE ALTAR stood and moved to a pew at the front of the cathedral. After a few moments, they walked down the aisle and out the front door. The cathedral was empty, except for Cathy and Matt and whoever was seated on the bench behind them. Perspiration beaded on Matt's forehead. He stared straight ahead, his jaw set, his heart racing.

He heard a shuffle behind him and then a voice, at once both quiet and urgent.

"Señor," the voice whispered.

This is it. Matt turned.

Seated behind him was Raul Silva. "I am happy to have found you. I have been looking for you," Raul said. "I need to know if you have found your daughter."

"No. No, we haven't. How did you find us?"

"I must confess that I have been keeping track of you."

Just then an elderly man walked into the cathedral and sank onto a bench near the front. He bowed his head. The three sat in silence until he left.

Then Raul leaned forward and whispered, "I am here to help you, but to do that, I need to know what you know. Will you tell me what brought you to Antigua?"

"I'm sorry, but I can't say anything," Matt said.

"I know what you must be thinking. You do not know me. You do not know how I can help you. You are wondering why I am here. Perhaps even you wonder if you can trust me. I understand this. But I assure you that you can. My only wish is to help you find your daughter."

Matt glanced around the cathedral again and dropped his voice to a whisper. "We have reason to believe Melissa is being held against her will."

"Will you tell me this reason?"

Matt shook his head. "I've said too much already, and I must ask you not to repeat it."

"Of course."

Cathy said, "When you left Tikal, you said that you were going to search for information. Did you find anything at all?"

"After I left you, I returned to Flores, and I learned that three men in the nearby town of San Andrés were hired to take a pack mule with supplies into the jungle two days before Melissa disappeared. They were hired by someone from Guatemala City to haul in supplies and set up a camp as part of an archaeological expedition."

"But you don't believe it?" Cathy said.

"It could be the truth. There are many ruins in the Petén."

"But two days before . . ." Matt said.

Raul nodded. "I will see what more I can learn, and then I will talk to you again."

* * *

Melissa opened her eyes; the sun was high in the sky. *I must have fallen asleep.* Her face felt gritty after four days without washing; her lips were parched, and her hair was matted. At least the palm trees provided shade. She could hear monkeys chattering in the jungle.

Carlos sat nearby, whittling a piece of wood.

"What are you making?" Melissa asked.

Carlos flushed and stuffed what looked like a figurine into his pocket. "You are awake, señorita." He stood and walked over to her. She asked for a drink of water, which he prepared and brought before sitting down beside her.

"Javier has gone into town to get more supplies," he said. "Only César and I are here."

Melissa looked around the campsite. She could see the older man dozing in a chair a few yards away, his head dropped forward on his chest.

"César?"

Carlos followed her gaze and nodded.

Melissa studied the older man before turning back to Carlos. "What are they going to do with me?"

"They don't tell me. But they won't hurt you."

Melissa glared at Carlos. "What do you mean they don't tell you? *You* brought me here. Why?"

"I am sorry, señorita. They told me they would give me money. I need money for my family. I had no choice."

"No choice! You could have said 'no.'"

"You have never been hungry, señorita. You do not know what it is to see your brother and your little sisters hungry. To see your mother beg for food. You do not know." His eyes flashed, and he stood to walk away.

"Don't go. Please, stay and talk to me."

Carlos turned and looked at her, shook his head, and moved away.

The afternoon passed slowly. Carlos avoided Melissa. The only time he came close to her was when he brought her water or a piece of bread, and then he refused to talk.

Melissa's back ached from sitting in one place. She longed to stand, to walk around and stretch her legs. She craved real food. As always, her thoughts returned to her parents and to Josh, and she wondered where they were and what they were doing. Mostly, she wondered if they would find her and if she would be alive when they did.

Late in the afternoon, Carlos again approached her. He handed her a drink and waited for her to swallow the lukewarm water. When he spoke, his voice was harsh. "You live in the United States. You have everything. You come to our country and then you go home to your big house and big car. How is it fair that you have everything and I have nothing?"

Melissa stared at him. "I don't know."

"You do not know because it is not fair. You were born there, and I was born here. You come here to see our country. You stay in fancy hotels and eat in expensive restaurants. You walk around in your fancy clothes and stare at us like we are animals in a zoo."

"That's not true. I am here because my father wanted me to see the land and people he loves so much. All my life he has told me about Guatemala."

"What does he know about Guatemala?"

"He spent two years of his life living here and helping people."

"Helping them? How did he help them? Did he give them his money?"

"No, he gave them something more important than money. He taught them about Jesus Christ."

"He did not help them." Carlos sneered.

"That's not true. He taught them where to find answers, how to find hope and peace in their lives."

"Hope?" Carlos laughed. "Hope for what? Money to buy food?"

When Melissa didn't answer, Carlos continued. "There is no hope when you are born in Guatemala. There is only getting enough food to live and to help your family live." He paused then added bitterly, "My father left when I was ten years old."

"You told me he died."

"He is dead to me. He left my mother without food, without money, without anything except his children."

"That must have been very hard."

"What do you know about hard? How could my father leave his family?" Melissa's voice dropped to a whisper. "I'm really sorry, Carlos."

"I am sorry too."

"But there is hope, Carlos. I know there is."

He looked away from her. His words came slowly. "It is easy to hope when you have everything you want. Your father works in an office and brings you on trips. My father left me without food to eat."

"God will help you if you ask Him to. I know He will."

"What has God ever done for me?"

"You have to ask Him for help."

"Does God help you? Is He helping you now? No, señorita, God will not rescue you."

"You don't know that. Miracles happen."

"Not in Guatemala."

"My father saw miracles happen when he was here. Miracles happened to people who had faith."

"What miracles? What people?"

"People he taught. His friends."

"Friends," Carlos mocked.

"That's how my father got into his business, from a friend in Guatemala."

"What business?"

"My father imports jade," Melissa said.

"Your father steals our jade? Maybe that is why they want him."

"What do you mean they want my father?"

Carlos shrugged. "I hear things," he said as he turned and walked away.

* * *

Cathy and Matt remained in the cathedral for several minutes after Raul left. Cathy's head was spinning. Most of the time, she felt like she was walking around in a fog, going through the motions. And then there were moments of sheer suffocating terror, moments when reality washed over her without warning and she felt as though she would collapse.

But now, she felt neither. Waiting for a madman to show himself had her on edge.

"Are you doing okay?" Matt said.

"Am I okay? Are you really asking that?" Her voice held more anger than she intended.

"You know what I mean." When Cathy didn't answer, Matt said, "Do you blame me for this?"

Did she? If he'd been with them in Tikal, maybe it wouldn't have happened. And he should have been there. She opened her mouth to say something and then closed it. It wasn't Matt's fault. It was just easier to have someone to blame.

"Let's go back to the hotel," Cathy said.

They walked to the hotel in silence. Matt unlocked the door and glanced around the room and then sat beside Cathy on the bed. "I'm sorry I wasn't here, Cathy."

"It's not your fault."

"But part of you thinks it is."

"That part of me is wrong."

Just then the phone in their room rang. Cathy froze. "Someone must have been watching for us to come in," she said.

The phone rang again.

"Put it on speaker," Cathy said. Matt nodded and pushed the button then picked up the receiver.

"Hola," an unfamiliar voice said.

"Who is this?"

"I do hope you are enjoying your stay here; it's a nice hotel, don't you think?"

"What do you want?"

"How is your wife, Mr. Miller? She looks very much like your daughter."

Cathy caught her breath. She covered her mouth with both hands and closed her eyes as she fought to control her breathing.

"What have you done with Melissa?" Matt said.

Silence.

"Please tell me what you want." Matt's voice dropped to a near-whisper. "Don't hurt my daughter, I beg you. Please don't hurt her. I'll do anything."

"Of course you will," the man said.

There was a long silence before the man spoke again. "I trust that you haven't spoken to anyone?"

"No. No, I haven't."

"Good. Now, don't leave your room again."

"I won't. Just, please, don't hurt my daughter."

Silence and then faint breathing on the other end of the line. Faint breathing and then a click.

CHAPTER 17

ELLA, BLANCHE, AND LILA WERE just finishing breakfast when Scott confronted them.

"You've got to understand that what they're doing isn't safe," he said, with more than a little annoyance in his voice. "Melissa is a needle in a haystack at this point."

Blanche looked Scott straight in the eye. "Now, you listen here. You may run this tour, but that doesn't mean you run us. And if our husbands want to help find a lost girl, well, I for one am proud of them."

Word of the men's disappearance spread like wildfire.

"I just wish I'd known about it and gone with them," expressed more than one of the remaining members of the group as they rallied around the three wives. Blanche relished the attention. She was proud of her man and happy to let everyone know it. Ella expressed confidence in the men's ability to be led by the Spirit and said she was sure they would be protected. Only Lila remained silent. Finally Blanche and Ella took her aside.

"You're being awfully quiet," Blance said. "Is something bothering you?"

Lila shook her head and turned away.

"Lila, this is me you're talking to. Are you sure you're okay?"

And then the tears came, first in just a trickle then in sobs.

"I really think they'll be okay," Ella said.

"It's not that." Lila sniffed.

"What's going on, my friend?" Blanche asked.

It took some prodding, but finally Lila opened up. They hadn't told anyone, but they'd had some bad news just before the trip. Lyle had gone to the doctor for a routine checkup, and the doctor had ordered an EKG. And it didn't look good. The doctor suspected a blockage and said Lyle needed surgery, but their tickets for the Book of Mormon tour were already bought, so the doctor agreed

to schedule it for three weeks from when the EKG had been taken, after Lyle and Lila returned from Guatemala. "One last hurrah before they cut me open," Lyle had said.

"He promised he'd take it easy," Lila said. "And now he's doing this. I tried to talk to him before he left, but he wouldn't listen. Said he was an old man who'd spent his life living for himself, and now it was time to do something for somebody else."

"Your husband is about the most unselfish man I've ever known," Ella said.

"I know, but I guess that's not how he sees it. And he wasn't about to sit on the bench for this one."

"The Lord will take care of him," Blanche said.

"If you walk in front of a train, you're going to get hit, no matter how good you are. That's what I told him before he left, but he just said if it was his time to go, then it was his time to go. He wanted to die knowing he'd done some good in the world."

"Oh, Lila, I had no idea."

"Nobody did. Maybe I should have told Gary, but Lyle made me promise not to, and he would have been so mad at me if I had. I couldn't bear to have him leave mad. I knew I couldn't talk him out of it, and I couldn't have him be mad at me, in case—" Her voice broke. "He said they needed him because he was the only one who spoke Spanish."

* * *

Gary suggested the three men head back to the airport. If Melissa was no longer in Tikal, she must have traveled through Flores. The sun was low in the sky, and they knew that little daylight remained.

No one in the airport remembered seeing Melissa. The answer was always the same: "No, no señores. A red-haired girl we would remember. She has not been here."

As they were leaving the airport, a man seated behind a counter beckoned to them.

"I think I remember seeing the girl you are looking for, but it was a few days ago. Are you sure she is still in Flores?"

"When did you see her?" Gary asked.

"Was she with anyone?" said Lyle.

"Do you know where she was going?" asked Vernon.

The man shook his head. "I cannot help you more. I am sorry, but I do not remember. Many people come and go every day. I only remember that I saw her."

Gary wrote his phone number on a piece of paper and handed it to the man. "We're staying at the Petén Esplendido," he said. "If you remember anything else, or if you see her again, please call us."

The man studied the number and then asked, "Why are you looking for this girl?"

Gary explained the situation to the man, ending with, "She'd met a boy in Tikal, and we think she was with him when she disappeared."

The man listened carefully. "What you want to know is where someone would go who did not want to be found." He waited for the men to nod before he continued. "Maybe it is not Flores."

The man reached under the counter and pulled out a map of Guatemala. He opened it on the counter in front of them and circled Flores with his finger. "We are here," he said. Then he pointed at each of the villages surrounding Lago Petén Itzá: Santa Elena, San Miguel, San Andrés, El Remate, and others. "If people want to sightsee, yes, they come to our beautiful Flores. But if they want to disappear, they go someplace else." He studied the map and then pointed at Santa Elena. "I would begin my search here." He leaned forward over the counter and whispered, "The authorities there—they would not pay attention to a girl. And even if there was a problem, they could be bribed to look the other way. It would be easy for someone to take her there and disappear." He nodded and sat up straight.

Gary pulled out his wallet to pay for the map, but the man at the counter held up his hands in protest. "No, no, señor. You take it. I want to help you find this missing girl."

They thanked him for the map and for his information, and then they stepped out of the airport and headed back toward their hotel.

***

A man carrying a briefcase and a newspaper approached the desk clerk in the airport. He folded his newspaper and mentioned casually, "You are a good man, señor. They were North Americans. They would have paid handsomely for that map."

The desk clerk nodded. "It is true, señor, but they are looking for a missing girl, and it is all I could do to help them."

"A missing girl? What is this about?"

The desk clerk explained what he had just been told.

Eduardo Guerrero pulled several coins from his pocket. "May I pay for their map, to honor you for your kindness to them?" he asked. "And perhaps you would be kind enough to let me buy another map from you as well."

"Of course."

Eduardo thanked the desk clerk and picked up the map. "Did the men mention where they are staying tonight?" he asked. "I need to find a place to stay, and perhaps I could help them."

"I believe they are staying at the Petén Esplendido."

Soon Eduardo Guerrero was settled in a room at the Petén Esplendido. He smiled to himself when he thought about how easily he had acquired this last bit of information. Now he had to decide what to do about the old men. He could silence them easily enough. A few quetzales to the desk clerk and he would have their room number. But that would draw attention. Better to let them poke around, at least for now. Left to themselves, he considered them to be little more than an annoyance. But they were an annoyance that had to be watched.

Unfortunately he couldn't be in two places at the same time.

Eduardo glanced at his watch. Sitting on the edge of the bed, he picked up the remote and turned the TV on, flipping through the channels, pausing occasionally. Finally he turned it off. He stood again and walked to the table where he poured himself a drink.

There was a knock on the door.

Eduardo cracked the door. His eyes narrowed when he saw Javier. "I expected César," he said as Javier entered the room.

"César sent me. He didn't want to leave the girl alone with Carlos."

"And why is that?"

Javier shrugged. "Carlos feels sorry for her."

"And the girl?"

Javier smirked. "We are taking care of her."

"See that you do. I need her alive. Now, do you have a friend who would like to make some money?"

"Sí."

"Good. Bring me your friend in an hour, and we will talk."

An hour later Javier returned with a young man he introduced as Alfonso. Eduardo motioned for the two men to sit across from him. "I need a man who can see things but not be seen and hear things but not be heard. Are you this man?"

Alfonso nodded.

"There are three men staying in this hotel," Eduardo said. "Older men from the United States. I want you to find them and watch them. I want to know where they go and what they do. Tomorrow night at eleven o'clock, you

will come to this room and wait for my call." He stood to dismiss the others. "I trust you will not disappoint me."

* * *

Cathy watched the hands on the clock move slowly from one number to another. All they could do was pray and wait.

"When this nightmare is over, I'm going to be a better father," Matt said. "I've been too hard on her."

"You've done the important things."

"Have I? I've worked hard and provided her with a house and food to eat."

"And braces and clothes and piano lessons and about a million other things."

"A dad is supposed to be able to fix everything. That's what dads do," Matt said. "I think deep down, underneath it all, I've been scared she would do something I can't fix."

"That's why you don't like Josh."

"Yeah. That's why I don't like Josh. I've never felt as completely powerless as I have in the last few months. It's like we've lost our girl."

The irony of his words washed over Cathy, bringing with them a fresh wave of pain.

Matt slipped his arm around Cathy and pulled her close. "We're going to find her, Cathy, and we're going to take her home."

They lay awake in the dark, each absorbed in their own thoughts. Sleep finally came, providing temporary relief.

Cathy awoke to Matt's moaning. She flipped on the light and shook him. "It's a dream, Matt, just a dream. It's not real."

His body was covered in cold sweat. She held him in her arms and stroked his hair. He clung to her; she listened for his breathing to slow and his body to relax. Finally he leaned back against the pillow.

"It was so real, so real."

"Was it Melissa?"

Matt nodded but didn't elaborate. "I can't stop thinking about her out there in the dark. At first I worried about jaguars and crocodiles. But now that I know—" His voice broke. "I can't get his voice out of my head. I keep hearing it over and over, taunting me."

Cathy held Matt until he drifted back to sleep. And then the panic came again, seizing Cathy, overpowering her. She was suffocating. She sat up in the bed and tried to breathe. *So cold.* Cathy pulled the covers high around her chin

and cuddled against Matt, but nothing could warm her. Shivering under the blankets, she tried to think of anything except the one thing her mind refused to forget. And she waited for dawn.

* * *

Carlos hardly spoke to Melissa the rest of the evening. She tried unsuccessfully to engage him in conversation, but he remained aloof and unwilling to talk. She ate her evening rations and then waited until the shadows deepened in the jungle and her inevitable return to the pit. When the time came, César approached Melissa and said something she couldn't understand. He motioned for her to stand and pushed her toward the hole and the ladder.

She lay on the stone floor, listening to the jungle sounds and waiting for morning. *How long?* As she lay in the dirt, filthy and bone weary, she thought about what Carlos had said earlier that day. *He's wrong,* she thought. *There is hope. There is always hope. Even for me.* The thought surprised her. It had been several months since she'd thought about such things, since she had prayed. But now she poured out her soul to the One Being besides her captors who knew where she was and could help her. Peace finally came, and she drifted off to sleep.

It was still dark when she awoke suddenly and knew she was not alone. She lay still, listening for any sound, her heart pounding in her ears. And then she heard a slight shuffle and felt a hand closing over her mouth, stifling her scream.

CHAPTER 18

Day 6

"Señorita," a familiar voice whispered. "It's me, Carlos." He was shaking Melissa's shoulder; she could feel his breath beside her ear. She tried to speak, but his hand tightened on her mouth. "You must be quiet and come with me now," he said, dragging her to her feet. He pushed her toward the ladder and up its steps. With his free arm around her waist, he gripped her arm and propelled her forward, past César lying asleep on the ground. Melissa stumbled on a tree root and cried out. César stirred and mumbled in his sleep. Carlos squeezed Melissa's arm, holding her completely still until César was breathing evenly again. Then steadily, stealthily, they moved toward the blackness of the jungle.

Far away, deep in the jungle, Melissa heard the roar of a howler monkey and shuddered.

They walked without speaking for nearly an hour before he relaxed his hold on her and spoke again. By then daylight was approaching and they were far from camp, surrounded by tall mahogany and ceiba trees.

"I was afraid for you," he finally said. "Those men—I do not trust them. I did not want them to hurt you."

"You rescued me?"

He stared off into the distance. "We must keep moving. They will be looking for us."

* * *

After a restless night of sleep, Vernon, Lyle, and Gary went in search of the breakfast buffet. They loaded their plates and found a spot outside where they could spread out the map.

"I've been thinking about the best strategy here," Vernon said. He pointed at Flores on the map. "Here's where we are." He traced the perimeter of Lake Petén Itzá with his finger. "We need to check out all these places. I was wondering if we should split up. Divide and conquer—"

"Except you don't speak Spanish," Lyle broke in.

"I think we should stay together and head straight for Santa Elena," Gary said. "We've got to start somewhere, and from what the man in the airport said, it's probably our best bet."

A few tables away, a young man sat with his back to the men. He finished his juice and prepared to leave.

* * *

Melissa and Carlos spoke only rarely as they pushed through the rainforest. The air was stagnant; humidity made the temperature almost unbearable. Carlos's canteen was nearly empty, and thirst was taking its toll. Giant trees sheltered smaller ones in a dim world where sunlight barely filtered through the dense canopy. The thick undergrowth made progress slow. The need to be quiet kept them both on edge. Finally Carlos directed Melissa to a small clearing where they could rest.

They sat in silence for several minutes before Melissa turned to face Carlos. "How do I know if I can trust you?"

Carlos didn't answer immediately. When he spoke, his voice was quiet and tired. "If they find us, what do you think they will do with me? I was promised money to bring you to them and then to make sure you didn't get away." He stared into the jungle. "I did not know what would happen to you. I only needed money for my family. I did not want you to be hurt. Do you believe me?"

She met his eyes and nodded. "Do you know where we are?"

"We are away from the camp. They will not find us here."

In every direction, Melissa could see nothing but green—thick green foliage everywhere she looked.

"No one will find us here," he repeated.

She turned back to him, panic rising in her throat. "No one will find us? Then how will I get back to my family? To the United States?"

"Maybe your God will help you."

She stared at him. Was he mocking her? "Maybe He will," she said, turning her face away from him so he could not see that tears had formed in her eyes.

It was a long time before Melissa and Carlos spoke again. The heat was stifling. Melissa licked her lips and tasted salt. Her hair hung around her

shoulders. It had been five days since she had washed it, five days of sweating during the day and lying in the dirt at night. She dragged her fingers through the tangled strands, pulling out twigs and pieces of grass. It was useless.

"I'm thirsty," she said.

Carlos nodded and looked away. He didn't answer at once, and when he did, his voice was pleading.

"Señorita, I brought you here because I was afraid for you. I thought it would be better for you to run away and be here than to stay there." He sought her eyes. "I know some things, how to survive—some things. I will do my best."

Melissa knew what he was saying. She had to be strong, had to be a part of this. They had to be a team. She watched as he studied the ground and waited for her response.

"Do you think we will be okay?"

He stared out into the jungle and shook his head. "I don't know."

"Do you know where we are?"

"I know that we are away from the camp."

"Are there any towns nearby where we could get help?"

"If we walk far enough, maybe we will find something."

"What about wild animals? My dad said there were jaguars."

"Your dad was right. There are jaguars, pumas, snakes, other things." He shrugged. "It is the rainforest."

"But you know how to keep us safe, right?" She tried to keep the panic out of her voice.

"I will do the best I can," he said again. "That is all I can promise you. Do you think I should have left you there?"

"I don't know."

Carlos nodded and looked down at the ground again. She thought of the men who had been guarding her. She thought of Javier and how he had looked at her. No matter how afraid she was now, she could not wish to be back in camp with those men.

* * *

César awakened and noticed that Carlos was gone. Strange. He slid out of his blankets, dressed, and walked to the duffle bag to pull out the last chunk of bread. It was a good thing Javier was coming with more supplies. César glanced around, but there was no sign of Carlos.

"Where has that boy gone to?" he muttered under his breath. "What good is he, leaving me here to do everything?"

He walked around the edge of the camp before plopping down on a stool to finish his breakfast. He chewed slowly, listening for voices or twigs cracking, sounds of Carlos returning from a morning stroll, but all he heard were the sounds of the jungle awakening.

He glanced toward the cenote. Something was different. The ladder. The top of the ladder was poking out of the hole. He was sure they'd removed it the night before. He walked to the edge of the cenote and called down, but there was no answer. Cursing, he climbed down the ladder steps. When he reached the bottom, he stood still, waiting for his eyes to adjust to the darkness. And when they did, he knew he was alone.

César climbed out of the pit and looked again for any sign of Carlos or the girl. He shouldn't have trusted Carlos; the boy had been getting too friendly with her. César should have sent him for supplies instead of Javier. He walked around the site, looking for anything out of place. Only Carlos's backpack was missing.

Systematically, he began checking the perimeter of the camp. He knelt on the ground and searched for broken twigs or bent branches. After examining the forest floor, he moved a few steps and repeated the process, continuing around the campsite until he found the place where Carlos and Melissa had left. He looked ahead into the jungle, mentally following their path.

The sun was climbing in the sky. Soon it would be too hot to make good progress.

César picked up his duffle bag, pausing to look around the campsite one last time. He stepped into the jungle and headed in the direction where he was sure he would find Carlos and Melissa; he walked quickly, confidently, following the trail they had not intended to leave. It was not hard. *Two people traveling together in the dark leave clues.*

CHAPTER 19

RAUL STEPPED OFF THE SMALL airplane in Flores and walked toward Petén Esplendido. He needed a place to store his things, even if only temporarily, and there wasn't any other choice but to get a room. *A shower wouldn't hurt either*, he thought. *And a change of clothes.*

An hour later, Raul was back on the street. He walked along the cobblestone sidewalk and caught a tuk tuk to cross the island causeway into Santa Elena. He walked through the marketplace, watching for someone he knew. And finally he saw him.

The man looked different. Older but much the same—his build, the way he carried himself when he walked. Adán was a few years older than Raul. Large for his age, he had used his physical prowess to intimidate the smaller boys when they were young. And Raul had been among the smallest.

Although he hadn't seen Adán in the intervening years, he had heard of him often enough. In just the last twenty-four hours, almost everyone he spoke with had mentioned Adán's name. It seemed Adán was deeply entrenched in Guatemala's underworld.

Raul watched as Adán moved through the marketplace, his eyes shifting from side to side, occasionally glancing over his shoulder. He was looking for someone. He stopped and turned toward Raul, as if he could feel eyes watching him. Raul stood in the shadow, waiting for the right moment.

As Raul watched, another man approached Adán from behind and greeted him. Then both men turned toward Raul, and he found himself facing a man he had tried not to think about for the better part of two decades. A man he could never forget.

Raul had always known this day would come, known he would see Marcos again. But he was unprepared for the icy stabbing in his chest. It had been nearly thirty years. Thirty years of praying to forgive. But now, now that he

saw him again, he wondered if it had all been for nothing. Memories flooded his mind, vivid pictures he thought he had erased. Tears stung at his eyelids, but he forced them back. And then came the anger, an anger that had nearly overcome him once before. Hatred filled his body. He felt his fists clench and forced them open again.

Sofia. Her name came to his mind unbidden and, with it, a surge of grief he'd thought he could no longer feel. And then, there she was in his mind— her smile, her eyes, dark and luminous. He closed his eyes and could smell her perfume, could feel the gentle brush of her lips on his cheek.

Raul turned away from the marketplace and took several steps toward the street. *I can't do this. I can't confront this man.* Not now, not yet.

But you must. Another girl's life may depend on it.

He heard the voice as clearly as if someone had spoken it, but he knew no one had. The words pierced him.

I can't do this.

Once more he heard the voice. *But you must.* And then he prayed, prayed again for the strength to forgive.

He didn't know how long he stood in the shadows battling feelings too raw to ignore. He had hoped for instant peace, but that didn't come, and he knew he couldn't wait much longer. Still, he hesitated, watching as people jostled past him, selecting, weighing, and paying for fresh produce from the tables piled with tomatoes, bananas, mushrooms, and peppers. Two black-eyed children smiled shyly at him from behind stacked bags of grain, and women near him bartered for pieces of woven cloth. He could smell the freshly slaughtered chicken.

It was time.

CHAPTER 20

LYLE DIDN'T TELL THE OTHERS when his chest started to hurt. He'd toughed out much worse things than a little pain. Why, he'd practically cut his leg off that time he'd let the ax slip from his hands when he was chopping wood for the stove. He hadn't stopped then, and he wasn't about to stop now. Instead, he led his friends through the streets of Flores and across the causeway into the ramshackle town of Santa Elena, where the streets were thick with dust and dirt. If he was more quiet than usual, nobody noticed.

Immediately they were approached by those who would sell them everything from sunglasses and watches to bootleg CDs.

"My wife would love this place," Vernon said, his attempt at a whisper undermined by his hearing loss. "She's always on the lookout for a bargain."

"Kind of glad the ladies aren't with us right now," Gary said.

Lyle moved straight ahead without commenting. The pain had moved into his shoulder and wasn't letting up. "I don't have time for this," he muttered under his breath.

"Did you say something, Lyle?" Gary said.

He shook his head and grimaced. He clasped his shoulder and squeezed it.

"Are you okay?" said Vernon.

Again he nodded and kept walking. The pain was getting worse, but he couldn't stop. He was the only one who spoke Spanish, and the others wouldn't get far without him. They needed him, a young girl needed him, and that was all there was to it.

As they made their way toward the marketplace, a little girl carrying a handful of jade necklaces approached him. He shook his head and moved on. *Just keep moving.* The pain worsened, and he gasped a little. Everyone around him was fading, their voices becoming fainter with each step.

Lyle stopped and tried to breathe.

Vernon and Gary paused beside him. "That looks like a bank," Vernon said.

"I don't think they went to a bank, Vernon, do you?" Gary said.

"Probably not. Well, then, this way looks promising," Vernon said, pointing to their right.

Gary nodded and turned to Lyle. "Hey, what's going on? You look terrible."

Gary's voice echoed in Lyle's head as he tried to respond. Everything around him was darkening, closing in. His head began to spin. He reached out to grab Vernon's arm as his knees buckled.

* * *

Cathy and Matt spent the day in their hotel room, waiting, rehearsing scenarios as they tried to think through any eventuality.

"I've prayed harder since all of this started than I've ever prayed in my life," Cathy said. "I keep telling Heavenly Father I'll do anything—anything at all—if we can just get her back."

Matt nodded. "I've been doing the same thing. Trying to strike a bargain, I guess. My life—my whole life—for hers."

"I've sat here and thought about every stupid, petty thing I've ever done. I've promised to be better, if—"

Matt reached over and took her hand. He traced the contour of her fingers. "He isn't punishing us."

"I know, but—"

"But you're not perfect?" Matt studied Cathy's face. "Don't be so hard on yourself."

"But this is my fault, Matt. You don't say it, but I'm sure you must think it. I turned my back on her. I walked away from them so I could have some privacy while I talked to you. I trusted her to do what I asked her to do, and I shouldn't have. I should have known she was impulsive and would take off with that boy. She's done things like that before. She didn't used to, but with Josh, she has. I should never have left her alone with a boy I didn't know."

Matt went to the window. He pulled back the curtain and stared at the grounds outside. Then he turned to face Cathy. "So why did you?"

Cathy's face crumpled.

"Blaming isn't going to do any good," he said. "Blaming you, blaming myself. It doesn't help anything."

Cathy escaped to the bathroom. Matt heard the bathroom door close and then water running. He balled his fist and smacked the window frame. After a few minutes, he heard the door open and turned to see Cathy emerge. Her eyes were swollen.

"I'm sorry, Cathy," Matt said.

"It doesn't matter."

"It does matter."

Cathy sat on the bed and glanced over at Matt's open suitcase. Her eyes widened. "Where did you get that thing?"

"I'm just trying to protect my family."

"And how is that going to protect your family? You've never shot a gun in your life."

"I just want to protect my family," Matt repeated.

"And you're going to do that by handing a gun to this person, this monster who has our daughter? You know that's what will happen, don't you?"

"Cathy, I don't want to fight with you. But I can't go into this without some way to protect myself if I have to. I know I don't have a lot of experience—"

"You mean any?"

"I know I don't have much experience, but it's the best I can do. Do you really want me to meet this madman without any way to protect myself?"

Cathy shook her head. "I'm sorry. I'm just so scared."

"I know. So am I."

* * *

Javier walked to the marketplace in Santa Elena where he bought fresh bread, fruit, and cheese. He paused to watch some boys playing with a ball. His eyes drifted to a group of girls laughing, and he thought of the girl back in camp. He remembered how she looked—so different from the girls before him.

Turning from the marketplace, Javier continued along the dusty cobblestone street until he saw Alfonso standing in the shadows, staring at something across the street. Javier followed his friend's eyes and saw the old men. Mr. Guerrero had been right—they were easy to find.

"Hola," Javier said as he approached Alfonso. "I see you found the *gringos*."

"You'd better get out of here. I don't want to make that guy mad."

"Ah, loosen up; nobody's watching us." Javier glanced around the streets. "So, are they doing anything interesting?"

Alfonso shrugged. "Not really. What do you think he's going to pay me?"

"You mean *us*, don't you?"

"Us? What're you doing besides keeping me from doing my job?"

Javier snickered. "Some job. Stand around and watch gringos all day. I expect to get a cut of whatever you get. Don't forget if it wasn't for me, you wouldn't have a job."

"What do you think they're doing?"

Javier followed his friend's gaze and watched as two of the men reached for the third and helped him sit on the sidewalk.

"We should move closer so we can hear what they're saying," Javier said with a broad smile.

"Aren't you supposed to be going somewhere today?"

"It doesn't matter when I leave. Nobody's going anywhere."

"It's your neck," Alfonso said as he pushed off the wall and moved toward the three men.

Javier followed. "Let's ask them if they need help. It'll be fun."

"Are you crazy? I'm supposed to watch them, not make friends with them."

"Yeah, well, something is wrong with that guy. He looks like he's dying. What if he dies? Then how are you going to feel?"

Alfonso shot a hard look at Javier. "Slow down." He stopped in the shadows just a few feet from the Americans. "I'm doing what I'm getting paid to do, okay? If he dies, that's his problem."

"I hope Mr. Guerrero sees it that way," Javier said. He knew he was playing with Alfonso, but he didn't care. When Alfonso didn't answer, Javier continued. "Well, if you're not going to do anything, then I am."

Javier walked over to the three men, glancing back just once to grin at Alfonso. *"Hola, señores. ¿Cómo están? ¿Les puedo ayudar en algo?"*

One of the men looked blankly at Javier. "We don't speak Spanish," he said. "Do you speak any English? Our friend needs a doctor—a hospital. Can you help us?"

"Yo no hablo inglés," Javier said.

The man lying on the ground moaned and grabbed the arm of the one who had just spoken. "No hospital." He swallowed and closed his eyes. "In my pack . . . medicine."

Javier watched as the second man rummaged through the pack until he found a bottle of tablets and said, "Nitroglycerin. Isn't that for his heart?" He opened the bottle and dumped a tablet into his palm.

"Put it under his tongue," the other man said.

Javier looked over his shoulder at Alfonso. The two men continued talking.

"Did you know he had a heart condition?" one said.

"Not a clue," said the other.

Javier raised his eyebrows. "Maybe he *is* going to die," he mouthed, clutching his chest.

Alfonso made a face; Javier laughed and called out to him. "You're too worried, my friend. The gringos don't understand a word I'm saying."

He turned back to the men. They were looking at him, their expressions a mixture of disgust and desperation. One reached out his hand. "Please help us," he said. "We've got to find a doctor."

He could help them, but why should he? It didn't matter to him if the man lived. He shrugged and repeated, *"Yo no hablo inglés."*

He looked at the sky and then back toward Alfonso. "It is time for me to go. *Tengo una cita con una hermosa chica pelirroja de cabello largo, ojos verdes, y piel blanca y suave al tacto."* Javier's eyes traveled back to the three men, who showed no reaction to his words. He kissed his fingers, touched the rim of his baseball cap in a salute, and grinned at Alfonso as he started to walk away from the three men. "You have fun here," he said and laughed then sauntered down the sidewalk toward the mule he had left in a side street. Swinging the pack onto the mule's back, he headed for camp.

CHAPTER 21

RAUL MOVED THROUGH THE CROWDED marketplace without taking his eyes off the two men. After the initial shock of seeing Marcos again, he had forced his feelings into submission. Now he studied Marcos and Adán. It was strange to see them here, to see them together again. Once, the three of them had shared a schoolyard and a soccer field.

As a child, Raul had attended a Catholic school, a rare opportunity for a Maya boy but a privilege offered him by Marcos's father in exchange for many hours of hard labor. Raul's father had been a hired hand, working the fields day after day. But children did not understand the price their parents paid. Raul did not know that he was different; he only knew that he and Marcos were boys. And so they grew up together, the best of friends.

And when the time came, together they joined the Guatemalan Army, where they were taught how to kill a man in less time than it took to ask his name, where boys became monsters who could destroy entire villages for no reason other than that they were told to.

Raul approached the two men. When he was within earshot, he paused to listen, but their voices were too low to be understood.

Just then Marcos turned to face Raul. Raul watched as Marcos glanced at him, recognized him. Marcos's face paled, and he stepped backward.

Raul moved toward him. "It's been a long time," he said, his voice low.

"Why are you here, Raul?"

Raul's eyes were unflinching. His short laugh held no humor. "Getting right to the point, are you, Marcos? Don't you want to know how I've been all these years?" The two men stared at each other, oblivious to the third man, who stood behind Marcos. When Marcos didn't respond, Raul shifted his gaze to Adán, the man he had come to find.

"I have been looking for you. Could we go somewhere to speak privately?"

"What do you want, Raul?" said Adán.

Raul dropped his voice. "I was told you could help me move merchandise through the Petén."

"And where did you hear that?"

"Here and there. Are you interested?"

Adán didn't answer at once. Finally he said, "I am busy now. If you want to talk, come to La Cueva de la Serpiente tonight at nine o'clock. There we will be undisturbed."

Raul nodded. He turned and stared straight into Marcos's eyes. Marcos returned his gaze, but neither man said anything.

Raul walked away. He forced his feet to move steadily through the crowd. Forced his eyes to focus on what lie ahead.

Turning from the marketplace, he walked down the street. He wanted to run, to scream, but he knew he couldn't. Waves of nausea threatened to overcome him, but he walked on until he could go no longer and took refuge in a side street. There, away from the crowd, he collapsed against the side of the building, his body retching again and again. He slid down the wall and pressed his face against the building. His shoulders shook as sobs wracked his body.

Just a few feet away, a woman pushed a cart piled with tapestries down the sidewalk. A soda truck drove by.

Raul didn't know how long he had been in the alleyway giving vent to his feelings, but the emotion had passed, and it was time to move on. He needed to think clearly; to do that, he had to stifle his feelings. He looked at his watch and calculated how long he had before he needed to meet Adán.

A young boy weaving through the people on the sidewalk caught Raul's eye. The boy was slim and ragged, with shaggy black hair, but unlike the other boys Raul saw, he appeared to be alone and without anything to sell. The boy approached each person, spoke with them, and then moved on.

Across the road, a group of men drew Raul's attention. They were congregated on the street corner, jostling each other and laughing raucously. His eyes were on them when the boy approached him.

"Señor, por favor." The boy held out a crumpled photograph. "My brother," the boy said. "I am looking for my brother. Have you seen him?"

Raul glanced at the photograph and shook his head. "I'm sorry, but I cannot help you." His eyes returned to the men. Beyond them, he could see a café. He wasn't hungry, but he knew he needed to eat.

Raul was nearly across the street when the impression came to go back. At first, he disregarded it, but then it came again, more forcefully. Turning,

he watched the boy moving down the sidewalk. When the impression came a third time, it could no longer be ignored.

"Please, could I see the picture again?" Raul asked when he reached the boy.

"Do you know him then? Do you know where he is?"

Raul took the photograph and studied it. "This is your brother?"

"Sí. He has been gone for six days, and my mother is worried. Always before he comes back." His voice dropped to a whisper. "She says she knows he is dead. She wails and says she needs to find him so she can give him a proper burial."

"When your brother left, did he tell you where he was going?"

"No, señor. He said he had a job."

Raul nodded as he memorized the photograph. "How old is your brother?"

"He is nineteen."

"And you?"

"I am ten, señor."

"And do you and your brother have names?"

The boy nodded. "I am Juan," he said. "And my brother is Carlos."

Raul handed the picture back. "I am sorry I cannot help you, Juan, but I have not seen your brother." Raul searched the boy's eyes and saw his disappointment. *Why did I feel I had to come back? To give this boy false hope? What do You want me to do?*

As the boy turned to leave, the feeling came again, compelling Raul to stop the boy once more. "If I do learn something, tell me where I can find you and your mother."

Raul listened as Juan gave him directions to his home and then watched as the boy continued down the street. *Why?*

Just then he heard his name and turned to see who was calling him. A man was hurrying toward him.

"Am I glad to see you," Vernon said. "You're from the Book of Mormon tour, right?" Vernon motioned for Raul to follow. Straight ahead, Raul could see Lyle lying on the sidewalk, with Gary squatted beside him. Raul forced his mind to focus on what Vernon was saying.

". . . his heart. We've got to get him to a hospital."

Raul knelt beside the man lying on the sidewalk. His skin was grayer than normal, but his breathing was relaxed and steady.

"What happened?"

"Not sure. Maybe a heart attack. We found nitroglycerin in his pack," Gary said.

"We can talk later," Vernon said. "We need to get him to a hospital now."

Raul leaned back on his heels. "He will need to go to Guatemala City for a hospital."

"Guatemala City? But . . ."

Raul looked down at Lyle again. The color in his face was improving. Raul stroked Lyle's cheek; Lyle grimaced and opened his eyes.

"Didn't expect to see you here," Lyle said.

"How are you feeling?"

"Good as new. What's everybody doing sitting around when there's work to be done?"

Raul looked up at Gary and Vernon. "Maybe it would be best to take him to a hotel where he can rest until I find a doctor." When the others nodded, he walked to the edge of the street and hailed a tuk tuk. He didn't need this. Not now. Not with everything else.

"You call that a taxi?" Vernon said as the red tuk tuk pulled up beside the curb. "That's a golf cart as I live and breathe. A golf cart with three wheels! How are we going to get back to our hotel in that?"

Gary climbed in the back and slid across the short seat. Vernon helped Lyle into the back then wedged in beside him. "At least he won't be able to go anywhere," Vernon said.

Raul climbed in front and directed the taxi driver to the Petén Esplendido in Flores.

When they reached the hotel, Raul handed the driver a handful of quetzales, and the three men eased Lyle out of the tuk tuk and into the building.

Raul saw the others to a room and then stepped out into the hallway to make a phone call. When he returned, Lyle was resting on the bed; his color was almost normal. Raul sank into a chair beside the bed and looked at the other men. "While we wait for the doctor, please tell me how you came to be here."

"We're looking for the girl," Vernon said. "Figured it was the best thing we could do."

"And have you had any luck in your search?"

Vernon shook his head. "Not yet."

"We flew in yesterday," Gary said.

Vernon pulled out the map they'd been given in the airport and pointed at the lake. "First we went to Tikal and talked to the park ranger. Next we headed to Flores and searched there. Nothing." He circled the area with his finger. "Our plan was to visit each of these towns and see if we could find anybody who'd seen her. I mean, how many girls with red hair do you find in these parts? None that I've seen. So we figured it was as good a shot as any."

"What brings you here, Raul?" Gary asked.

"The same as you—looking for the girl, asking questions."

Before Gary could ask Raul to elaborate, Lyle cleared his throat and they all turned to look at him.

"I thought you were asleep," Vernon said. "Now I'll have to watch what I say."

"There's something," Lyle said, his voice barely audible.

"Don't talk; you need to rest," Gary said. "A doctor is coming."

"Something . . ." Lyle lay still for a few minutes, his eyes closed, his brow furrowed. He worked his mouth, as though he was trying to formulate words that wouldn't quite come. "Man . . . talking . . . said . . ." He closed his eyes for several seconds. "Something . . . girl." Lyle's voice was weak. He grimaced and pressed his hand against his chest.

Raul pulled a chair next to the bed and sat down. "Someone said something about a girl? Did you think he was talking about Melissa?"

Lyle opened his eyes and tried to sit up. "Yes. Said he had . . . date . . . red hair . . . girl with . . . red hair . . . white skin. Soft . . . white skin." His face contorted in pain then, and his hand went to his shoulder.

Gary reached for his arm, easing him down again.

"Did he say anything else?" Raul asked. "Anything at all?"

Lyle barely shook his head. "Can't . . ." His eyes closed. His face was again gray and clammy. "Tell Lila I love her," he said just before he lost consciousness.

The three men moved quickly. Vernon searched for the nitroglycerin while Gary ran for a wet cloth from the bathroom. Raul felt for his pulse and nodded at the others when he found it. Vernon forced Lyle's mouth open and slid the nitroglycerin under his tongue. Gary pulled a vial of consecrated oil from his key ring and motioned for Vernon and Raul to help him give Lyle a blessing.

When they finished, Vernon turned to Gary and asked the question that was on all their minds. "Do you think he's going to make it?"

Gary shook his head. "We need the doctor to get here."

"He said he would come as quickly as he could," Raul said. Lyle's face was ashen, his breathing shallow. Raul walked to the door, opened it, and looked out. *Where is the doctor?* He glanced at his watch. It seemed callous to talk about other things now, but he needed to know what the others remembered. Any detail could be important and, in the next few hours, could easily be forgotten. He returned to the others and said, "While we wait for the doctor, please tell me what you remember about the man Lyle heard."

Gary and Vernon described Javier as well as they could, but their attention had not been on the young man speaking Spanish. They remembered that he

wore a baseball cap, but neither man was sure he would recognize him again, and neither had noticed anyone else the young man might have spoken to.

Lyle regained consciousness just as the doctor arrived. The doctor listened to his heart and then agreed that they needed to get Lyle to Guatemala City as soon as possible. But travel was risky. They had to balance his need to rest and recover before making the trip with his need to get to better medical facilities. The recommendation was that they remain in Flores until tomorrow then fly to Guatemala City and check Lyle into the hospital there for a few days before making the flight home. They all knew that his best chance at recovery was to be found in a hospital in the United States.

"Looks like other people are going to have to find that little girl," Vernon said.

CHAPTER 22

ALTHOUGH THE STIFLING HEAT SLOWED them down, Carlos and Melissa kept moving throughout the day. They didn't know where they were going, but staying in one place too long could mean being found by the wrong people. Carlos walked silently in front of Melissa, his shoulders hunched, his eyes scanning the terrain. He pushed the branches out of the way for Melissa, who followed closely behind him. Only occasionally did she break the silence when a branch snapped back, whipping her across the face. Then she would wince and cry out, and Carlos would try harder to make the path easier for her to follow.

"What are you thinking about?" Melissa asked when they stopped to rest.

"I'm not thinking; I'm listening," he said.

"Are you scared?"

"Why would I be scared? Are you going to hurt me?" Carlos laughed and looked away.

"I'm scared."

"Well, that's because you're a girl."

"I think you are scared, but you just don't want to admit it."

"I'm not scared. I'm stupid."

Melissa watched him for several seconds. Finally she spoke softly. "You aren't stupid. You're brave. You could have stayed there in the camp and let those men do whatever they wanted to me. But you risked your life for me. And now you're trying to keep me safe." She saw his eyes narrow as he stared into the woods. "I'll bet you wish you hadn't done it. I'll bet you wish you'd stayed in camp and collected your money."

She stared at her hands, waiting for him to disagree. But he didn't. A lump formed in her throat.

"We need to keep moving," he said, raising his eyes to the sky.

"What are you looking for?"

"Clouds." He turned his eyes toward her. "There aren't any."

"Is that good or bad?"

Carlos shrugged. "Clouds mean rain, and rain means water. Let's go."

As evening approached, Carlos and Melissa were able to move more quickly through the brush. The cooler air brought some relief but, with it, the knowledge that they needed to find a safe place to spend the night. They looked forward to resting, but even that brought little comfort. They were hungry; the food that Carlos had brought with him was long gone, and they knew tomorrow meant another day trudging through the mass of dense jungle branches and facing the punishing heat.

There was little to hope for, yet they forced their legs to move forward. Finally, before it was too dark to see, they stopped. Carlos had found a small cave where they could spend the night. It smelled like decaying vegetation, but it appeared to be empty. They crawled inside. Melissa lay on her side, closed her eyes, and fell asleep almost immediately.

When she awoke it was dark. She sat up. For a moment she thought she was still being held captive in the underground room. But then she remembered. She closed her eyes again. With her eyes shut, she could see her home and her family.

And Josh.

The last time she'd seen Josh, he was angry and sulky. He'd made it clear he didn't want her to leave and didn't understand why she was taking this trip, why she couldn't stand up to her dad and refuse to go. Melissa had sided with him that day, but now it all seemed insignificant. Why had he made such a big deal out of her leaving? She wondered if he missed her, if he even knew anything about what was happening to her. Probably not.

She heard a faint fluttering above her. Her body tensed as she concentrated, and then she heard the sound again, louder and closer.

"Carlos!"

He didn't answer.

"Carlos, wake up. Something's in here!" Still there was no answer. "Carlos, where are you?"

Suddenly there were hundreds of tiny wings flapping all around her. She screamed and waved her arms. Her hands connected with a soft body. Then there was another one, and another. She flailed at them and screamed again and again, covering her face with her hands, but still they came.

Then through her screams, she heard a voice calling to her and saw a light coming toward her. It was Carlos—Carlos there beside her, holding her,

pulling her out of the cave, away from the bats. He wrapped his arms around her and held her close, shielding her, stroking her back, murmuring that everything would be okay. She felt her body grow limp and sag against him as panic was replaced by despair. He held her as she cried against his shoulder.

When her tears subsided, he said softly, "Señorita, do not be afraid. They're only bats. They will not hurt you. And look what I have brought for you."

He reached down and picked up an oval-shaped fruit he must have tossed aside a few moments before. Shining his flashlight on it, he grinned and held it out to her.

"I found papaya for you to eat," he said, placing the fruit into her hands.

"Papaya?"

"I found a papaya tree not far from here."

Melissa wiped her eyes and watched as he drew a knife from his pocket and sliced the fruit into small wedges. He gestured for her to take a piece, and when she hesitated, he picked up a piece and held it to her lips. The papaya was sweet and juicy. She chewed the fruit, savoring its flavor.

After they had eaten, Carlos turned his attention to their shelter. "We need to go into the cave," he said. "The bats will not hurt you."

"I won't go back in there."

"It is safer in the cave than out in the open."

"I won't go back in there," she said again. She walked over to a tree and sat down.

He shook his head and began searching for something. He picked up some pieces of dry bamboo then knelt in front of the cave and lit the wood with a lighter. "The fire will keep the bats away."

"So you're a Boy Scout too," Melissa said.

"Boy Scout? What is this?"

"Don't they have Boy Scouts in Guatemala?"

He added kindling to the fire. "What are these Boy Scouts?"

"Not what, silly—who."

"*Who* are these Boy Scouts?"

"It's like a club that boys have."

"A club? What is that?"

"A bunch of boys get together and do things. Boy things. Like tie knots and build fires."

"This is what boys do in your country? Tie knots and build fires? This is Boy Scouts?"

"Well, sort of." She yawned and felt her eyes close. She forced them open, blinked several times, and then leaned back against the tree. "I guess there's more

to it than that. They go on campouts." She yawned again. "I don't really know much about it because I've never been a boy."

Melissa fought to stay awake but finally lost the battle.

***

After a time, Carlos slid his arms beneath her, carried her into the cave, and laid her down. Then he sat next to her, pulling her head onto his legs for a pillow. Eventually, he too closed his eyes and went to sleep.

Sometime during the night, Melissa bolted upright. "What was that?"

"What was what?" he asked groggily.

"I heard something."

They listened, and then they heard the roar again.

"What is that?" Melissa asked.

"It is a jaguar, señorita."

"A jaguar?"

"But you do not need to be afraid. Jaguars do not attack people."

Another roar. Carlos reached over to put his arm around Melissa. She shuddered as the roars became louder.

"It's so close," she whispered.

Carlos pulled her to him. "Do not be afraid," he said. "I will keep you safe."

She leaned against him as they waited, listening for the jaguar. It was almost silent for a few moments before they heard the bellow of a howler monkey followed by a crash and a fierce yowl.

CHAPTER 23

JAVIER ENTERED THE HIDDEN CAMPSITE and looked around. *Where is everyone?* His eyes swept the area, but there was no sign of César or Carlos. He hurried over to the cenote; the ladder was still in place. He climbed down the ladder into the dark hole where Melissa had spent the last four days. It was empty. His flashlight cast eerie shadows on the walls of the pit. He didn't like it below ground. He had heard that human skeletons had been found in other cenotes in the Yucatán Peninsula. People said that the ancient Maya used the cenotes for human sacrifices to the rain gods. Of course, he hadn't told the others he was afraid, but now, alone in the dark, he felt nervous. Grasping the sides of the ladder, he climbed back to the top.

Not sure what else to do, he sat on a tree stump and pulled out a slice of cheese and a chunk of bread. He stared up at the thick canopy. The light was fading. Soon he would be alone in the dark jungle. He stood and walked around the camp perimeter.

Maybe they had killed the girl. No, they wouldn't have done that. But there could have been an accident. Maybe one of them had decided to have some fun and she had fought back and then he had killed her by accident. Or maybe they were scared that she'd talk and Mr. Guerrero would be mad.

Last night Mr. Guerrero had warned him to keep her safe. What would he do if he found out she was dead?

But maybe she wasn't dead. Maybe Javier had just got cut out of the deal. Maybe they had left while he was gone so they wouldn't have to split the money with him. Maybe that's why César had sent him out of camp.

But they needed supplies. He was sure they did.

Maybe someone had found them. He glanced around the clearing again, looking for anything that would indicate a struggle. Nothing.

It would soon be dusk, and he had to make a decision. He could wait at the site for them to return. But what if they didn't? He would be alone all night in the rainforest, and they would be somewhere else laughing at him.

He could cut his losses and disappear. He thought of the money he was supposed to get. He earned that money; it was his, and he wanted it.

Or—he could tell Mr. Guerrero what he had found at the campsite. Mr. Guerrero would be furious. But he couldn't hold Javier responsible since he'd been with Mr. Guerrero the night before. Maybe Mr. Guerrero would realize that it was he, Javier, who could be trusted and would reward him for that trust. If César was trying to cut him out of the deal, Javier would make sure it didn't happen.

His decision made, he swung the pack back onto the mule and started down the trail the way he had come.

It was well after dark when Javier reached Flores, hid the mule, and headed for the Petén Esplendido. He would go to the room where he had met Mr. Guerrero the night before and wait with Alfonso for the phone call.

He slipped in the door and walked down the corridor, retracing his steps from the previous night. Occasionally he passed a well-dressed tourist carrying a suitcase.

Javier was nearly to the room when he noticed Alfonso sitting alone in a chair in a corner. He approached his friend from behind and poked his back. Alfonso jerked and whirled around to face Javier. Javier laughed at his panicked expression.

"Be quiet," Alfonso said, glancing around the hall. "I'm not supposed to be seen, remember? What are you doing here anyway?"

Javier slumped into the chair next to Alfonso. "Change of plans. Anything interesting happening here?"

"Not much." He nodded at the door across the hall. "They're in there. When you left, there were three of them, right?"

"Sí. The one on the ground and the other two."

"There are four now. The new one's local. Maya. This guy showed up right after you left. They talked and then came here. After a while, a doctor came. Then the new one left for a while and came back with food. I should have jumped him and taken his food. At least it would have added some excitement to the day." Alfonso leaned back in his chair, yawned, and stretched his legs.

"You're complaining about easy money? When's the last time you made money sitting around in a hotel watching some rich old men's door?"

"I haven't seen any money yet, and I'm hungry."

The door to the room they were watching opened a few inches. Alfonso motioned for Javier to move into the shadows and be quiet as they listened to the voices coming from within the room. The fourth man stepped out of the room, glanced toward the young men, and continued down the hallway.

As soon as the man was out of sight, Javier stood. "We've got to follow him."

"You follow him if you want. I'm staying here and watching the gringos, like I'm being paid to do."

"I'm going to find out what that guy's doing." Javier could almost hear the coins from Mr. Guerrero jingling in his pocket.

It wasn't hard for Javier to follow the fourth man. He had been following people all his life: his mother when he was small, his big brother when he got older, and street gangs after his brother disappeared. He'd learned how to keep one eye on the street and one eye on the person he was following. He kept to the shadows as the man walked briskly down the streets of Flores. Javier watched him catch a tuk tuk and grabbed the next one, telling his driver to follow at a distance. They traveled back across the causeway into Santa Elena and then turned left at the edge of town and then right again.

"You've come to the Cave of the Serpent," said the tuk tuk driver as he stopped and looked back at Javier. "You know, it is the gateway to the ancient subterranean earth monster."

Javier had heard the story, and he didn't like it, but he wasn't about to let on. Instead, he snickered. "It's a superstition, Old Man," he said as he watched the man he was following climb out of his tuk tuk, pay the driver, and walk toward the cave.

"Maybe, but I wouldn't be going in there after dark."

After the driver pulled away, Javier found a comfortable place to wait.

* * *

Raul walked toward the wire fence that blocked the entrance to the cave. The gate was shut. He tugged on the gate and was surprised when it opened. It was almost nine o'clock; the cave had been closed for nearly four hours. Pulling out his flashlight, he stepped into the entrance of the cave. Systematically, he moved the light back and forth, illuminating each area as he listened for approaching footsteps. Water trickled somewhere deep in the cave. Above, stalactites hung from the ceiling, forming eerie shadows on the walls. Twisting the flashlight back and forth, he made his way through the winding passages, stopping frequently to listen. Once, he thought he heard faint footsteps from the direction he had come. He turned around and shined his light but could see no one. His light dimmed. He shook the flashlight. The battery must be weak. Where was Adán? He turned off the flashlight to preserve the battery and was immersed in darkness. He stood still, listening for a sound, and then he heard

faint footsteps again, moving toward him. They were slow, hesitant. He turned the flashlight back on.

"Adán?"

There was no response.

"Adán, is it you?"

Raul rotated the flashlight around the room, pausing to bathe each corner in light, but there was no sign of anyone. He listened for footsteps but could hear none. He continued moving through the cave, ducking to pass into an area with a lowered ceiling.

His light flickered again. He looked back, memorizing the way he had come. Again he had the uneasy feeling that faint footsteps were following him. Again he called out and heard nothing.

And then his light went out, leaving him in complete darkness. He flipped the switch back and forth, but nothing happened. Several seconds passed as he waited to see if his eyes would adjust and debated what to do. Reaching behind him, he could feel the cave wall and stepped backward to lean against it. He slid his foot over the uneven floor of the cave and felt his way along the wall toward what he thought was the cave entrance. Again, he called for Adán but heard only an echo coming from deep inside the cave.

Suddenly a light turned on, flooding the room, blinding him. Raul shielded his eyes against the brightness, and the shaft of light dropped to the floor. There, standing before him, was Marcos.

"My father is dead," Marcos said.

Raul recoiled from the words. Whatever had come between Marcos and himself, he had loved Marcos's father like a second father. "Where is Adán?"

Marcos shrugged but did not answer.

Raul stared at the other man. "Why did you come here?"

Marcos's voice dropped to a whisper. It was almost pleading. "We were like brothers," he said.

"You took everything from me," Raul said.

"I had no choice."

"Everything I ever cared about."

"I was following orders." Now Marcos's voice trembled.

"Following orders? You killed them all—women, children, old people. Village after village, house after house. When you came to her village, her house, you didn't stop. You forced her to walk out of her house and into that building with all the other young women. You made her go there, and you knew what they would do to her."

"Do you know what that has been like for me, knowing that? I had no choice, Raul. I had to do it, or they would have killed me."

"It would have been better if you had died."

Slowly, Marcos nodded his head. "You are right. You were always right. It would have been better if I had died that day. And that is something I have had to live with all these years."

Neither man spoke for several moments. Finally Marcos broke the silence. "Will you ever be able to forgive me?"

Raul didn't answer. He looked into Marcos's eyes and could see his pain.

"When I saw what you had done, I wanted to kill you. I wanted to kill you with my bare hands. But that would not have brought her back. Nothing, nothing could bring her back to me." Raul's voice broke. "I have tried to forgive you, Marcos. I have tried for thirty years. And I thought I had succeeded, until today. But when I saw you there, in the marketplace . . ."

Marcos nodded. His voice was almost a whisper. "I don't blame you, Raul. I can't forgive myself either." It was several moments before he spoke again, but when he did his voice was quiet, weary. "You must know that my death would not have saved Sofía that day."

They heard footsteps.

Marcos turned to face the sound. "That must be Adán," he said.

They waited as the steps grew louder; finally Adán stepped into the light. Adán nodded at Marcos and then approached Raul.

"What do you want, Raul?"

"Hello, Adán."

"Why don't you tell me what you're looking for, because I don't believe you're into drug trafficking."

Raul nodded. "Six days ago, three men were hired to set up a camp, supposedly for an archaeological expedition in the lowlands. I need to find the men. I thought you might know something."

"Why do you need to find these men?"

"A young woman disappeared the day after they were hired to set up a camp. I thought there might be a connection."

"And why would I help you?"

Raul looked at Adán. He had aged, yet, in some ways, he was the same. Only his eyes looked truly old—old and merciless. Gone was any passion or excitement. Raul watched Adán without flinching or speaking.

Finally Adán spoke again. "Many girls are missing in Guatemala. They are foolish. They go where they don't belong, and they never return. Then their families weep and wail and wonder where they are. What is this to me?"

Raul didn't answer.

"Who is this girl?" asked Marcos.

"Her name is Melissa Miller. She is from the United States, on a vacation here with her parents. She was taken from Tikal several days ago." He met Adán's eyes. "And I can assure you, she has done nothing to deserve this. I'm trying to help her parents find her."

"You should let the police handle it."

"You know as well as I that the policemen turn their backs on these things."

"The police are busy," Adán said. "They have more important things to do than to chase after a girl." Adán turned to leave. "I know nothing," he said, glancing toward Marcos.

Marcos nodded. He stared at Raul for a moment before he walked away. Raul listened to the crunch of footsteps as the two men moved through the cave.

CHAPTER 24

IT WAS SOME TIME BEFORE the men emerged from the cave—first the two men Javier didn't recognize and then the man he had been following. The night was clear and warm. Javier trailed the man through the streets of Santa Elena, confident that Mr. Guerrero would be interested in what he had to tell him.

The man walked at a steady pace a block in front of him. Lost in his own thoughts, Javier didn't notice when the man stopped and looked back or when he slowed his pace. It wasn't until Javier had nearly caught up to the other man that he realized what had happened.

"Hola," the man said. "Do I know you?"

"No, señor." Javier kept his face down as he approached the man. "I have never seen you before."

"Where are you going so late at night?"

"What is this to you, where I am going? It is not your business."

The man studied Javier. "I was curious, but you are right. It is not my business." He turned and continued down the street.

Javier moved more slowly then, deliberately increasing the distance between the man and himself. When Javier arrived at the Petén Esplendido, the man was no longer in sight. Javier walked through the entrance and across the lobby then through the darkened corridor until a dark shape sprawled on a chair at the end of the hall drew his attention. It was Alfonso, and he had fallen asleep.

Javier had almost reached Alfonso when the man he'd been trailing stepped out from behind a plant and blocked his way.

"I knew I recognized you," the man said. "I saw you and your friend here hanging around the hotel earlier this evening. I wondered then what you were doing. *Maybe you were selling something,* I thought. Then I saw you on the streets of Santa Elena, following me. Now, here you are again. Why? Why would two young men be here in this hotel?" He drew his wallet from his pocket and

removed several bills. Flipping through them, he looked up at Javier. "Perhaps we could discuss this further in my room?"

Javier shrugged and looked at Alfonso then followed the man down the hall and into a room.

"After I spoke to you on the street, I kept thinking about you," the man said. "You seemed so familiar, but I couldn't think of where I had seen you." He turned on the light in the room and motioned for Javier to sit down. Returning to the door, he glanced out into the hall and then shut the door and locked it. "Then I remembered. I had seen you here, in the hotel." The man crossed the room to the window and closed the drapes. "Then I remembered something else." He opened a drawer in the nightstand and withdrew a set of batteries. He continued talking as he replaced the batteries, checked his flashlight, and then pulled up a chair beside Javier and sat down. "My friends who are staying in the room your friend is watching—they said they saw you on the street earlier today." The man looked straight into Javier's eyes. "That was you, wasn't it?" It was more a statement than a question, but he waited for a response from Javier.

Javier's mind raced. He could feel the man's eyes boring into him. "What do you want from me?"

The man thumbed through the bills and then casually laid them on the table between them. "I thought perhaps you would be so good as to tell me why you are here in this hotel, watching my friends."

Javier shifted positions and glanced at the money.

Silence hung between them. Finally the man spoke again. "There is something else I remembered, and I wondered if you could help me answer a question. You see, my friend heard you say that you had a date tonight. A date with a girl with red hair and white skin." The man chuckled. "I have looked around, but I do not see a girl with red hair. Perhaps this is where you were tonight in Santa Elena?"

The man picked up the money and fanned the bills out on the table. "But there is a red-haired girl who is missing. I am looking for her, and if you could help me find her, it would be very good for you." He tapped the money with his finger.

Javier shifted. "I don't know what you're talking about."

"I think you do." The man again fingered the money on the table. "But maybe you are afraid."

Again, the man waited.

When Javier didn't respond, the man leaned forward in his chair and said, "This girl is a United States citizen. Her parents are searching for her. The

Guatemalan government is looking for her. The United States government is looking for her. When she is found—and she will be found—it will not be good for those who took her. Or those who withheld information about where she is."

Javier's jaw tightened. He could feel his pulse racing. He had to think. There was a knife in his pack. If he could distract the man, he could get to it. By the time they found the man, Javier would be gone with all the money. Nobody knew he'd been here tonight. No, that wasn't right. The men Alfonso was watching had seen him. They would remember they told this man about him. And Alfonso might talk.

Alfonso might tell Mr. Guerrero Javier had been at the hotel tonight. Mr. Guerrero would wonder why he wasn't back at the camp. He'd want to know about the girl.

Javier didn't know where the girl was—that was the truth.

If he answered the man's questions, he could take his money and disappear. Or maybe he wouldn't have to disappear. Maybe he could still tell Mr. Guerrero about the girl and about the conversation he overheard tonight at the cave. Maybe he could get money from both of them.

Javier licked his lips. "I don't know where the girl is."

"But you have seen her."

"I said I don't know where she is. She's gone."

"What do you mean, she's gone?"

"How many ways do I have to say it? The girl's gone. I don't know where she is."

"When did you last see her?"

"I never said I saw her."

The man tapped the money again. "This person you're working for—do you think he will protect you when everything goes down? He doesn't care about you. You're just a kid he's using to get what he wants. So what do you think he's going to do when he's finished with you? You think he's going to pay you a big bonus and thank you for helping him out? You're a bigger fool than I think if you believe that. You're a witness to a crime, and he will not leave a witness. Now why don't you tell me what you know."

Javier took a deep breath and blew it out. "I'm telling you the truth—the girl's gone. Yesterday morning they sent me into town for supplies, and when I got back, she was gone. Everybody was gone. The whole camp—empty."

"Who was with her when you left?" The man fingered the money on the table and repeated his question.

Javier shrugged. "There were two other men. Carlos and César."

"So these men sent you into the city to get supplies, and when you returned, they were both gone."

"That's what I said. Except that Carlos didn't send me anywhere."

"And you have no idea where they might have gone?"

"I already said I don't know where they went," Javier said.

"Why don't you tell me what you do know. Let's start with your name and how you kidnapped her."

* * *

Raul sat for a long time after he let Javier go. The combined emotions of the day washed over him, leaving him drained and weary. Seeing Marcos and Adán after so many years had awakened feelings he had long since buried. He leaned back in the chair and closed his eyes.

It was March 1982, at the height of Guatemala's thirty-six-year civil war. The military had staged a coup, and General Efraín Río Montt had just taken office. Raul had been hopeful that this lay pastor would put an end to all the violence in his country. When General Montt gave his inaugural address, he'd even said that his presidency was the will of God. Surely a God-fearing man will make good decisions, *Raul had thought.*

Before the month was over, Raul had deserted the army.

The night Sofía had come to him, her eyes were wide with terror. She had heard things. The army had invaded the village of Río Negro and once again demanded that the residents abandon their homes. Once again the people had refused to leave, but this time, the military did not take no for an answer. One hundred forty-three Maya were slaughtered, almost all women and children. The rest had fled to the hills.

"The military has been asking those people to leave for years," Raul said. "They need the land so that they can build a dam to produce electricity."

"Are you defending the army? That was the land of the people. *You can't force people to leave their land just because you want it." Her voice dropped to a whisper. "They say that the women were violated. And the children—"*

Raul pulled Sofía against his chest and felt her body shudder as she relaxed against him.

She raised her face to look at him, her eyes wet with tears. "They say that the men in the next village over were forced to help with the killing."

"That can't be true," Raul said. "I'm sure it's just a rumor."

He enveloped Sofía in his arms. She was warm and soft, and she begged him to leave the army and take her away from all the horrors of war. He tilted her chin up and gazed into her eyes. A man could drown in those liquid-brown eyes.

"I'm so afraid for our people," she said.

Raul walked to the hotel window and pulled back the curtain. It was dark outside. As he stood staring into the darkness, he could almost feel Sofía there beside him. The longing to see her, to hold her once again, was almost more than he could bear. If only he had listened that night. He should have taken her and fled, leaving everything behind.

But he had wanted to offer her more than his hands and his heart. He'd wanted to accumulate a little money so they could start out right, without having to struggle the way his parents had always struggled. And so he'd waited, promising her that it wouldn't be long—just a few months.

Four months later, she was dead.

Raul walked over to the bed and pulled down the covers. He sat on the edge of the bed and slipped off his shoes. Leaning back against a pillow, he closed his eyes, but the memories refused to be silenced.

It was a Sunday in July, market day in Rabinal, and he was going to see Sofía. The paths into the neighboring village of Plan de Sánchez were crowded with people on their way to market. Raul had stopped at the marketplace in Rabinal to look for a gift to surprise Sofía when he heard two thunderous explosions followed by a spray of automatic gunfire. He pushed through the people, sprinting down the path toward Plan de Sánchez as the gunfire continued.

Then he heard his name. He stopped and scanned the crowd until he saw a pair of eyes nearly hidden behind the trees lining the trail. He stepped toward them, and a hand reached out, clutching his arm, pulling him into the surrounding woods. Gabriela, Sofía's younger sister, stood before him. Tears streaked the young girl's face as she blurted out her account.

Three days before, soldiers had come to her house and demanded to see everyone. They said they were doing an inspection and wanted to talk to her father. They threatened him, accusing him of harboring insurgents.

"They went to every house in the village," Gabriela said. "Then today, the soldiers came back. We tried to hide under the bed, but they found us and made us go outside. The soldiers were separating everyone. The children had to go one place; the older men and women had to go someplace else. They made Mother and Father go into a building. Then they forced Sofía and me to go with all the other girls in the village." Gabriela's breath came in short gasps.

"Where is Sofía now, Gabriela?"

Gabriela shook her head. "Just as we got to the building, Sofía whispered that she was going to distract the soldier and told me to run as fast as I could and hide in the hills. When I looked back, I saw her step into the building." Gabriela raised her eyes to Raul's and whispered, "What are they going to do to her, Raul?"

Bile rose in his throat. He shook his head and motioned for Gabriela to come with him. Together, they ran toward the village, but as they approached town, he saw a military blockade preventing anyone from entering or exiting Plan de Sánchez.

Raul beckoned for Gabriela to follow him into the woods where they would not be seen. They paused just inside the forest and watched the soldiers. Suddenly Gabriela pointed at one of the soldiers.

"That's him. That's the one who found us and forced us to leave our home."

Raul felt the blood drain from his face as the soldier turned to face them. "No, it cannot be."

"Do you know that man?"

Raul shook his head and turned away. "No, I do not know him."

Gabriela grabbed his arm. "Look!" she said, pointing at the sky.

Raul looked up and saw smoke curling above the trees.

"Don't follow me," he said. "You must hide. I will find Sofía."

Raul ran toward the blockade and forced his way between the soldiers who blocked the entrance. Just as he pushed past the last soldier, he turned and stared straight into the eyes of his childhood friend Marcos. Surprise and fear crossed Marcos's face as Raul turned away and raced toward the flaming buildings.

Now, as Raul lay awake in the dark, the crushing agony of that day returned; he turned his face to the wall and wept.

CHAPTER 25

JAVIER FOUND ALFONSO SPRAWLED ON the bed in Eduardo Guerrero's hotel room, flipping through the channels on the TV. He paced the floor as he waited for the phone to ring.

"Why are you so nervous?" Alfonso said. "Mr. Guerrero isn't expecting you to be here."

"I don't like sitting around."

"Relax. Have some wine."

"Wine doesn't solve everything."

Alfonso laughed. "It does for me."

"Look, Alfonso." Javier's lips hardened. "You met Mr. Guerrero. I don't think he likes to be messed with."

"Who's messing with him? Do you have something going on I don't know about?"

"What are you talking about?" Javier shook his head and reached for the wine on the table.

The phone rang. Alfonso looked at Javier before picking up the receiver. "Hola."

"What do you have for me?"

Alfonso recited the day's events: how he had followed the three men into Santa Elena and watched as one of them became ill. He described the man who had joined them and returned with them to the hotel. He told Eduardo about the doctor who had come and reassured him that he had watched everything just as he had been instructed to do.

"*Bueno,*" Eduardo said. "It seems our friends from north of the border will not be making any trouble for us."

Javier took the phone.

"Mr. Guerrero, this is Javier," he said. "I have news for you." He described his arrival at the campsite only to find it devoid of people. Eduardo's sharp

intake of breath told Javier that this news was unexpected. Javier explained how he had searched for clues, but finding none, had returned to Flores to report his findings. Finally he described how he had followed the man to La Cueva de la Serpiente.

The only thing he failed to include was his conversation later that night with the man.

* * *

Eduardo Guerrero continued to hold his phone long after he had finished his conversation with Javier. He hated complications. Despised them. And this job seemed to be nothing but complications. But he would handle it.

He pressed the numbers on his phone.

"I have a job for you," Eduardo said.

"Who is this, and where did you get this number?"

"La Cofradía."

The line was silent. Finally the man on the other end of the line spoke. "What do you need?"

* * *

Just after ten o'clock, Matt's phone rang. His hand shook as he picked up the receiver.

"Come to the ruins of Santa Clara at midnight tonight. Come alone. I will find you there."

* * *

The phone began ringing just after the blond man had climbed into bed. Pulling a robe over his silk pajamas, he made his way down the darkened hallway to the study, flipped on the light, and walked to the large cherry-wood desk.

"Hello," he said, as he sat in the leather desk chair.

"I overheard something tonight that I believe will interest you."

"I'm listening."

"I was having a drink with an associate from the Instituto de Turismo when he received a call from a member of La Cofradía asking about a missing person in the rainforest near Tikal."

The blond man withdrew a sheet of paper and a pen from the desk drawer and placed it on his otherwise empty desk. "And why did he contact your friend?"

"He said he had been hired to track a missing American girl. He was looking for information about the search for her: their current location, which part of the rainforest they have already searched—that kind of thing."

"I see. Did he say anything else?"

"Just that he was going to be cleaning up somebody else's mess."

The blond man replaced the phone and made a few notes on his paper. Absentmindedly he twisted the ruby on his finger and then folded the paper exactly in half and slipped it into the desk drawer.

He smelled a rat, and it was time to find out what was going on.

CHAPTER 26

SLIDING HIS ARMS AROUND HER waist, Matt drew Cathy close and hugged her, breathing the scent of her hair, memorizing it, just in case. He could feel her body trembling against his, her arms tightening around his neck. He stroked her hair and kissed her forehead and then her lips. "I don't like leaving you here alone. What would I do if something happened to you?"

"Nothing's going to happen to me."

"Promise me you'll keep the door locked until I get back. And don't let anybody in."

"I'm a big girl. I'll be fine."

Matt leaned back, lifting her chin until he could see into her eyes. They were brimming with tears. "I know, but it's my job to take care of you. And I haven't been doing such a hot job of that lately."

"When you get back with Melissa, I'll give you a chance to make it up to me."

"It's a deal." He pulled her into another tight embrace and whispered against her ear, "I don't want you worrying about me. I'm coming back, and I'm bringing Melissa with me."

"I'm going to hold you to that."

Matt squeezed his eyes shut as tears threatened. He held her for a moment longer before releasing her. "Okay. I guess it's time."

"I'll be praying for you."

"I'm counting on it."

He held her one last time, cupping her face in his hands and kissing her lips. And then he left. He knew she was fighting to maintain control as he walked from the room and pulled the door shut behind him. Matt walked out of the hotel into the dark night.

Once outside the room, Matt took out his map. He had memorized every detail, yet he checked again to be sure he was going the right way. When he

reached the corner, he looked at the street sign: *Avenida Norte*, just as he read on the map. He turned and followed the street four blocks until he came to the back side of the old convent, Santa Clara. He looked at his watch. It was 11:40 P.M. He felt for the gun inside his pocket. Forcing himself to breathe evenly, he studied the surrounding area, orienting himself in case he needed to get away quickly. Then he moved around the block to the front of the convent and made his way into the ruins.

He walked through the complex of long narrow corridors and stairwells, stopping frequently to listen for footsteps. He paused when he reached an arch that opened onto a cloister and stepped out into the fresh air. A fountain stood in the middle of the cloister, with high arches on all sides. He slipped back into the corridor and continued making his way around the ruins, his senses alert.

He never heard footsteps, but a voice spoke to him in the darkness. "Mr. Miller, it is good to see you."

Matt spun around. No one.

"Where are you?"

No answer.

"What have you done with my daughter?"

Silence.

"What do you want from me?"

Finally the voice came again. "I want you to take me to the jade field."

Matt stood motionless, beads of sweat forming on his brow. "I don't know how to get to the jade field." He heard the click of a gun being cocked. He swallowed. His mouth was dry. "I've only been there once, and then I had a guide. There's no way I could find it again." He stared into the dark corners of the corridor, his eyes straining to see past the shadows. His heart pounded as he waited for a reply. When none came, Matt's voice dropped to a whisper. "I'm telling you the truth. I can't take you there. Now, please, tell me what you've done with my daughter."

"Of course you can take me there, Mr. Miller. You want your daughter. You will find a way."

Matt's mind raced, searching for alternatives, but he knew, even as he sought another choice, that there were none.

"Even with a guide it would take days to get there." Matt's voice broke and he waited for several seconds, trying to gain control, before he continued. "Please, I beg you, please give her to me. I'll do anything. Just give me my daughter."

"Of course you may have your daughter—after you have taken me to the jade. We will take our little trip together, and there, your daughter will be waiting for you, waiting to leap into your arms and give you a little kiss. And

one last thing, Mr. Miller: we need to hurry. Your daughter is very beautiful, and I do not know how long my men will be able to resist her charms."

Matt forced himself to remain silent as he battled the raw fury that shot through him. He didn't want uncontrolled anger playing to the enemy's advantage. Finally he spoke again. "You have to let me talk to her."

"You are not in a position to make demands. I have your daughter, and if you ever want to see her alive again, you will do exactly as I say." The man stepped out of the shadows and approached Matt. He held a gun in one hand.

"It is good to finally meet you, Mr. Miller. My name is Eduardo Guerrero."

He was shorter than Matt and stocky. A dark mustache framed narrow lips. Brown eyes looked at Matt, his eyebrows raised, as though he were waiting for Matt to respond to a joke.

"We will go now," Eduardo said.

"I can't take you there without my guide."

"Then let's get your guide."

"He lives in Salamá."

* * *

Cathy held herself together as well as she could until Matt closed the door. Only then did she allow herself to give vent to her fear. Collapsing on the bed, she wept. When the tears were spent, she slid off the bed and onto her knees, burying her face in the bedspread. She prayed, begging for her husband and daughter to be protected. Sobs wracked her body as she pled for comfort and peace. As she prayed, a quiet assurance came, calming her. She basked in the warmth and love that enveloped her. It was as though some unseen Being had wrapped her in a soft warm comforter and held her in His arms.

Eventually, she stood and walked into the bathroom to look in the mirror. Her eyes were red and swollen. She blew her nose and then returned to the bed, where she curled under the blanket.

Sleep evaded her as she tossed and turned and waited for Matt's return. In the early hours of the morning, exhaustion overcame her, and she drifted into a restless sleep.

CHAPTER 27

Day 7

It was barely dawn when Matt and Eduardo Guerrero came to the village of Salamá. Matt stared out the car window at the orange and olive trees as he drove into town, the peaceful setting in stark contrast to the turmoil he was feeling. He could see the bright-blue house as soon as they turned onto the street. Like many of the houses in Salamá, it had cinderblock walls, with a fence across the front of the yard. A single light burned in the house. María must be up early making tortillas. Matt glanced over at Eduardo, who was leaning back in his seat, a lit cigarette dangling from his mouth.

"This is it," Matt said.

Eduardo nodded, and his eyes closed as he drew on his cigarette. Rolling down his window, he crushed the cigarette and threw it onto the road then pulled the gun from his pocket and cocked it.

"No mistakes," Eduardo said as he stepped from the car.

Matt walked to the door and knocked. He could feel Eduardo's gun pressed against his back as he waited for the door to open.

"Señora, it is Matthew Miller," he called.

"Elder Miller, is it really you?" Even after twenty-five years, she still insisted on addressing him by the name she called him when they first met: his missionary title. She held the door open for him. "Please, please come in."

Her eyes shifted to the man beside him and her smile faded. "Is there a problem, Elder Miller?"

"I need to talk to your husband."

Just then Santiago stepped to the door. "Do I hear my good friend?" He stopped when he saw the man beside Matt. "Welcome to our home," he said, his eyes moving between the two men. "What brings you here?"

Matt turned to María. "I apologize for the intrusion."

"It is no problem. You are welcome here anytime, Elder Miller."

She moved back into the kitchen, and in a moment he could hear the rhythmic pounding as she kneaded and shaped corn tortillas. It was a sound Matt had heard every morning, from every kitchen he had visited in Guatemala.

"My friend, I need you to help me," Matt said to Santiago.

Santiago nodded. "Of course. Anything."

"We must go to the jade field."

Santiago looked from Matt to the man beside him, his eyes full of unanswered questions. "To the jade field?"

Matt felt the gun push deeper into his back. "I'm sorry, but we have to leave right away."

Santiago glanced between the men. "I will get my things."

Eduardo nudged Matt to follow the man through his small home. They watched him gather a few supplies and kiss his wife goodbye. Then the three walked out to Eduardo's car. Eduardo motioned for the others to get in the front seat.

"You will not be hurt if you do what I say," Eduardo said as he climbed into the back and laid his gun across his lap. "And now I'll take your phones," he said.

Matt and Santiago handed Eduardo their phones and watched as their only links with civilization were tossed out the window.

"And now, Mr. Miller, you will give me your gun."

"I don't know what you're talking about," Matt said.

"Give me the gun, or you will never see your daughter again."

* * *

Melissa and Carlos had huddled together through the remainder of the night, listening for the jaguar to return and waiting for daylight. Carlos fed the small flame bits of kindling as long as he could, which provided a little light. Just before dawn, Melissa had dozed off to sleep, and Carlos left the cave to explore the area.

He returned within an hour to find Melissa still sleeping. He knelt beside her and watched the purple shadows dance on her face as sunlight trickled through the jungle canopy. He hated to wake her, but they had to get moving. All too soon the sun would be high in the sky and the heat would be unbearable. He shook her shoulder.

"Señorita, we must go now," he said.

She sighed as her eyes flickered open.

Carlos held up another papaya and smiled at her. "I bring you breakfast," he said, "and I bring you good news." He paused for effect. "I heard water not far away."

Melissa scrambled to her feet. "Are you serious? Water? Then what are we waiting for?"

"Don't you want to eat first?"

"I'll eat on the way."

Carlos grinned and motioned for her to follow him back into the maze of trees and fern entangled with vines. The rush of the river grew steadily louder as they moved toward it. Finally they could see emerald-green trees ahead bathed in a splash of sunlight. Melissa squealed, and Carlos reached for her hand, pulling her through the last stretch of forest before they reached the crystal-clear stream threading its way through the lush foliage. The water sparkled in the light, illuminating vibrant orchids lining the riverbanks. A fallen mossy log lay partly across the river. Downstream an egret waded in the water.

They slid down the bank to the edge of the river, knelt by its side, and scooped handful after handful to drink. It was cool and delicious, soothing to their parched lips. Their thirst satisfied, they pulled off their shoes and stepped into the river. It had been six days since either of them had bathed; the water felt cool and refreshing. Carlos watched Melissa submerge then bob out of the water again, water streaming from her face. She giggled as she splashed him and then lay back in the water and closed her eyes. Her hair floated around her face, and he thought how relaxed and happy she looked.

Eventually, they returned to sprawl on the riverbank, wet and rejuvenated. With the sun hot on their faces, it was not long until Melissa fell asleep. Carlos watched her sleep for a while then got up and began to search for fallen logs.

Sometime later, Carlos looked up and saw Melissa awaken. He stood several feet away, lashing the logs together with vines. Melissa stretched, rolled onto her side, and opened her eyes. Carlos grinned at her.

"I'm making a raft," Carlos said. "For the river. The river will take us to help." He pointed at the flowing water. She nodded and sat up. Her hair was nearly dry from the sun; she combed through the tangles with her fingers.

"Look," Melissa said, motioning to a wild turkey on the other side of the riverbank.

Carlos nodded. He finished fastening the logs together, grabbed two extra logs, and slid the raft gently into the water. Beckoning for Melissa to join him, he jumped on and held it steady while she climbed onto the raft and sat down. He pushed the raft into the current. Handing one of the thinner, extra logs to

Melissa, he demonstrated how to steer before settling down for the slow ride. As they floated down the river, Melissa watched birds flying overhead, and Carlos pointed out an occasional monkey he glimpsed hanging from a tree. It was so idyllic and beautiful they almost forgot they were lost.

CHAPTER 28

CATHY WAS STILL ASLEEP, WEARING the clothes she'd been wearing the day before, when the phone rang in her room. She rolled onto her side and sat up with a start. Where was Matt? Her chest constricted as she turned on the light and walked to where she could see into the darkened bathroom. Frantically, she spun around, taking in the entire room. A sob caught in her throat. He wasn't there. The phone rang again. She stared at it, and when it rang a third time, snatched it up.

"Hello?"

"Hello, is this Cathy Miller?"

"Who is this? What have you done with my husband?"

"Cathy, this is Nick Slade."

Cathy sank onto the bed. "I'm sorry. I thought you were—"

"It's okay. I've been worrying about you guys ever since I listened to Matt's voicemail the other day. I thought I'd call to make sure everything was okay."

"It isn't." Her voice broke.

"Cathy, what's going on?"

"Melissa's missing and now Matt—"

"Then she hasn't been found. I was hoping when I didn't hear from you again that she had been. I'm so sorry, Cathy."

Cathy squeezed her eyes shut. The sympathy in his voice was going to be her undoing.

"But I interrupted you. You were saying something about Matt?"

"He's gone," Cathy said. "He left last night and hasn't come back."

"Do you know where he went?"

"No, I don't. He was supposed to—I'm sorry, I can't think."

"It's okay. When did Matt leave?"

Cathy took a deep breath. Nick's calm voice was helping her focus. "He was supposed to meet a man at midnight, so a little before that, I guess. I thought he'd be back by now."

"And you don't know where he was going? Do you know why he was meeting the man? Was it about Melissa?"

"Yes, and that's all I know."

"Have you contacted the authorities?"

"No," Cathy said. "I guess I should do that, but . . ."

"But?"

"We were told not to talk to anyone. I shouldn't be talking to you. And who would I call?"

"How about the embassy?"

"We tried to talk to someone there before, and he totally blew us off."

"Okay, listen, Cathy. You just hang tight. I'm going to come, and I'm going to help you figure all this out. And I promise you, nobody's going to be blowing me off."

"You don't have to do that."

"I know I don't. But I want to come. Matt's not only a valued employee, but I consider him to be a good friend." Nick paused before continuing. "I'm not a man who sits around and waits for things to happen. I make things happen. And Cathy"—his voice softened—"I don't know how else to say this, except to say it, but it's not safe for you to be there alone. Under the best of circumstances, it's not safe, and now, with all this going on, it's really not safe. I'm going to come, and I'm going to get to the bottom of this."

* * *

Vernon paced the floor in the Guatemala City airport. The flight out of Flores had taken forever to get off the ground. And now it was practically dinnertime, and they still hadn't gotten to the hospital. Apparently nobody in Guatemala owned a clock. Patience had never been his strongest suit, but today, when he had a man trying to die on him, he was fit to be tied.

He glanced over at Lyle, who was sitting on a bench with his head leaned back and his eyes closed. Lyle didn't look good. His skin was sallow. Vernon's eyes shifted to Gary standing in a line in front of the counter. They shouldn't have been so dang independent. It would have been easy enough in the United States to rent a car and get to the hospital.

Vernon surveyed the airport again, wishing Scott would walk through the door, even though he knew it wasn't going to happen. Raul had all but insisted they contact Scott, but Vernon had told him they'd take Lyle to the hospital. After all, Scott had a tour to run and a missing girl to find, and there was no reason he needed to drop everything else for something as simple as getting Lyle to the hospital. Lots of people had paid good money to see the lands of

the Book of Mormon, and Vernon could do his part to see that their money wasn't wasted. It's not like Scott could do heart surgery on Lyle.

And, sure as could be, Scott would have told Lila, and Vernon didn't want Lila worrying herself half sick when there was nothing she could do about it. Plenty of time for worrying later. She was probably worrying enough as it was. *That is, if she even knew about his heart trouble.* Knowing Lyle, he probably hadn't even told his wife about it.

No, it was better this way. They'd get Lyle settled in a bed before they called his good wife. No point in her missing any more of the tour than she had to.

Vernon walked over to Lyle and sat beside him on the bench. Lyle opened an eye and looked at him. "You look awful," Lyle said.

"Thanks; you don't look so great yourself."

"At least I have a good excuse." Lyle tried to laugh but grimaced instead. "This is a lousy way to spend a vacation."

Vernon reached over and patted his arm. He couldn't think of anything to say. It just wasn't in him to be all warm and fuzzy, so he cleared his throat. "I'm going to go check to see what's holding Gary up."

It was an excuse, and he knew it. Vernon had never learned how to be soft. He figured that was his wife's job. His job was to be tough. "Tough as nails," he always said. But today, when his throat started hurting every time he looked at Lyle, he didn't know how to be tough.

He looked at his watch. Another hour. They could have crawled faster than this. He walked over to where Gary was standing in line and asked what was taking so long. Gary looked straight through him, the way he'd always done when he sat across from him in his office at the church. "He's going to be all right," he said. Just as if he'd asked about Lyle instead of getting a car. Gary always did know too much. Vernon turned back toward Lyle and ran straight into an American carrying a briefcase and wearing the kind of clothes Vernon only wore on Sunday. Except nicer. He looked like the kind of man who'd never gotten dirt under his fingernails, the kind of man who belonged in an international airport. Vernon offered a quick apology, and the man extended his hand in greeting.

"It's good to talk to someone who speaks my language," the man said.

"Hey, you don't happen to know Spanish, do you?"

The man shook his head. "Not very much, I'm afraid. What do you need?"

"We need to get a car. You wouldn't think that'd be too hard, would you?" Vernon nodded at Gary, who was a few steps closer to the counter. "I'm just not sure how good he is at charades. Can you tell if that's the place where you rent a car?"

The man looked around at the signs. "Looks right to me."

Vernon nodded. "We need to get my friend to the hospital." He cleared his throat and looked away. He'd taken care of sick cattle for years, but heart problems—that was out of his range. He didn't like feeling helpless.

"I hope it's not too serious."

When Vernon didn't answer, the man spoke again. "Is there anything I can do to help?"

"'Preciate that, but I don't suppose there's anything you can do."

The man extended his hand again. "Nick Slade," he said. "And you are?"

"Vernon Taylor, from Wayne County, Utah."

"I'm glad to meet you, Vernon. What brings you to Guatemala?"

"The wife," Vernon said. "She talked me into this trip. Got our friends to come too."

"Your wife? Why did your wife want to come here? Most women I know would've signed you up for Hawaii."

"No kidding." He looked over at Lyle before he continued. "She saw this tour advertised, and it caught her fancy. Who'd a guessed it'd turn into something like this?" He lowered his voice. "A girl in our group's missing. We think she got nabbed. So here we are, trying to help find her, and then my friend goes and decides to have a heart attack. Not exactly the trip we planned."

"Did you say a girl's missing? You don't mean someone on the tour?"

"That's right. Pretty little thing, too. We were up visiting Tikal National Park, and next thing you know, she's gone. The authorities are trying to tell us she ran away, but I don't believe it. I think somebody up and took her."

"Why do you think there was foul play?"

"It's what my gut tells me." He stared across the crowded airport and shook his head. "She's a good girl. Sure, she might've had her differences with her parents, but underneath, she's a good girl. You can tell those things, you know."

"Yes, you can," Nick said. "Do you mind if I ask the girl's name?" Before Vernon could answer, he added, "That's actually why I'm here. I came to help find my friend's daughter who's missing. It has to be the same girl."

"You don't say," Vernon said. "Her name's Melissa. Melissa Miller. That the same girl?"

Nick nodded. "That's her."

"Well, I'll be danged," Vernon said. "What're the chances?"

"I just talked to Melissa's mom this morning and decided to come. Matt's a good friend of mine, and Melissa—she's their only daughter, you know? I can't even imagine what they must be going through."

"That's why we couldn't sit still either. We were tired of sitting and doing nothing but eating and following our wives around. We had to do something." Vernon cleared his throat. "Didn't expect it to end up like this, though." He looked across at Gary. "Well, it looks like he's finally at the front of the line, but it was sure good to meet you, Mr.—what did you say your name was?"

"Slade. Nick Slade. And I'm serious about helping you. I can at least help you get your friend to the hospital."

Vernon shrugged and walked over to where Lyle sat on the bench. He sat beside his friend and patted his knee. "Ready to go traveling?"

Lyle opened one eye again. "Well, I sure don't want to stay in this joint."

Gary returned to the three men and wiggled car keys. "Men, we're in business." He looked at Nick and extended his hand. "Should I know you?"

"No, I don't think so. I'm Nick Slade. I met Vernon here a few minutes ago, and he told me a little about your predicament, so I thought I could offer you a hand and help you get your friend to the hospital."

"Well, thank you," Gary said. "I certainly won't turn down an offer of help right now." Gary turned back to the other men. Vernon had Lyle on his feet and was holding him by the arm. "Let's get out of this place," he said.

Neither Gary nor Vernon argued when Nick offered to drive the car. After all, even a little Spanish was better than no Spanish when it came to reading street signs.

"This is it," Nick said as he pulled into a parking spot. He saw them into the hospital and offered to return the car for them. "You're probably going to want to take a bus when you leave here. Driving in Guatemala City can be pretty nerve-wracking if you're not used to it. If you take a tuk tuk or bus, just close your eyes and hang on, and you'll get where you're going safely."

Gary and Vernon thanked Nick for his help. "Good to know there's people like you helping now that we can't," Vernon said, "and I'm glad for that."

* * *

The light tap startled Cathy. She stared at the door. The tapping came again, this time more loudly.

"Who is it?"

"It's me, Cathy. Nick Slade."

She blew out the breath she'd been holding and then slid the lock open and turned the knob to let Nick in. Without saying a word, he held out his arms and hugged her for a long moment before she pushed away. "Thanks so much for coming."

"I'm glad to be here. You look like you've been through the wringer."

Cathy smoothed her hair and attempted a smile. "I'm sure I look awful," she said. She crossed the room to a mirror and stared at her reflection. "I look so old. Old and tired."

Nick had found a chair and motioned for Cathy to sit beside him.

"Now, start at the beginning, and tell me everything."

"I don't know how much Matt told you."

"Not much. He left a voice message saying Melissa had disappeared and that he was leaving to find her. Honestly, Cathy, if I'd realized she was still missing, I'd have come sooner. I just assumed you'd found her. So—you think she was abducted?"

"We weren't sure at first. The authorities thought she ran away. I guess it makes sense they'd look at that first."

"Yeah, it makes sense from their shoes, but it must have been pretty frustrating for the two of you."

She nodded slowly. "But then Matt got a text message. It told us to come to Antigua, to this hotel. Then there was a note, and the phone calls began. Matt was supposed to meet this man last night."

Nick reached over and touched her arm. "Go ahead and cry, Cathy. Let it out."

"It's okay. I think I'm all cried out." Cathy pushed herself out of the chair and walked across the room to the window. "I was just thinking. What if Matt was mugged on the way to the meeting place? What if he didn't even meet the man?"

"I guess that's possible. Do you know where they were supposed to meet?"

"Some ruins," Cathy said. "I'm trying to remember the name. There are ruins all over this city. Even this hotel is built on ruins. Santa Clara. That's it."

Nick stood and joined her at the window. He turned Cathy's shoulders to face him. "I am so sorry. I feel responsible for all of this."

"Why would you be responsible? That doesn't make any sense."

"Sure it does. I've been thinking about it all the way here. If I hadn't left town when I did, Matt wouldn't have stayed behind to take care of things when you went on your trip. If he'd been with you, Melissa probably wouldn't have been taken."

"You didn't tell Matt to stay behind. That was his decision. He's always put work ahead of everything else." She shook her head and moved away from Nick to sit on the bed. "And even if you *had* told him to stay home, there's no way you could have known everything that was going to happen. Nobody has ever blamed you in all this."

"I've blamed myself."

"Well, don't," Cathy said. "If anybody is to blame, it's me. I'm the one who was with her . . ." Her voice drifted off, resigned. It was all old ground.

A noise from outside the room attracted Cathy's attention. She could hear footsteps as someone walked down the hall. Cathy stiffened, her eyes glued to the door. The footsteps approached and stopped in front of her room. When the steps began again, she exhaled slowly and closed her eyes.

"I'm so afraid," she said. "I don't dare leave the room. Matt asked me to promise him I wouldn't go anywhere. Actually, he told me to not even open the door. It was one of the last things he said to me before he left."

"I think you do need to be careful. But listen to me, Cathy. I'm going to do everything I can to protect you and help you find Matt and Melissa. That's why I came here. I don't want you to be afraid. If someone tries to hurt you, they're going to have to get past me first."

"You have no idea how much I appreciate your saying that. This morning, after you called, I felt so relieved. I started writing things down. Everything I could remember about the boy Melissa was with. What he looked like, what he was wearing, everything he said. I've been going over every detail, trying to come up with something that would give us a clue. I don't know what else I can do. I feel like I should be out there searching for them, but where would I even start to look?"

"Have you eaten anything today?"

"I don't feel like eating."

"I know, but you've got to keep your strength up."

Nick picked up the phone, pushed a button, and spoke into the receiver.

"I didn't know you spoke Spanish," Cathy said.

"I don't really. I just know enough to order food."

Cathy sat farther back on the bed and closed her eyes. "After all this is over, I don't know how we're going to repay you."

"You can repay me by helping me find your husband and get him back to work. You're doing the best thing you can do. If anybody can come up with a clue, it's going to be you because you're the last one who was with Melissa and you're the only one who knows what the boy looks like. So keep thinking, keep remembering and writing things down."

"I will. And thank you. Again."

They sat in silence for several minutes, absorbed in their own thoughts, until they heard a knock on the door. Nick opened the door and brought in the food he had ordered. "You need this even if you don't feel like it. And then

you need to get some sleep. We'll look at your list in the morning when we're both fresh."

Cathy nodded. "Thanks for coming, Nick. It really helps to have someone to talk to."

"I'm in the room right next door if you need me."

After Nick left, Cathy picked at the sliced cucumbers, tomatoes, and onions on her plate. Ordinarily vegetables marinated in a vinaigrette dressing would have appealed to her, but tonight nothing tasted good.

She was glad Nick had come. It felt so good to talk to someone and have him just understand. Compassion had never been Matt's strong suit. She'd misjudged Nick. Matt had always said he had a heart, but she'd been so frustrated over Matt's long hours away from home that she'd assumed he was getting pressure from Nick. "Always trying to squeeze more juice out of a dry orange," she'd said to Matt on more than one occasion.

Pushing the plate away, she climbed back onto the bed and propped the pillows behind her back. Now what? Matt had been gone for almost exactly twenty-four hours. She remembered how last night he had held her and promised he would return with Melissa. Her throat began to ache. *I'm not going to do this.*

Cathy slid off the bed and walked over to the patio doors. She pushed the curtains back. It was dark outside. She opened the door and stepped onto the terrace. Another balmy evening. The weather really was perfect here. Matt always said he'd move to Guatemala if it wasn't for the unstable government.

"High's going to be in the thirties here today," he'd say after he checked the weather. "What do you think the temperature is today in Guatemala City?"

"Oh, let me guess. Seventy-five. Am I right?"

"Close. It's seventy-two."

Cathy stepped back into the room and noticed her camera on the dresser. *I wonder.* She picked up the camera and scrolled through the pictures she'd taken in Tikal. Melissa next to a ceiba tree, Melissa beside a stela, the two of them in the Great Plaza, Melissa striking a pose in front of the ladder, Melissa and Cathy hugging on the top of Temple IV.

Nothing of Carlos.

She climbed onto the bed once again and pulled the covers up over her lap and then picked up the camera again. This time she scrolled through the pictures more slowly. She paused to study the last picture, taken at the top of Temple IV right before Melissa disappeared. She and Melissa were laughing; their arms were around each other, their faces pressed together. Cathy studied Melissa's face. She looked radiant. Carlos was responsible for that.

Carlos, what did you do with my daughter?

CHAPTER 29

THE BUS TO TIKAL WAS due to arrive, and there was still no sign of Javier. Maybe it had been a mistake to let him go, but Raul wasn't in the habit of keeping hostages. He figured the young man's lust for money would keep him coming back. His instincts told him Javier would try to play both hands in this game.

Just as the bus arrived, Javier appeared. Following Raul's instructions from the night before, Javier climbed onto the bus and chose a seat near the back. Raul sat across and slightly behind him. It gave him a good vantage point, and no one would suspect they were traveling together. Javier slumped against the window and pulled his red baseball cap down over his eyes.

As the bus pulled away from the curb, Raul noticed a boy with large sober eyes watching him. Raul smiled, and the boy smiled back. An older man snoozed in the seat next to the child, his eyes closed and his mouth open. Across the aisle was another, older, boy. Probably brothers. As Raul watched, the older boy leaned forward, reached across the aisle, and tapped his brother on the leg. Then he twisted to face forward. The boy with sober eyes spun around and reached across to tap the other boy. Raul watched in amusement as they continued their game. It reminded him of a time he and Marcos had ridden the bus with Marcos's father.

It was the fall they'd both turned ten, and Marcos's father decided to take them to the festival of All Saints in Todos Santos Cuchumatán. He bought them straw hats, candy-stripe pants, and thick cotton shirts with huge flapping pink collars. "It is the traditional costume," he told them, "which you have to wear to be able to go." Raul smiled as he remembered the delicious fiambre, the music of the marimba band, the dance of the conquistadores, and of course, the race.

The riders, most of whom had spent the previous night drinking hard liquor, were instructed to follow a course around the town, pausing at each lap for another swig of aguardiente. The winner of the race was the jockey who could stay on his

horse the longest, although everyone who participated was rowdily praised. Marcos and Raul watched the drunken stampede in delighted amusement. It was like nothing Raul had ever seen before.

Raul's conversation with Marcos as they rode the bus home was boisterous. They imagined growing up and returning together to ride in the streets of Todos Santos Cuchumatán.

"I will stay on my horse longer than you," Marcos had said.

"But you forget, all the best jockeys are small," Raul said. "And I am smaller than you."

"But I will be able to hold my liquor better than you."

"Says who?"

"Says me."

Raul and Marcos never returned to Todos Santos Cuchumatán. Instead they grew up to be soldiers.

Marcos wanted to join the army, and he convinced Raul to join with him. They knew nothing of war. They listened to speeches denouncing Communism and were entranced by the khaki uniforms and the idea of change. They could not have known that the military's efforts to wipe out the threat of Communist insurrection would turn into a virtual slaughter of the Maya. In years to come, people would call it genocide. At the time, though, it was called following orders given by the Guatemalan Army, and in the end, more than six hundred villages had been destroyed, 200,000 people killed or missing.

At first Raul worked side by side with Marcos, enjoying the camaraderie and the discipline, but after the massacre at Río Negro, Raul realized that he was in a place he could not be, so he deserted and Marcos continued. Marcos's people were not the targets.

Raul thought back to his recent conversation with Marcos and, for the first time, wondered about the burden Marcos had carried with him. He imagined trading places with Marcos and was grateful to be in his own shoes. Better to be the hunted than to be the hunter. But could the hunted forgive the hunter?

The bus pulled into the parking lot and stopped. Raul would be the last person off the bus, as he always was. Habit. Years of studying people, assessing them, occasionally seeing what no one else saw, what he was paid to see. Today was no different. He scrutinized each person as they exited and then followed Javier down the steps and onto the path leading to Tikal.

They walked through the jungle, past the park entrance and the reservoir. They continued past the courtyard and on toward Temple IV before veering off the path and away from people. Only then did Raul speak to Javier, and then only in hushed tones. They hiked for nearly two hours, stopping occasionally for a brief rest before continuing on through the dense jungle vegetation.

Finally Javier came to the campsite. "This is it."

Raul's eyes scanned the area. "Where did you keep the girl?"

Javier led Raul to the cenote, where the ladder still stood in place. Raul motioned for Javier to climb down first then followed. Once they were at the bottom, Raul turned on his flashlight. Squatting on the ground, he studied the area where Melissa had lain. He saw a strand of red hair and put it in his pocket.

After exploring the cenote, they returned to the surface and Raul began a methodical search of the clearing. It wasn't long until he found where Carlos and Melissa had stepped into the jungle. "We begin our search here," he said.

* * *

César pushed back the branches and stepped into a clearing. Carlos and Melissa had been there. He was sure of it. He moved slowly, his eyes scanning the ground. After a few minutes he noticed a pile of papaya pits and picked one up. Turning it over in his hands, he saw bits of fruit meat still clinging to the pit. It was fresh. His eyes surveyed the area again, pausing by the cave entrance. He stooped to look inside. It was empty. He knelt in the dirt and studied the floor. He could see the remnants of a fire. He touched the blackened soil. The cave had been recently occupied. Turning away from the cave, he studied the clearing again. He retraced his steps around the perimeter, halting when he saw the bent branches and undergrowth.

They can't be far, he thought as he stepped into the jungle. He took a few steps and stopped to listen. The sound was unmistakable. Running water was just ahead. Carlos would have heard the water too.

César followed their inadvertent trail through the rainforest, pausing just long enough to listen for the water flowing in the distance. Finally, he parted some reeds and saw the stream. He studied the banks of the river and the area nearby, noting the matted grass and pieces of bamboo strewn on the ground.

He looked at the sky. The sun was dropping on the horizon. He would need to keep moving if he hoped to find them before dark.

* * *

The sun beat down on Melissa and Carlos as the hours passed and evening approached. They spoke now and then but mostly floated in silence, occasionally using their poles to steer around a rock or away from the riverbank. Progress was slow.

More and more often, Melissa's thoughts returned to her parents. She wondered if they had given up looking for her. Whenever she thought of them, guilt

washed over her followed by a resolve to be better if they found her. *When* they found her.

She turned her head and caught Carlos watching her. His look was disquieting, his voice low. "When you go back to Los Estados Unidos, will there be a boyfriend waiting there for you?"

Josh. She didn't answer at once. Finally she said softly, "I don't know."

He waited, his black eyes challenging her to continue.

"What I mean is, I had a boyfriend, but I don't know if . . . Things are different."

His lips twisted, mocking her. "How different?"

"Everything is different. I'm different." She dropped her head. "You wouldn't understand."

"Maybe not, but I am a boy, and I am sure your boyfriend will still want you."

She flushed at his bold insinuation and looked away. "It's not just that."

"Then what?"

"I don't know if I will still want him."

Carlos grinned. "Ah, I see how it is. Now that you have been with Carlos and see what a real man is like, you no longer love your rich boyfriend in Los Estados Unidos."

Melissa pulled a face at Carlos. He was closer to the truth than she wanted to admit, even to herself. His eyes refused to leave her face, and she could feel her cheeks burning.

"Tell me about this boyfriend."

Her lips curved into a smile. "His name is Josh, and he's very attractive."

Carlos looked away. "Then why don't you love him anymore?"

"I didn't say I don't love him anymore."

"But you didn't say that you do."

Melissa sighed. "It's just that I don't know what I think anymore." That was simple enough to say. She stared into the jungle. "My parents don't like him. They don't think he's good for me."

"What do you think?"

"I don't know. Maybe they're right."

Her eyes shifted back to Carlos, expecting to see sympathy or understanding, but his expression had changed, and he was staring over her shoulder.

"What's wrong?"

"Sit still and don't talk," he said, grabbing the pole and pushing it against the bottom of the river.

Melissa turned to follow where Carlos's eyes were focused.

"What are you looking at?"

He watched a spot in the water without blinking while he maneuvered the raft downstream.

"What's going on, Carlos?"

"Señorita, you must be quiet," he said, his voice low, any hint of flirtation gone.

"I'll be quiet if you'll tell me what's going on."

A moment passed before he answered. "There's a croc."

"A crocodile?" Her voice rose, panicked.

"You have to be quiet," he said again, sharply this time.

She turned to follow his eyes and then saw it. The crocodile was swimming just under the surface, a few yards from their raft. Her eyes fixed on the dark line in the water as Carlos labored to steer the raft away from it. Neither spoke. Melissa gripped the side of the raft. In the distance she could hear the loud throaty squawk of a macaw. After a few moments, the line disappeared under the water, and Carlos looked at Melissa and exhaled audibly.

"That was close," he said.

Melissa nodded. Her heart was still hammering. She reached across the raft to touch Carlos's hand. "Thanks," she said.

"Hey, no problem. Remember, this is Carlos you're dealing with." He tried to smile, but Melissa could hear the shakiness in his voice.

Just then she looked over his shoulder and saw a dark line under the water, closer than before. Her throat constricted. She tried to talk but couldn't. Instead, she grabbed for Carlos's shoulder and pointed. He twisted around and gasped then grabbed the pole and propelled the raft downstream, away from the approaching crocodile.

Melissa watched as the dark line drew closer. Each time Carlos maneuvered the raft, the crocodile changed directions, narrowing the distance. Then the crocodile lifted out of the water and opened its jaws to reveal jagged rows of teeth and snapped them shut again. Melissa screamed and lost her balance, falling near the edge of the raft. Carlos scrambled to grab her and pull her back from the edge, but not before the crocodile swam to the side of the raft and snapped at her moving body. Carlos grasped the pole and jabbed the crocodile. The crocodile lunged for the pole, snatched it from Carlos, and crushed it between its powerful jaws. Melissa screamed again as she watched Carlos stumble and fall. He caught himself and pushed away from the edge as the crocodile's jaws closed next to his leg. The crocodile bumped his nose against the raft repeatedly. Carlos pulled his

knife from his pocket; he and Melissa clung to the sides of the raft as it rocked in the water. The crocodile lifted a webbed foot onto the raft, and they felt it tip toward the reptile. Carlos stabbed at the crocodile, missed, and stabbed again and again. Each time, he barely escaped its snapping jaws as Melissa hung on to the raft and tried to keep it from capsizing. She felt her fingers slipping and screamed again. Carlos looked back at her, his face stricken but determined.

"You have to swim," he said.

The crocodile lifted its foot again, tilting the raft and plunging Melissa into the water. She surfaced and saw the crocodile swivel its head to see the sudden movement. "Swim!" Carlos yelled as he plunged the knife into the crocodile. The crocodile whipped around to face Carlos, the knife embedded in its neck. Carlos grabbed for its mouth, his hands closing around the crocodile's jaws. The crocodile shook his snout back and forth as Melissa watched in horror then forced her body to move toward the shore. Glancing back, she could see Carlos's muscles bulging as he struggled to contain the crocodile's razor-sharp teeth. Then the crocodile gave a final jerk, and Carlos lost his grip on the creature's mouth and fell into the water. The crocodile whirled around and snapped at Carlos's arm. Carlos grabbed the raft and tried to push it between himself and the crocodile. Just as Melissa reached the riverbank, the crocodile's jaws closed on Carlos's leg and pulled him under the water. Melissa watched Carlos thrash, fighting to keep his head above the water, and then the crocodile began to roll, forcing Carlos under the current.

CHAPTER 30

IT WAS ONLY A FEW miles from Salamá to the pueblo of Chilasco—a few battered homes and a large playing field—where Eduardo directed them to an unobtrusive place to leave the car.

Being there reminded Matt of another day, several years before, when Santiago had brought him to Chilasco. On that day, they had visited the jade pillar that sat in the school yard. The locals told him it had been found buried in the ground about thirty years before, and it had taken three hundred villagers to haul it there. They had once used it for hanging criminals, the men told him.

But on this day, there was no sightseeing. A light misty rain had started to fall, and the sky was gray. The three men gathered their supplies and began the hike into the cloud forest of the Sierra de Las Minas. The dirt trail quickly became muddy and slick as the rain continued in a steady drizzle. They pulled their shirts up over their heads and kept their eyes on the ground as they stepped around the large mossy stones embedded in the path.

They hiked for more than two hours, often in a steep descent. Clinging to the guide ropes, they gingerly made their way down the loose, wet rock. More than once, Matt lost his footing and slid down the incline. Progress was slow as they sloshed through the mud. Matt kept his eyes on the trail, glancing only occasionally at Santiago, who was hunched against the rain directly in front of him. He could hear Eduardo breathing behind him. At another time, he would have noticed the orchids lining the trail, water glistening on their petals. He would have stopped to admire the water lilies and the ferns. He would have seen the iridescent green-and-red quetzal birds in the trees. But today his mind was occupied with one thing only.

If Eduardo needed to be shown the way to the jade cache, then Melissa would not be there. She couldn't be. Eduardo didn't know where it was.

Why he wanted to go there seemed obvious enough. If Eduardo knew the jade's location, he would also have the ability to excavate and sell it. Eduardo's

motive had to be money. But that left unanswered the whereabouts of Melissa, and that gnawed at Matt.

Santiago paused in the path to call over his shoulder. "I hear the falls. They're just ahead."

Matt stopped and listened; he too could hear the rush of water. As they trudged on, the noise from the cascade grew louder and louder until they had to shout to hear each other.

A few more moments and they could see the falls. The water was immense, spilling down the mountainside as if in slow motion, bouncing from rock to rock. They stopped to gaze at the falls and could feel a fine mist on their faces.

Matt was breathing heavily, but Eduardo ignored him and pointed at Santiago. "Keep moving," he said.

"We need to refill our canteens before we move on," Santiago said.

Santiago moved closer to the pool at the base of the waterfall. Large rocks lay around the edge of the falls and in the water. Santiago stepped onto one, testing his footing, before he knelt and dipped the canteen into the pond.

Matt moved to join Santiago. He could feel Eduardo's eyes on him. The stones were wet and slick. He stepped from one rock to another, his foot slipping each time it met the wet surface. *Just a little farther.*

"That's enough; let's go."

Matt lost his balance. His foot slid off the rock, catching the toe of his shoe between two stones. His legs buckled, and he heard a distinct crunch as his ankle twisted. Stabbing pain shot through his calf. Collapsing on a rock, he bent forward and took several deep breaths as he waited for the throbbing to subside. Just then he felt a sharp kick in his thigh, sending fresh waves of pain through his leg.

"Get moving."

Matt clamped his eyes shut and tried to move. Beads of perspiration formed on his brow. He pushed himself up, wincing as he tried to stand. Then he felt Santiago's hand grasping his arm, lifting him, steadying him. Santiago supported his weight as they moved across the rocks.

Matt heard a gun being cocked and felt Santiago stiffen. Bracing himself against the pain, Matt forced himself to move more quickly. Once across the water, Santiago helped Matt sit on the bank and knelt beside him to look at his ankle. It was bruised and swollen.

"He sprained his ankle," Santiago said. "He cannot walk on it."

Eduardo leveled the gun at Matt's head and looked at Santiago. "Then we will go on without him," he said. "You will take me to the jade."

"We have an agreement," Matt said. "I take you to the place, and you give me back my daughter."

"Yes, this is an unfortunate turn of events. But, you see, I need the location, and your friend will take me there. I no longer need you, Mr. Miller."

Santiago stepped between the two men. "If you kill him, you will never find the jade," he said.

Eduardo turned his gun toward Santiago. "You will take me there."

Santiago stared at Eduardo without flinching. "No, señor, I will not take you there."

"Then you will die."

"So be it."

Eduardo narrowed his eyes and laughed. "Ah, such bravery, to die for your friend. I wonder if you will be so brave when the gun is pointed at your wife and children."

"NO!" Matt pushed himself up against the searing pain. "I can keep going. We will take you."

Eduardo turned his eyes back to Matt. "We will see. But remember, you are expendable."

Matt nodded. Santiago slipped his arm around Matt's waist and held him as they moved away from the falls.

CHAPTER 31

MELISSA GRABBED THE WEEDS ALONG the shore and pulled herself out of the water. When she turned back to look for Carlos, she could still see the crocodile thrashing and rolling.

She screamed again and again until her screams were stifled by rough hands that clamped her mouth shut and jerked her into the woods. Struggling against the strength of the hold, she felt the muzzle of a gun in her ribs. She froze, waiting. After a few seconds, the man lowered his gun and relaxed his grip. Her heart pounded in her ears. Then she felt a blow on the back of her head. Her legs buckled, and everything began to whirl. She was only vaguely aware of hands pulling her, jerking her backward, and rope scratching her wrists before everything went black.

It was dark when she regained consciousness. She could see the flicker of a small campfire a few feet away and could smell burning wood. Men's voices reached her. For a moment she thought she was back in the camp with Carlos. Then she remembered, and the awfulness of that memory swept over her. *Carlos.* Her throat constricted; she was choking. She fought the urge to scream. Squeezing her eyes shut, she forced herself to breathe. She had to think. Lying on the ground, she tried to reconstruct what had happened after the crocodile attack, but it was gone.

The men's voices grew louder. She lay still and listened, trying to make out what they were saying. She opened her eyes again and could see two men. The one facing her was taller and more thickly built, his hair cropped short. The other man's hair hung below his shoulders. Their voices grew more heated until the long-haired man stood and pointed toward where she was lying on the ground. He spit and swore under his breath.

"*La chica es mía,*" he said. "I have a deal."

A chill went through Melissa's body. *The girl is mine.* They were arguing about her.

"You *had* a deal. That was before you lost her."

"Yeah, okay, there was a problem, but I took care of it."

The man with closely cropped hair laughed. "If you're smart, you'll take off and never show your face again." He stood and walked toward her, his back to the other man. His lips were curved into a mirthless smile, and his eyes were cold steel.

Just then the smaller man turned to face Melissa; she gasped as she recognized César. César lunged at his rival, but not before the other man pulled a gun from his belt and fired. Melissa screamed again as she watched César fall to the ground.

The man checked César's pulse and then walked over to the smoldering coals and stomped on them. He picked up his pack, slung it over his shoulder, and returned to where Melissa was lying on the ground. He yanked her to her feet and pushed her in front of him. They marched in silence for what seemed like hours. The darkness in the jungle amplified every sound. Melissa was terrified, but still she forced her feet to move forward. Finally the man parted some branches, and they stepped out onto a narrow road. Eventually, they came to an abandoned truck, hidden among the trees. He surveyed the area, opened the truck door, and thrust Melissa inside, closing and locking the door behind her.

* * *

Raul and Javier tracked Melissa all afternoon and evening, pausing only when they came to the cave where Melissa and Carlos had spent the night and again when they reached the river. Raul studied the pieces of broken bamboo.

It was growing dark, but they kept moving, following the riverbed. They pushed on through the oppressive heat, the hunger, and now the overwhelming fatigue. Finally they stopped to rest.

They had just started to move again when they heard the gunshot.

Beside him, Raul heard Javier's sharp intake of breath. They waited, but there was no other sound. They began again, more cautiously than before. An owl hooted far in the distance.

After a few moments walking in silence, Raul stopped. His instincts told him something was wrong, but the only sounds were the steady flow of nearby water and an occasional rustle in the jungle undergrowth. He surveyed the area with his flashlight, pausing on a makeshift raft caught against a deadfall in the river several yards downstream. From across the clearing, Raul heard Javier make a quiet but distinct sound. "Ch-ch."

Raul turned and hurried to where Javier stood staring at the ground. A man lay facedown, dead.

"This explains the gunshot we heard," Raul said. "Do you know him?"

"Yeah, I know him. That's César," Javier said.

Raul searched the area. He found pieces of charcoal, still warm to touch, and cigarette butts. Then he returned to the place where he had seen the raft and systematically combed the riverbank with his flashlight. After a few minutes, he saw something that chilled him: a body caught in the reeds along the shore. Raul shined his light on the face and heard Javier gasp.

"It's Carlos," Javier whispered. "A gun didn't do that to him."

Raul shook his head. "No, this was most likely a crocodile attack." His eyes narrowed as he studied the surrounding area. "Which means Melissa is either alone or with the shooter."

"Or in the river."

Without answering, Raul pulled what remained of the body out of the river and placed it beside the other body.

He could hear Javier pacing. Otherwise, the only sounds were those from the nearby river and the jungle wildlife.

"Give me my money," Javier said. Raul glanced at the younger man; his face was scared but determined. "If Carlos didn't kill César, then there's somebody else out there. Whoever killed César will kill me. I'm getting out of here."

"I still need your help."

"You're not listening. They're both dead, and I'm next. I'm done. Give me my money, or I'm going to take it from you."

"Tell me why they want Melissa."

"I don't know what you're talking about." Javier's eyes darted around the area.

"You know something, and as soon as you tell me, I'll give you the money. Why did they choose her?"

"It's not her; it's her father."

"Her father? What are you talking about?"

"I was just paid to keep her. That's all."

"But you said something about her father."

Javier exhaled. "César said we were keeping the girl until they got her father to do something. That's all I know. Now give me my money."

Raul stared at Javier. Finally he reached into his pocket, opened his wallet, and withdrew some cash. Javier snatched the money from Raul and fled back the way they had come.

Raul searched the perimeter, looking for a break in the foliage. Finally, he found what he was looking for and was about to leave the clearing when an image came into his mind, and with it, a feeling that compelled him to walk back to where he and Javier had left the bodies. Kneeling beside the young man's remains, Raul focused the flashlight on his face. It seemed familiar. Why? Raul closed his eyes and concentrated. And then, in his mind, he could see the image of a photograph as clearly as if he was holding it in his hand. The boy in the marketplace. The brother who had gone on a job and hadn't returned. Raul studied the young man lying on the ground before him. The boy's name had been Carlos. It all fit.

Raul lifted his face toward the sky. He needed to be on his way. Already he had spent too long. There was nothing more he could do.

His mind returned to Juan, the ten-year-old boy with hopeful eyes, awaiting his brother's return. His mother, who must be desperate with worry. He had to give them something he had been denied. He had to give them answers.

He moved both bodies into the clearing and covered them with river rocks. That should keep them safe from wildlife until the authorities were notified. Satisfied that he had done all he could, Raul stepped into the jungle, away from the river, following the trail left by the unidentified gunman. It was easy to follow and eventually led him to a narrow road.

He walked south toward the nearest town. Although the road was sparsely populated, especially this late in the evening, eventually an old rusted green truck pulled up beside Raul. The driver offered to take Raul to Santa Elena.

As they drove, Raul called the local police to report finding both Carlos and César in the rainforest. He shared what he believed to be Carlos's identity and explained where their bodies could be recovered. Then Raul dialed Matt's cell phone number. When no one answered, he called the hotel and asked them to connect his call to the Miller's room.

* * *

They drove through the night without stopping. Melissa begged the man to tell her where he was taking her and what he was going to do with her, but he remained silent. Finally she gave up, turned her face toward the door, and closed her eyes.

Her thoughts drifted to Carlos. She pictured his hair curling around his ears, his eyes flirting when he quizzed her about her boyfriend. She felt the sun baking her skin as they floated down the river; the warmth of his arms around her when she was afraid.

Another memory came: Carlos flailing against the crocodile. She tried to block out the image as grief swept over her. Melissa's throat ached; tears trickled onto her cheeks. She wiped her face on her sleeve. And then another image invaded her mind—Carlos's mother at home, his younger brother and sisters. A moan caught in her throat as she mourned for a mother she hadn't met who would never know why her son hadn't come home, siblings who would never again hear his voice or feel his hands rumpling their hair. They would never know he had sacrificed his life for her.

Melissa cried until exhaustion overcame her and she fell asleep.

When she awoke, sunlight was streaming into the truck. They were following a white Toyota pickup with at least a dozen young black-haired boys standing, jammed together, in the truck bed. A framework fastened across the top of the truck kept the boys from falling off the pickup. The road curved, and Melissa watched as the boys leaned over the sides of the truck, laughing and jostling each other. *That's something my parents never would have allowed.* She turned her face toward the side window. Trees with occasional small purple flowers lined the road.

They entered a town built on lush green rolling hills with palm trees dotting the landscape. They passed yellow, purple, and blue houses with sheet metal roofs. On the horizon, she could see a steep mountain range.

They passed a soda machine standing next to an aqua-blue building. Two women sat on the sidewalk holding an umbrella for shade. Another woman walked along the street, a round woven basket loaded with tapestry on her head. In front of her a man walked, pushing a cart filled with peeled oranges.

The truck slowed, turned into a parking lot, and stopped. Her captor pulled a satellite phone from his pocket and typed a short text message then climbed out of the truck and walked around the side to Melissa's door. Melissa could hear the crunch of his boots on the gravel. He opened her door, grasped her arm, and pulled her out. Twisting her arm behind her back, he shoved her forward, toward the motel.

CHAPTER 32

Day 8

CATHY SLEPT RESTLESSLY, HER SLEEP interrupted by dreams. She saw herself running mile after mile on an ancient stone road high in the mountains, pursued by an unseen foe. Melissa's voice called to her, luring her on in a desperate chase. At each turn in the road, she expected to see Melissa, but instead the road stretched farther ahead, higher, steeper, the footsteps behind her pounding in her ears. She awoke in a cold sweat.

Climbing off the bed, she walked to the mirror and splashed water onto her face. Her face was gaunt. What a lousy way to lose weight.

The ring of the phone startled her. She stared at it while it rang three more times before she picked it up.

A voice she didn't recognize asked for Matt. Before she could respond, the man spoke again. "*Hermana*, this is Raul Silva, and I must talk to your husband right away."

"Matt isn't here," Cathy said. "The day after we talked to you in the cathedral, this man called and told Matt to meet him in the Santa Clara ruins. He left that night, and I haven't seen him since."

"I'm very sorry to hear this," Raul said.

"Yes—it's . . . But that's not why you called. Do you know something about Melissa?" Cathy said.

"Only a little. I spoke with a man who had seen her."

"Then she's alive? She's all right? Please, tell me everything you know."

"I am sorry; I do not know any more than that," Raul said. "But now, hermana, I need you to think carefully. I need you to think of any reason why someone would want your husband. Any reason at all. Is there something they might want from him. Money?"

"No. I mean, Matt makes a good living, and we have a little savings, but not like that."

"Hermana, what does your husband do for a job?"

"He imports jade. Why?"

"He imports jade to the United States from Guatemala?"

"Yes, that's right. Do you think that could have something to do with this?"

"I do not know, hermana. Can you tell me if there is someone he does business with here? Someone I could talk to?"

"He works with a man named Santiago. But I'm sure Santiago isn't involved in any of this. Matt taught and baptized him when he was on his mission. Surely you can't suspect him."

"No, of course not, hermana. I'm sure your friend is not involved. But maybe he knows something that will help us find your husband. Do you know where he lives?"

Cathy glanced around the room. "His address must be here someplace. I can look through Matt's things and see if I can find it."

"Yes, that would be good. But for now, please tell me what you remember about this friend."

"I know he lives near the jade, in a small village. Somewhere near the mountains."

"And his surname?"

"I'm sorry; I can't think of his last name. I should know it. It's a common name."

Cathy heard a light tap on the door. "Someone's here."

"Are you expecting anyone?"

Cathy swallowed, her eyes fixed on the door. She heard the knocking again and then a voice. "Cathy, it's me—Nick. Are you all right?"

She exhaled. "It's okay. It's Nick."

"Nick? This is someone you know?"

"Yes, he's Matt's boss. He called yesterday morning to see how we were doing, and when I told him Matt was gone, he offered to fly down to help search."

"Then maybe he would know about Santiago."

"Yes, he might know something. I'll ask him." Cathy stepped to the door and opened it. She smiled at Nick and motioned for him to come inside.

"I'm trying to get information about Santiago. You wouldn't happen to know his last name or where he lives, would you?"

"Santiago?"

"Matt's supplier here in Guatemala."

"Oh, I'm sorry, Cathy, but I'm afraid Matt handles all of that. Who is looking for him?"

"I'll explain in a minute," she said, returning to her conversation with Raul. "I guess he doesn't know, but I'll look as soon as we hang up and call you back if I find something."

Cathy wrote down the cell number and finished her conversation with Raul before turning to face Nick. "That was Raul Silva."

"Raul?"

"He was the guard on our tour bus. He's been trying to help us find Melissa, and he told me just now that he talked with someone who has seen her."

"Really? What did he say?"

Cathy reviewed her conversation with Raul. After she finished, Nick was silent for several seconds and then said, "Do you think it's a good idea to talk so freely to someone you don't really know? I'm not trying to scare you, Cathy, but weren't you warned not to talk to anyone? For all you know, this guy could be involved somehow. Did he give you any real information?"

"I told you; he talked to someone who has seen her."

"Who? What did they say?"

Cathy sank onto the bed and cupped her face in her hands.

"He didn't tell you, did he?"

"No, he didn't. He wanted to know about Matt."

"What about Matt? From what you told me, he wanted to know about Matt's business. Doesn't that seem a little odd to you?"

"I trust Raul, Nick."

"And I'm not saying you shouldn't. Well, maybe I am. The truth is we don't know whom we can trust right now. Raul is probably just fine, but how do you know? If he *were* involved—think about this—what better way would there be than to pose as a guard on a tour bus? Who is going to suspect him? I know you don't want to believe he could do something like that, but the point is we just don't know. We can't know. And we can't risk giving information to the wrong people."

"Of course. You're right. So what do I do?"

"Don't take any more chances. Stay safe in this room, and don't answer the phone."

"But Nick, what if Matt calls? Or Melissa? I can't agree to that!"

"What could you do if one of them did call?" He touched her arm. "I know you're really frightened, and I know you want to help them, but the best way you can help them is to stay safe yourself. You need to trust me to figure things out. We don't want anything to happen to you."

Cathy walked to the window and stared outside at the blue sky. She felt like she'd been punched in the stomach. Nick joined her at the window. When he spoke, his voice was soft, almost tender. "Hey, I'm just trying to take care of you, you know?"

"I know," Cathy said. "And I do appreciate it. So what's next?"

"If you're okay here, I thought I'd head over to the embassy in Guatemala City and see what I can find out there," Nick said.

Cathy nodded.

"We're going to get through this, Cathy. Use your cell phone if you need to call me while I'm gone." He paused. "Is there anything you need before I go?"

"No, I'll be fine."

Cathy listened for the door to close before she turned from the window and walked across the room, stubbing her toe on the corner of a chair as she moved past it. Tears sprang to her eyes as pain shot through her foot. *That's right, kick me when I'm down.* She flopped onto the bed, pounded her fist on the pillow, and wept. *I can't do this.*

After the tears subsided, she lay quietly on the bed for a time before she sat up and wiped her eyes. She needed to find Matt's planner.

What if Nick was right? Maybe she shouldn't trust Raul so implicitly. But Scott trusted him; the tour company had hired him. Surely that meant something. Nick was being protective, but he didn't know Raul. And he was wrong.

Cathy yanked the suitcase up onto the bed and unzipped it. *Matt's clothes.* Choking back a sob, she squeezed her eyes shut. *I don't have time for this. I can't keep falling apart.* She took a deep breath, opened her eyes, and forced herself to look at the pile of hastily folded clothing. Matt's planner had to be there. She rummaged through his clothes, feeling along the edges of the suitcase until her fingers closed on something small, hard, and rectangular.

She slid the book out and stared at the black leather. She stroked the cover of the book before she opened it and saw his handwriting. She always teased him that he should have been a doctor because no one else could read anything he wrote.

She sat on the edge of the bed and turned the pages. They were largely blank, with an occasional note about a deadline or meeting scrawled under the date. The last notation was written on February 7, the day Melissa had disappeared: Dinner at Chili's.

Cathy flipped to the address book at the back of the planner. She ran her finger down each listing until she found the name she was looking for: Santiago Gonzales.

Just then her cell phone rang. Maybe it was Raul.

She answered the phone, but instead of Raul, she heard Nick's voice. "Hey, didn't I tell you not to answer the phone?"

Cathy knew he was teasing, but his words still bothered her.

He continued. "I just got to the embassy and thought I'd give you a quick ring while I'm waiting to talk to Mr. Whittaker."

"I hope you get more out of him than we did."

"I intend to." Nick paused before adding, "I noticed a man outside your room this morning."

"What was he doing?"

"He wasn't really doing anything; that's the thing. I watched him for several minutes and—I don't know—it was weird. It's probably nothing; I just want you to be extra careful while I'm not there. I don't want to come back tonight and find you missing too."

"I'll be fine."

"I know you will. Well, I need to go. It looks like Mr. Whittaker is ready for me."

After double-checking the lock on her door, Cathy walked to the window. A couple stood in the courtyard together. *Could have been Matt and me.* She had to call Raul.

* * *

She couldn't stay in the bathroom long, or he would get suspicious. Melissa retrieved her phone from where it was hidden beneath her clothes. It was supposed to be water-resistant, but would it be enough? *Please, please, please.* She pressed the button and held her breath until the light came on. *Thank you!* It took forever for the phone to power on. One percent battery. One bar. *Please, let it be enough.* She touched the compose text box and typed a message.

No bars. Melissa moved the phone around until one bar showed again and pressed send.

Send failed. Retry?

Yes.

She watched the dial go around and around. *Hurry. Please hurry.*

Send failed. Retry?

Yes.

The screen went dark. The battery was gone.

CHAPTER 33

IT HAD BEEN NEARLY TWENTY-FOUR hours of hiking through the cloud forest. Matt, Santiago, and Eduardo stopped for the night along the path, where they took turns watching for animals. When dawn broke, they began their march again, moving steadily and slowly toward the misty peaks of the Sierra de Las Minas. Santiago supported Matt as much as he could, but the pain in Matt's ankle was excruciating. Their only rest came when Eduardo wanted a cigarette, and that wasn't often enough.

"How much farther is it?" Matt asked Santiago as they paused on the path. Beads of perspiration had formed on his upper lip. His eyes were weary but determined.

Santiago studied the sky and shook his head. "Maybe we get there late tomorrow. Maybe the next day. It is still far."

"I can make it," Matt said, grimacing as he shifted his weight to lean against a mossy boulder. Balancing on one leg, he elevated his injured foot on a nearby rock and pulled up his pant leg. His ankle had doubled in size, and the bruising extended halfway up the inside of his calf.

"Are you sure that Melissa is okay?" Santiago asked.

Matt shook his head.

Eduardo had paused to take a swig from his canteen. He replaced it in his pack. *"Vamos ya."*

"How do we know you have his daughter?" Santiago asked. "Or that she is okay?"

"You don't. Now let's get moving," Eduardo said.

"We must see her," Santiago said. "We're not going any farther until we see her."

"You're not in a position to make demands," Eduardo said.

"I think I'm in a very good position. Without me, you won't find what you're looking for."

Eduardo's eyes narrowed. He looked back and forth between the two men.

"It is not too much to ask to know that his daughter is okay," Santiago said. "Then we will do what you want."

Eduardo pulled the gun from his belt and cocked it.

"There is no need for this," Matt said. "We just have to know Melissa is okay, and then we'll take you where you want to go."

Eduardo pointed the gun at Matt. "I don't need you," he said.

"If you kill him, I will never take you to the jade," Santiago said. "We wait here until we see his daughter—alive and unharmed."

Matt's heart pounded. He could see anger in Eduardo's eyes. He glanced sideways at Santiago and was surprised at how calm Santiago looked. Calm and resolute.

After what seemed like an hour, Eduardo pulled the satellite phone from his pocket. Matt watched as Eduardo studied his phone. He saw a slight smile cross his face and an almost imperceptible nod. Not sure what it meant, he waited and silently prayed.

Finally Eduardo replaced his phone and opened his pack. He withdrew a rope and tossed it to Santiago. "Tie him up," he said. "You're coming with me to find a signal."

After he was bound, Matt listened to the retreating footsteps. His hands and feet were tied and his leg ached. He leaned back against the boulder and tried to relax.

The cloud forest was mostly in shadows, with sunlight barely penetrating the dense canopy and pervasive mist. Trees were shorter and more thickly built there; their leaves dripped moisture onto the boggy forest floor. Moss and ferns carpeted the ground and any fallen logs. Matt breathed in the damp green aroma of rotting vegetation.

He thought about Cathy and wondered how she was doing. He pictured her in his mind, the way he had left her, her eyes full of tears, her chin quivering, trying to be brave. She must be going crazy. He'd always said she worried enough for both of them. Matt shifted his weight. He couldn't stay comfortable in one place for very long. Just like in life. He liked variety, challenge—needed it, even. Cathy used to like that about him. Now she liked stability. She said that life threw enough curve balls; she wanted to be able to count on some things. What she meant was she wanted him to do the same thing day after monotonous day. She didn't understand why he couldn't do that.

He remembered when Nick had first approached him at a buying show and offered him a chance to make more money. "Right now you're doing it

all," Nick had said with a handshake and a smile. "Let's get you doing what you do best and let other people take care of everything else."

Nick owned a multimillion-dollar business marketing precious gems all across the globe. But he didn't have jade, and he thought the gem would add an interesting and profitable branch to his company. So he'd offered Matt a position. Matt would have autonomy, and he'd get rid of the paperwork that had occupied so much of his time before. He could concentrate on new product design—which he loved—and discovering new clientele. Instead of the small ma-and-pa business he'd been building, he'd now be international. The new challenge had excited him almost as much as the promise of a bigger paycheck, so he'd called Santiago. The demand for jade was about to increase, and he wondered if Santiago could keep up with it. Santiago had agreed—he was willing to work harder if it meant more money for his family.

Matt had gone home that night with a bouquet of flowers and the good news. But Cathy hadn't seen it as good news. All she'd seen was Matt spending more time away from home. With a little time, though, Cathy had warmed up to Nick. Nick certainly knew how to charm a woman. Maybe a little too well.

Matt looked over at the hillside surrounding him. It was covered in wild flowers—orchids and bromeliads. Yellow, orange, purple, pink. *Fuchsia,* he corrected himself.

"Get it right, Matt," he could hear Cathy saying, her eyes twinkling. "There are lots of shades of pink in the world. Which one is it?"

They'd met in an art class they'd both taken to fill a general education requirement. He'd been in his last semester and desperate for any class that would work with his schedule. She was actually interested in the subject and amused by everything he didn't know. They were so different. She'd looked at him that day, her eyebrows raised, her lips tilted in a mocking smile, strands of her auburn hair falling around her face, and life had never been the same since. She taught him about the nuances of color, and he taught her about—what? Patience, mostly.

Their first three babies had died before they were born, and something died in Cathy along with them. She'd gotten scared. When Melissa had finally come, Cathy clung so tightly to her, as if she thought she could keep bad things away if she just held her close enough.

And now this.

The low hum of the forest was shattered by the distant shriek of a howler monkey. He wondered what time it was. Not that it made any difference.

Melissa had tolerated her mother's protectiveness fairly well until the last few months. Until Josh. But even with Josh, Cathy managed to maintain

closeness. Of course it hurt her when Melissa pushed her away, but she dealt with it.

Better than he did.

It wasn't so much that Melissa was pushing them away as what she was pulling toward. Matt didn't like Josh, flat and simple. Didn't trust him. He was a kid going nowhere fast, and he was taking Melissa with him. And Cathy, Cathy who always gave everybody the benefit of the doubt, thought they should just wait it out. But that wasn't Matt's style.

He'd tried to talk to Melissa, but she wouldn't listen. She'd slammed the door on the way out of his study and skipped dinner. He'd thought about going to her bedroom and trying to talk to her again but didn't. She wouldn't have listened anyway, and he figured she'd get over it eventually.

Cathy had been quiet that night.

The next morning, Cathy and Melissa had left for Guatemala.

Matt watched a bird on a branch across from him. It held perfectly still and stared at him. Melissa loved birds. Matt had given her a birdfeeder one year for Christmas and hung it in a tree in their backyard. All winter she'd sat with her nose pressed against the window and waited for the birds to come.

Evening was approaching. Before long, the fog would descend, settling into pockets all around him. Santiago and Eduardo should be getting back.

He rotated his foot. If Cathy were there, she'd have his foot in Epsom salts. She always took care of him; her nurturing was so much a part of her that he hardly noticed what she did, and now he wondered if she knew how much he loved her.

The first time he told her he loved her they'd been standing outside in the rain for an hour, waiting for her roommate to show up with a key. He always wondered if that was an excuse. Finally, when he couldn't think of anything else to say, he'd stared at the ground and mumbled, "I think I'm falling in love with you."

She'd laughed and said she wondered when he was going to get around to figuring it out. "I love you too, Matt," she'd said as she encircled his neck with her silky arms and pulled his face toward hers. He'd kissed her then, a soft, sweet kiss. He'd felt the dampness of her cheek against his as he held her close and thought that moment was the reason for the rest of his life. Five months later, they were married.

Matt heard a rustle in the brush. *They're back.* He hadn't allowed himself to contemplate what he would do if they didn't return—or if only Eduardo returned. He strained to see into the deep green leaves, but the foliage was too

thick. Scanning the surrounding area, he waited, and then he heard another sound. He twisted, struggling against the rope that bound his arms. A young cat stood in the clearing, staring straight at him. It was small and pale, with dark spots on its flank. An adolescent puma, probably hunting with its mother. Matt's throat constricted. Slowly he pulled his knees up to his chest, wincing as pain shot through his leg. The cat watched him, unblinking. The mother wouldn't be far away, and she would protect her baby.

Like Cathy.

Matt held his breath as long as he could and then exhaled. He pressed his wrists against the rope, using first one arm and then the other, trying to loosen it, but to no avail. The young puma observed him curiously. It took a few steps toward him and stopped. Matt forced himself to sit still; only his eyes moved as he tried to think and fight the panic that rose in his chest. He shrank against the rock behind him. *Run away, little kitty. Run away to your mama.*

Matt heard movement behind him. His muscles tensed. He felt his pulse pounding in the roof of his mouth. The hair on the back of his neck stood on end. Slowly he rotated his head and then stopped, forcing himself once again to sit completely still. Directly in front of him, a fern glistened in a patch of sunlight.

Matt heard a hiss and a low growl.

He swallowed. His breathing was shallow and rapid, his mouth dry. He licked his lips and closed his eyes. The drone of insects was deafening. His ankle throbbed. Silently, he prayed.

Another sound, this time closer. The young cougar stretched and yawned. Matt's heart pounded, and he felt dizzy. This was it. After everything, this was it. He wondered what would happen to Cathy and Melissa. He saw a bead of water form on a leaf and drip onto the forest floor. He closed his eyes and waited.

And then the sound came again. A hiss followed by a low growl. Matt opened his eyes and almost imperceptibly moved his head until he could see the large tawny puma standing no more than thirty feet away from him, poised with one paw held off the ground, her ears flattened, her tail perfectly still. The puma stared at Matt with steady green eyes then slowly replaced her foot. Matt sat motionless and waited. The puma's tail twitched. Matt watched as she hesitated and then took another step closer and stopped again.

Matt heard movement to his side. The mother puma jerked her head toward the sound. Her baby was moving. Then she looked at Matt and hissed, her lips pulled back to reveal sharp canines. Matt heard another low growl.

The puma crouched, ready to spring.

CHAPTER 34

RAUL WALKED TOWARD THE MARKETPLACE where he had first seen Marcos and Adán. The square bustled with activity as people bargained for produce. A young woman selling peppers and tomatoes sat on the ground nearby, her woven turquoise-and-green skirt nearly covering sandaled feet. Her long black hair was pulled into a knot at the back of her neck, the way Sofía used to wear hers. She turned, as though she could feel his eyes on her, and smiled at him, and he looked away. His eyes surveyed the crowd, but there was nothing out of the ordinary.

The smell of pork steaming in banana leaves wafted by Raul as he walked along the cobblestone sidewalk. It was nearly noon, and he was hungry. He paused at a street vendor to buy some pork-filled paches, tamales made with potato dough.

Just then Raul's phone rang. It was Cathy. Raul listened, thanked her, and hung up the phone. He pulled a notepad from his pocket and jotted down the name: *Santiago Gonzales*. He needed to get to an Internet café.

He had just finished eating his paches when he heard a man approaching from behind. Raul knew even before he turned to face the man that it would be Marcos.

"Why are you here?" Raul asked. It was impossible to keep the bitterness from his voice.

"I want to help you find the girl," Marcos said. "I have been watching for you to come."

Raul turned to walk away.

"Please, let me do this for the girl. I can help you find her."

Raul spoke slowly, deliberately. "I asked for help. You were there with Adán. There was no concern, no help—not for me, not for the missing girl."

"I did not expect to see you again, Raul. Not ever. Seeing you . . ." Marcos shook his head. "I thought I would go to my grave without ever seeing you again, without having to look into your eyes and know what I had done."

"I wish that had been true."

"I do not blame you for your feelings toward me, but think of the girl. I can help you find her. I have connections." When Raul didn't answer, Marcos continued. "Would you refuse my help because of your hatred for me? Think of the girl. What do you need right now?"

"I need to find an Internet café," Raul said.

"Then, please, come to my house. I have a computer you can use. It is only a short distance from here."

Raul wanted to refuse, but if Marcos had a computer in his home, it would save time. Reluctantly, he nodded at Marcos. "If you will let me use your computer, I will accept your offer."

Raul followed Marcos through the streets of Santa Elena. Marcos stood more than a head taller than Raul and moved like a man who was used to being in charge. He approached a house and pushed the door open. The house was empty. Marcos directed Raul to the computer and then walked to the refrigerator and pulled out a bottle of orange soda. He offered a drink to Raul.

"I can get you access to vital records, military records, police records," Marcos said as he typed in his password.

There were hundreds of birth records for men with Santiago's name, fewer marriage records. *To have been baptized, Santiago's marriage would have had to be legal,* Raul thought. He opened a new search engine, scanned the monitor, typed a few words, and began to scroll through the screens. He minimized the website and pulled up a map of Guatemala. Boulders of jade were scattered throughout the Sierra de Las Minas, he had heard.

Returning to his previous page, he modified his search criteria. A list of names and addresses appeared on the screen. He studied them, finally narrowing the list to one: Santiago and María Gonzales, currently living in Salamá.

It would take several hours to get to Salamá. He turned to Marcos, met his eyes, and forced his voice to be cordial. "Thank you for your help."

"What happened to you, Raul? Where did you go?"

Raul didn't answer immediately. "I joined the insurgents," he finally said.

"You wanted to fight back."

"I wanted to destroy the army."

"My father hoped you would come back. He wanted to see you again. Even at the end, he wanted to see you."

"Did you tell him? Did you tell him why I never came back?"

"I couldn't."

"Instead you let him die believing I didn't care?" Raul stood and walked to the window of the house and looked outside.

"What is this girl to you?" Marcos asked. "Tell me about her."

"She is a United States citizen traveling in our country with her mother. They were visiting Tikal when she disappeared. Her parents—they're good people. They don't deserve this." Raul turned to face Marcos and saw his eyes shift. "What do you know, Marcos?"

Marcos poured himself a drink. "The night we met you in the cave, there was a phone call. I do not know what was said, but afterward Adán said he had a job to do. He said he would be playing an interesting game of chess with a young girl and an old friend. He left right away and has not come back."

"You think Adán is involved? She was taken several days before I talked with you."

"I do not know, Raul. But I know Adán. If he is involved, he will care nothing for the life of this girl."

"I came to him for help—"

"Adán helps no one but himself and La Cofradía."

"He belongs to La Cofradía?"

Marcos nodded. "We must get on our way. We can take my car and talk on the way."

"You are not coming with me."

"I can help you, Raul. I can help the girl. Let me do this. You know we can travel faster in a car, and if Adán is involved, you will want to have someone with you."

Raul again looked out the window. Finally he nodded his consent.

Marcos grabbed his keys from the top of his desk. Raul followed him to the car parked in front of the house. "Can you leave so quickly?"

"There is no one who will care that I am gone," Marcos said. "I live here alone."

"You never married then?"

Marcos climbed into the driver's seat and turned the ignition before answering. "I married once, but it did not last."

"And Adán?"

"Adán is a dangerous man." Marcos glanced at Raul. "I don't think he has ever had much use for women, except . . ."

"Except what?"

"Adán has been implicated in crimes against women but never convicted. La Cofradía protects him." Marcos paused and looked out the windshield. "All the violence he saw during the civil war—I think he developed a taste for it."

"Tell me about La Cofradía."

"Surely you have heard of it."

"Of course I know of it," Raul said bitterly. La Cofradía was an elite club, doing its business in the shadows of the night. Its members, trained by the military to kill, now used their talents for drug trafficking and organized crime.

"They defeated the Marxist guerrillas."

Raul turned to stare at Marcos. "You defend them? They massacred the people in more than six hundred Maya villages. My people."

Neither man spoke for several moments. Then Raul said, "Are you also a part of this group?"

Marcos didn't answer right away. Finally he said, "There are many things in my life I am not proud of."

* * *

The Guatemala City offices had been open for a couple of hours. The morning rush—if they had such a thing in Guatemala—should be over; it would be a good time to make an unobtrusive visit to an unobtrusive office and get some answers.

The blond man walked briskly through the building until he reached the door that read *U.S. Commercial Service* and tapped on the door. Impatiently, he ran his fingers through his hair while he waited. Finally a man opened the door and motioned for him to step inside.

"I trust your trip was uneventful."

"I'm not here to make small talk. What do you have for me?" He sat in the chair across from the desk.

The man returned to his chair. Leaning across the desk, he said, "Two bodies were found in the rainforest west of Tikal. Two men. The man who discovered them identified one of the men as Carlos Serna, a punk kid out of San Andrés; we don't have a name for the other man."

"When were they found?"

"The local authorities received a call last night."

"How were they killed?"

"Looks like the kid was attacked by a crocodile. The other was a gunshot."

"La Cofradía?"

"It's possible."

The blond man played with his ruby ring as he considered the possibilities. "You said a man discovered them. What was he doing?"

"I don't have that information."

"Do you know his name?"

The man seated behind the desk nodded. "That will cost you more."

"I understand."

"His name is Raul Silva."

"What do you know about him?"

The man turned to his computer screen and tapped a few keys. "Raul Silva. Ex-military. Defected in 1982. Disappeared, presumed to have gone underground for a time. Currently a guard on a tour bus."

"And what was Raul Silva doing in the rainforest yesterday?"

"As I said, I don't have that information."

* * *

It was well past dark when they drove into the village of Salamá and found the address they were looking for.

A woman cracked open the door and peered out at Raul and Marcos. "My husband is not at home," she said, pushing the door shut.

Raul stepped close to the door. "Please, señora, we have come to talk with your husband about a Matthew Miller from Los Estados Unidos." He watched her eyes, saw recognition in them, as well as uneasiness and fear.

"How do you know Elder Miller?"

Raul smiled and held his hand out to her. "Hermana Gonzales, I am Raul Silva, a friend of *hermano* Miller. He and his daughter are both missing. I was hoping your husband might know something that would help us find them."

María caught her breath. "Melissa?" she whispered. "She is missing?"

"You know her then?"

"No, señor, but hermano Miller speaks of her and shows me her picture. She is a beautiful girl." She turned her attention to Marcos. "And this man? Who is he?"

"He is a friend. He is helping me find them." María couldn't know what those words had cost him.

She nodded and opened the door.

They stepped inside and crossed the tile floor to a couch and some chairs. A teenage boy was sprawled on the couch, watching the television set. A small picture of Christ hung on the wall in an inexpensive frame. The boy sat up when the two men approached him. His eyes shifted from his mother to the men. A girl scampered into the room from the kitchen. She smiled shyly and ran to her mother.

"Miguel, take Ana out of the room while I speak to these men."

The boy remained on the couch. "I want to stay here with you, Mamá."

"It is okay. These men are here to help Elder Miller. Now go, and take Ana with you."

Miguel stood. He was taller than his mother, lanky. His straight black hair was cropped short above his ears, the top longer, tousled. Reluctantly he beckoned to his sister and left the room.

María motioned for the men to sit in the chairs and turned off the television. "Can I get you something to drink?" she asked, as if it were a social call.

"No, hermana. We are imposing on you enough in coming so late." Raul waited while she perched on the edge of the couch and then continued. "As I said, we are searching for hermano Miller and his daughter. We believe they have been taken hostage."

She gasped. "They are together?"

"No, señora. Hermano Miller was looking for his daughter when he disappeared."

She nodded and bit her lip. Raul noticed that her hands were trembling. "Where is your husband, hermana?"

Tears formed in the corners of María's eyes, and she brushed them away. "What did you say your name is, señor?"

"I am Raul Silva, and I am your brother in the gospel."

María dabbed at her eyes with a tissue. "My husband has been gone for two days," she said. "Yesterday morning, very early, Elder Miller came to our house with another man. He told my husband that he needed him to take them to the jade. They had to leave right away. My husband gathered his things, and they left. I have not seen him or heard from him since."

"This man who was with hermano Miller—did you know him?"

"I have never seen him before."

"Can you describe him to us?"

"He was a little shorter than Elder Miller, and he had a mustache. His eyes frightened me. They looked . . . dead."

"And where is the jade?"

María looked up at him sharply. "Is this why you are here? Are you looking for the jade also? You would take away our livelihood? Well, you have come for nothing, because I do not know where it is. Only my husband knows the way."

"No, hermana, let me reassure you that this is not our purpose. We only want to help you and the Millers."

María looked away. "I am sorry for questioning you. It is a hard time. Now, please, will you tell me what you know?"

"Of course."

Raul explained that he met the Millers on the tour and how Melissa had disappeared from Tikal. "I followed them to Antigua and talked to them there. They did not say much—only that they had reason to believe their daughter

was being held against her will. I could tell they were afraid. I supposed they had been threatened. That was almost four days ago. Since then, I have been searching for Melissa around Tikal." Raul then explained how he had met Javier and how they had followed Melissa's trail through the rainforest. He ended with his conversation with Cathy. "From there it was simply a matter of finding you."

The three sat in silence. Miguel wandered through the living room and into the kitchen where he poured himself a drink.

"I told you to stay with Ana," María said.

"She is asleep, and I want to know what is going on."

"Miguel, I asked you to leave us alone. I want to talk with the men privately."

"I am not a child, Mamá."

She sighed. "I don't have the strength to fight you."

Miguel walked to where the others sat and plopped down next to his mother.

"How old are you, *hijo*?" Raul asked.

"Fourteen."

"Your mother is lucky to have you to take care of her."

Miguel shrugged. "What is this about?"

"These men are looking for Elder Miller and his daughter. The man who came here yesterday with Elder Miller wanted your father to take them to the jade."

"He wants to rob us? And Elder Miller is a part of this?"

"No, *mijo*. The man has Elder Miller—" Her voice broke. Miguel looked from his mother's face to Raul's.

"We think the other man is holding hermano Miller as a hostage to force your father to take them to the jade," Raul said. "We are trying to stop him before someone gets hurt. We were hoping your mother could tell us where they might have gone. But she says she does not know how to get to the jade."

"I know the way."

"No, Miguel. I will not allow it." María's voice was sharp.

Raul looked straight at Miguel. "You know how to get to the place?"

"Of course. I have been there many times with my father."

María stood and walked to the door. "I am sorry, but I will not allow this. He is my son. My husband is missing, and I—no, it is out of the question."

"Mamá, Papá may be in danger. I have to help these men." Miguel lowered his voice. "Papá went with them because of his love for Elder Miller. I love Papá. It is the same. I must help him."

"But your father is not a boy."

"All my life you have taught me about the courage of the stripling warriors. They were also boys, and God protected them because of their faith in their mother's teachings. I have faith, Mamá, and He will protect me too."

"Miguel, listen to me. The jade is spread across four hundred kilometers. Even if you lead these men into the Motagua Valley, how can you know where to find your father?"

"God will show us the way, Mamá. I have faith that He will."

Raul blinked back the tears that came to his eyes. "You must be very proud of your son, hermana. We will take good care of him and bring him back safely to you. I give you my word of honor. I will protect him with my life."

María crumpled. She buried her face in her hands and wept. Miguel put his arm around her and pulled her head onto his shoulder. "I will be okay. You must have faith."

CHAPTER 35

SANTIAGO AND EDUARDO HIKED IN silence. As they reached higher elevations, Eduardo glanced at his phone with increasing frequency. It was dark when they reached the top of a knoll and Eduardo found a signal and dialed the number.

"I want to talk to Melissa before I do anything else," Santiago said.

Eduardo cast a dark look at Santiago then turned away and spoke to the man on the other end of the line. After a few moments, he pressed the speaker button and held the phone toward Santiago.

"Señorita," Santiago said. *"Me llamo* Santiago Gonzales. *Soy amigo de su papà, Matthew Miller. ¿Está usted bien?"*

"What?" He could hear the fear in Melissa's voice.

"That's enough," Eduardo said.

Santiago could hear a man's voice in the background.

"Now, if you want to see her, tell him how to find us," Eduardo said.

"I beg you not to harm the girl," Santiago began.

"Give him the directions."

Santiago did as he was told and then added, "Please, I beg you—"

"You talk too much," Eduardo said and disconnected the phone.

Eduardo found a comfortable place to sit, opened his pack, and withdrew a chunk of bread, some fruit, and a bottle of wine. The conversation between a terrified girl who couldn't speak Spanish and a determined man who couldn't speak English had been amusing. *Didn't think about not being able to understand the girl when you insisted on talking to her, did you?*

"We need to get back," Santiago said.

"There's no reason to hurry. It will take them at least a day to reach us. We'll stay here until daybreak."

After he finished eating, Eduardo picked up his phone again. There wouldn't be a signal once they left this place. He punched the numbers into his phone and waited.

"Just checking in," Eduardo said into the phone.

"That's good, because I've been hearing things."

Eduardo turned his back to Santiago and spoke quietly into the phone. "Everything is under control."

"Then why would a member of La Cofradía have been hired to track the girl?"

"We've had some snags, but I took care of them."

"Do you call dead bodies snags?"

"I don't know anything about that."

"Two men were found in the rainforest west of Tikal. Both dead. One was identified as Carlos Serna."

"He was disposable."

"And the girl?"

"She's been recovered."

"I'm going to need more than that."

Eduardo hesitated. He knew Santiago was listening to every word. "It was a minor complication, but I handled it and everything is under control."

"What about the location?"

"I'll have it soon."

"And I'll be waiting. Just remember, if you decide to try something, you've got more to lose than money."

"I don't like threats."

"And I don't like complications."

* * *

Melissa watched as the man replaced his phone, turned off the television, and picked up his bag. He motioned for Melissa to follow him out of the motel and back into his truck.

They drove through the town and into the countryside, gradually climbing in elevation, heading toward the mountain range directly in front of them. Melissa stared out the window as they drove. Tears trickled down her cheeks. Hearing her father's name had unleashed a torrent of emotion.

She tried to remember what the man on the phone had said. *Su papá, Matthew Miller.* Why had he said her father's name? Carlos had mentioned her father too. He'd said it was because of her father that she had been taken.

Again, she tried to remember the words the man on the phone said. *Su papá. Soy amigo de su papá.* A friend of your father.

A friend of my father knows where I am.

She glanced at the man seated beside her. His forearm muscles were taut as he gripped the steering wheel. His profile was hard; stubble covered his chin. His neck and shoulders were thick. His eyes bore into her whenever he looked at her, which was not often. There was no hint of warmth or kindness.

They came to a tiny village. Melissa saw the scattered homes dotting the landscape, the terraced gardens. Men and women walked along the road, pulling carts or carrying assorted goods on their backs. They drove through the village and a little farther before the man turned off the side of the road and parked. He climbed out of the truck and stepped around to the back to remove a pack. Slinging the pack over his shoulder, he walked around to her side of the truck and opened the door. Melissa stared straight ahead. She could feel his eyes on her, could smell his acrid breath. He grabbed her arm and pulled her from the truck.

"Where are we going?"

He looked at her—a hard look that made her wish she could take back her question. He pushed her toward a trail leading into the forest.

She forced her feet to move forward, following him along the wooded path. They walked for what seemed like hours. Sweat poured down her forehead, leaving muddy trails on her face. Blisters formed and broke on her feet, but still they walked. She feared stopping as much as continuing, so she concentrated on moving her feet one step at a time. When it was too dark to see, they stopped.

The man tossed her a piece of bread, and Melissa chewed it, savoring the sweet taste as it dissolved in her mouth. She closed her eyes and let her thoughts wander to home. She imagined a real meal, one with fried chicken and mashed potatoes. She could hear the chicken sizzling on her mother's stove, could smell the hot oil as the meat fried. It had been nearly a week since she had really eaten, and her stomach ached for food.

After she was finished, the man tied her hands behind her back. Then he settled against a rock and fell asleep, his gun held loosely across his lap. She listened to the rhythm of his breathing and to the occasional yowl of some wild cat in pursuit of prey. Every few minutes she looked at him and eyed his gun. She imagined taking it, feeling its weight in her hands, even leveling it at his head and firing it.

But then she would be alone. Alone in the darkness, in the forest. Alone with the wild animals. Alone and lost.

CHAPTER 36

"I'VE BEEN ON PINS AND needles ever since you left," Cathy said as she opened the door and stepped aside to let Nick enter. "I'm anxious to hear about your visit with Mr. Whittaker."

"I thought you might be hungry," Nick said, "so I went through the buffet and got a little bit of everything for you to taste. Let's eat while we talk."

"Thanks for looking out for me. I really appreciate it."

"Are you doing all right?"

Cathy nodded. "All things considered. So tell me about your conversation with Mr. Whittaker."

"Well, after he fumbled around at his desk for a while, he pulled out a file and read through it. Then he reassured me that the U.S. Embassy was working hard toward Melissa's recovery and he was confident that they would find her. He was just like you said he would be—very full of himself."

"He isn't doing anything to help us, is he?"

"I sure didn't get the feeling that he was. I almost wondered if he could somehow be involved in all this."

"Involved? What do you mean?"

"It's a gut feeling. Something about him isn't right."

"You don't really think he could have kidnapped Melissa," Cathy said.

"No, of course not. But I just wonder if he's holding back. Maybe he knows something he's not telling us. Maybe someone is blackmailing him. I don't know. All I know is it doesn't make sense for a representative of the United States to be so nonchalant about this."

Cathy considered his words.

"And I'll tell you what," Nick continued. "If that man is involved somehow, when all this is over, I'm going to make sure he goes down and goes down hard. It makes me furious to think my tax dollars are paying that slime ball to do

absolutely nothing. Anyway, I gave him a piece of my mind before I left, but I doubt it will make much of a difference. I told him I'll be back in the morning to check on what he's done. So what have you been doing?"

"Not a lot. Mostly trying to reconstruct exactly what happened, sifting through random facts, looking for connections—anything that might help us."

"Come up with anything?"

"Not yet. Do you realize that in the last twenty-four hours, you've suggested three different people who might be involved?"

Nick laughed. "Have I?"

Cathy nodded. "Raul, Mr. Whittaker, and some guy in the hall."

"I'm just trying to be careful. I want to find Matt and Melissa, and I don't want anything to happen to you. I don't want to get blindsided by trusting the wrong person."

"So you don't trust anyone?"

"I trust you, and I trust myself." His voice softened. "*Someone* took Melissa. We don't know who, and we don't know why. Until we know those things, I'm going to suspect every person I see. This could be completely random, but statistically, it's more likely to be someone who has had some association with you. That's why we can't trust *anyone* else."

After Nick left, Cathy walked over to the gas fireplace and turned it on. Settling on the floor in front of the fireplace, she picked up her notebook and scanned her notes until the lack of sleep over the past week caught up with her and she dozed.

Again the dream came. Again she saw the stone road leading higher and higher into the mountains. Again she heard Melissa's voice calling, the footsteps close behind. In her dream, she followed the path through the woods, past an old mining area and on to a tomb site that was littered with clay shards. She ran as fast as she could, but no matter how fast she ran, Melissa was always just ahead of her, beyond her reach.

When Cathy awoke, the room was dark except for the flicker of the fireplace. The dream had been so real it took a few moments for her heart to stop pounding. She was cold. How long had she been asleep? She looked at her watch; it was the middle of the night. She pulled the blanket off the bed and wrapped it around her shoulders. Moving to the window, she pushed back the curtains to look at the black sky. Just like the night Matt left. She swallowed and felt the familiar ache in her throat. Returning to her place in front of the fireplace, Cathy picked up her notebook and recorded the dream as well as she could remember it. She put down her pen and closed her eyes.

She needed to call Raul. The thought was accompanied by such certainty that she didn't question it. Instead, she walked over to the nightstand where Raul's number was written on a piece of paper next to her cell phone. She sat on the edge of the bed and picked up her phone. A new text message. She touched her screen.

I am okay. A man brought me to a motel in the mountains. We drove all night to get here. I think the people who took me are trying to get to Dad. I'm sorry for everything. Please find me. I love you.

Cathy read the message over and over again. Melissa was alive! She was okay! Cathy slid onto her knees and prayed, pleading that her family would be protected and that she would be inspired to know what to do next. Images from her dream came again and, with them, the persisting thought that she needed to call Raul.

CHAPTER 37

Day 9

ONCE THE DECISION TO TAKE Miguel with them was made, María no longer attempted to dissuade them. Instead, she threw herself into preparations, packing food and water for them to take. Occasionally, Raul saw her eyes grow misty as she looked at Miguel. She would reach up to touch his face and study his eyes before returning to her tasks.

It was after midnight when they finished their preparations. María insisted they sleep before starting their journey into the mountains. It was a small concession for an anguished mother.

Raul was barely awake the next morning when his cell phone rang. He looked at the screen before answering. *Cathy Miller.*

"Raul—" Cathy's voice broke.

"Hermana, what has happened?"

"Raul," she began again. "I just got a text message from Melissa. She says she's okay!"

"Then your tears are happy tears. That is wonderful news, hermana. From the beginning, I have felt that this was true. When did she send the text, and what exactly did it say?"

Cathy repeated the message. "What do you think about what she said about Matt?"

"This is the conclusion I have come to myself, hermana. It is what makes sense."

"But why? Why would anyone want to kidnap Matt? What do we have that would make someone want to do all this?"

"I'm not certain, hermana, but I think it may have something to do with the jade."

"Really? Did you find Santiago?"

"I found his family in Salamá. I am here with them now. Santiago is not here," Raul said. "He is with your husband. His wife, María, told me that your husband came here with another man. They asked Santiago to take them to the jade field. Santiago left with them yesterday early in the morning."

"Matt was there?" Raul could hear the strain in her voice.

"Yes, hermana," Raul said. "I am leaving this morning to follow them and find them. Now I must go and finish my preparations."

"There's something else I need to tell you before you go. I had a dream the last two nights—the same dream. I don't know what it means, but I feel compelled to tell you."

Cathy relayed her dream to him, the stone road leading high into the mountains, Melissa's voice calling for her, the footsteps. She described it all in detail, ending with the final place she had seen where the pathway had ended.

After she finished, Raul thanked her. "We are on the right trail, hermana. With Heavenly Father's help, we will find both your husband and Melissa."

Cathy's news was both relieving and concerning. Raul hadn't allowed himself to consider that Melissa might have been lost in the river, but still it was a relief to know that she had sent the text after he'd found the bodies in the rainforest. The fact that she was being held in a motel with a man was not surprising given the evidence, but it was disconcerting.

He could hear María in the kitchen, making tortillas. Miguel sat at the table, tying his shoes. Raul watched as the boy stood and walked to his mother, casually draping his arm around her shoulder. He saw María bury her face in his chest, saw Miguel wrap his arms awkwardly around her. Raul turned away then and waited until he heard the rhythmic kneading of the dough before he entered the kitchen.

"Are you ready?" Raul asked, trying to keep his voice light.

Miguel smiled at him, a broad grin that lit up his face. "I am ready. Today we begin our journey to rescue my papá and his good friend Elder Miller."

"That is right. We are undertaking a great rescue mission, and we will succeed."

María turned to face the sink, but not before Raul saw her chin quiver. Although her face was hidden, he could see her hands shake as they shaped the tortillas, could see them pause to wipe her eyes. He tried to find the right words to offer reassurance and comfort but in the end said nothing. There was nothing left to say.

When Raul returned to the living room, he found Marcos zipping up his pack. "We need to get on our way," Marcos said.

"You cannot leave until you eat breakfast," María said as she placed plates of black beans, scrambled eggs, and tortillas on the table.

"We will be back as soon as we can," Raul said when they finished eating.

Miguel hugged his mother one more time. She whispered in his ear and kissed each cheek then turned away, her face wet with tears.

Once they were in the car, Marcos asked Miguel to explain everything he knew about the journey that lay ahead. Raul told the others about his early morning phone call.

"You see, God is helping us." Miguel grinned at Raul. "I have been to the place in hermana Miller's dream. I will take you there, and there we will find my papá and Elder Miller."

Miguel's eyes shone with the excitement of anticipated adventure. Raul had seen those eyes a long time ago reflected in his own mirror. He had been wearing a brand-new khaki uniform and, like almost all youth, he had felt he was invincible.

Raul watched out the window as the road curved around the contours of the green hills, slowly climbing toward the Sierra de Las Minas. Miguel said he knew a shortcut to the road and to the jade. "It's a steeper climb, but we will get there faster," he said as they parked the car.

* * *

As soon as she ended her call with Raul, Cathy dialed Nick's number.

"I'm sorry if I woke you up, but I have some good news!" Cathy said. She told him about her text from Melissa. "I am so relieved. I know it's not over yet, but at least we know she's okay."

"Or that whoever has her phone says she's okay. Sorry, I didn't mean to cast a shadow over your good news. That's the skeptic in me talking. Hopefully everything is just as it seems." When Cathy didn't respond, Nick said, "Let me pull on some clothes, and I'll be right over."

It wasn't more than twenty minutes before Nick tapped on the door. He greeted her with a broad smile. "Good news today, huh?"

"Assuming it's real."

"Do you mind if I look at that text?"

"Not at all," Cathy said, handing him her phone.

Nick read it over carefully.

"Any hidden clues?"

Nick shook his head. "I don't think so, but I'm going to forward it to my phone, just in case there's something there."

"And I have more news," Cathy said. "Raul knows where Matt is."

"When did you talk to Raul?"

"After I got the text, I called him."

"I thought I warned you about talking to other people."

"Are you trying to scare me?"

"No. Well, maybe, yes," Nick said. "Two members of your family have already disappeared, and I don't want anything to happen to you. So what did Raul have to say?"

"That he's following Matt's trail. He's going to find them."

"Slow down! How does Raul know where Matt is?"

"He'd been to Santiago's house."

"Santiago? Matt's supplier?"

"Right," Cathy said. "Raul went to Santiago's house and talked to his wife. She told him Matt had been there. Apparently Matt and another man left with Santiago to go to the jade field, and Raul is following their trail. He's closing in on them."

"Wow! What a difference a day makes, huh?"

"So now you can stop telling me not to trust Raul. He's going to find Matt," Cathy said. "Look, I know this doesn't mean everything is going to be okay, but I feel really hopeful that we're near the end of this ordeal and that . . ."

"That Melissa and Matt are all right," Nick finished when Cathy couldn't continue. His voice was gentle.

"Yes, and that we're going to find them and this nightmare can be over and we can go back home and be normal again."

"I hope you're right. That all sounds very hopeful," Nick said.

"I know. It's hard to believe after all we've been through this week that it really might be almost over."

"I had planned to go to Guatemala City this morning to meet with Mr. Whittaker again, as promised. See if a night's rest made him more cooperative."

"I think you should still go."

"I agree. We need to have a Plan B, just in case."

"You can show him Melissa's text and see if he still thinks she's having a party."

"I'll do that. Definitely."

"And maybe he could send some reinforcements to help Raul."

"That's a really good idea—but do we know where Raul is?"

Cathy hesitated. "I'm trying to remember what he said. I think it was Salamá. Pretty sure that's right. Any idea where that is?"

"No, but I'm sure Mr. Whittaker will know. Actually, who knows what that man knows? But we can always look at a map, right?" Nick glanced at his

watch. "Well, I'd better get going. I'm not sure how long I'll be, but I'll check in with you as soon as I get back. Be careful while I'm gone, okay? I know it's hard to sit tight, but that's what you need to do."

"I'm being careful."

"No more talking to other people. Even if you think they're fine. We just can't take any chances."

"Got it."

"I've put a lot of things on hold at work and come a long way to help you, but I can't keep you safe if you ignore what I tell you."

Way to make someone feel guilty. "I know. I appreciate your concern."

"No more talking to other people, okay?"

"Thanks, Nick. I'll call you if I need anything."

Cathy closed the door behind Nick and locked it. She *was* being careful, and she refused to let Nick scare her. Melissa was alive, and Raul was going to find Matt. Cathy walked to the window. It was bright outside; the sun was high in the sky. A shower would feel good about now.

* * *

Eduardo pulled another cigarette from his pocket and lit it. He watched Santiago pace back and forth like a caged animal. Finally he ground his cigarette into the dirt and stood.

"Let's see if your friend is still alive," he said.

Traveling through the brush and vines was tedious. Santiago led the way through the forest, pushing between branches and climbing over fallen logs and stumps, flailing against the wet ferns that slapped his face. The two men slid more than hiked back to the trail.

He's scared, Eduardo thought. *As he should be.* Eduardo touched the cold metal in his pocket.

As they approached the place where they had left Matt, Eduardo saw the paw prints. He bent over and examined them. Not big enough for a jaguar; most likely a puma.

They stepped into the clearing. As Eduardo scanned the area, he heard a sharp intake of breath beside him and glanced sideways at Santiago. Following Santiago's eyes, Eduardo looked across to where a lifeless lump lay nearly hidden behind a boulder.

CHAPTER 38

Santiago sprinted across the clearing, knelt in the dirt next to Matt's body, and gently rolled him over onto his back. Matt lifted his head.

"I thought you were dead," Santiago said as he untied Matt's hands.

"I should have been. A mother puma nearly had me for dinner. Luckily she changed her mind at the last minute." Matt grimaced as he pushed himself into a sitting position. "Did you talk to Melissa?"

Santiago nodded. "She's alive."

* * *

Raul, Marcos, and Miguel spoke little as they hiked. During the long hours in the sweltering heat, Raul could almost forget who he was hiking beside and what had happened. The years vanished, and it was as if he and Marcos were boys again, playing games in the forest.

At other times, he would look at Marcos, and the pain of what had been and all that might have been would pierce his heart again. And yet he continued on, fighting his private battle.

They would hike for as long as they could see. Although they never said it, each knew they were on a short timeline, and the enemy was more than a day ahead of them.

* * *

It started to rain in the middle of the afternoon, a light misty rain Santiago called *chipi-chipi*. As evening approached, the fog rolled in, making it bone-chillingly cold. Matt and Santiago huddled together against a boulder as they tried to stay warm.

Eduardo sat across from them, wrapped in a wool blanket. He tugged his jacket hood over his head, pulled a cigarette from his pack, and leaned back against the rock to smoke while they all waited for Melissa's arrival.

Matt watched Eduardo. There was nothing else to do. He and Santiago said little through the long hours of the night. Sleep came intermittently, but when morning approached, he felt no more rested than he had at the beginning of the night. He moved his foot, wincing as pain shot through his calf. He slid his pant leg up and studied his swollen ankle. Bruises nearly circled his foot, extending halfway up his leg. Gingerly, he pressed on the ankle. He considered removing his shoe but rejected the idea; he knew he'd never be able to get the shoe back on again. He sat back against the boulder, closed his eyes, and drifted off to sleep.

The morning passed slowly. The only food they had was what Eduardo had brought with him, and Eduardo was unwilling to share. Clearly, he intended hunger to be their punishment for refusing to go on.

Through the foliage canopy, Matt could see the gray sky. The rain continued in a slow, steady drizzle. Matt lifted his face to the rain and tried to catch a few drops to wet his dry mouth, but it left him thirstier than before.

Eduardo paced back and forth along the path, pausing only to glare at the other two men and spit on the ground.

Finally Santiago stood and walked away from where they sat together and began methodically combing the area, gradually moving farther and farther away. Eduardo watched him; his hand fingered the gun.

"I'm going to find something for us to eat," Santiago said to Eduardo as he walked toward the woods.

Eduardo stood and leveled the gun at Santiago's head. *"¡Detènte!"*

"You can shoot me if you want, but I'm going to find something to eat."

"If you do not return in five minutes, your friend will die," Eduardo said.

"I will be back as soon as I find something for us to eat, and if you want me to take you to the jade, you'll make sure that nothing happens to my friend."

When Santiago returned, he held dark round gourds in his hands. He presented them to Matt with a flourish. "These will help the inflammation in your ankle. They are called *Crescentia alata*. If we can break into them, we can eat them."

He smashed the fruit on the edge of a rock, splitting it open, and held it out to Matt. "Here, eat the seeds. It tastes better than it looks."

Matt scooped out the dark pulpy mass of seeds and placed them between his lips. "It tastes like licorice."

Santiago nodded and cracked another fruit.

"I wish I could do more to help you." Santiago focused his eyes on Eduardo. Lowering his voice to a whisper, he said, "Do you think he will let us go after we take him to the jade?"

"I don't know. I want to believe he will."

"I want to believe that too. But I do not believe we can trust this man to do what he says he will do." Santiago watched Eduardo as he twisted around and reached into his pack. "He is working for someone else. I heard them talking."

Matt shifted positions. His foot throbbed at the jarring motion.

When Santiago spoke again, his voice was nearly inaudible and Matt strained to hear him. "If we want to live, we must escape."

"But Melissa—"

"Yes, of course we wait for Melissa. But then we watch, and when the time is right, we go." Santiago's eyes scanned the surrounding area. "I know this place very well. It would be easy for someone to get lost. But if we can get away, I can get us home again."

Matt was silent for several seconds before he responded. "He knows where you live, my friend. And he knows where my wife is. The only way we can protect our families is to see this through to the end. No matter what that means."

* * *

The cold boot jarred Melissa from sleep. She moaned and felt the boot again, shoving her, rousing her. Her body was stiff from lying in an awkward position through the long hours of the night. She had been awake more than she had slept, the night punctuated by the cries of wild animals. She met the morning relieved to have survived.

The man kicked her again and said something she couldn't understand. His voice was cold. She pushed herself up from the ground, ignoring the dull ache behind her eyes. He offered her something to drink, which she refused, and a piece of bread. Too quickly the food was gone, and he was ready to move. The path was muddy and slick from recent rain, and she fought to keep up as he hiked down the trail. Every step brought pain from the previous day's blisters.

Melissa found this man more frightening than the others who had held her hostage. When Javier looked at her, she had seen a desire in his eyes that had terrified her, but he at least had seen some value in her life, even if only as an amusement for him. This man showed no sign of anything but icy contempt. Her instincts told her that he considered her no more than a rag doll to be discarded without thought or feeling.

They hiked throughout the day, until she thought she could move no more, and still they hiked. Finally he stopped abruptly and motioned for Melissa to turn around. He tied her hands behind her back then ripped a strip of cloth from the bottom of his shirt and stretched it across her mouth.

"Your daddy would like to see you," he said, in near-perfect English. "Walk straight ahead."

CHAPTER 39

CATHY FINISHED DRESSING AND TIDIED the hotel room. A small white business card had slipped beneath the dresser. Cathy picked it up and studied the unfamiliar name. *Must have been a former occupant of the room,* she thought as she dropped it into the wastebasket. She sat on the edge of the bed. The brief euphoria she'd felt when she heard Raul was on Matt's trail was gone, replaced by a restless urge to do something. What, she didn't know. But she did know she'd go crazy if she sat in the hotel room, staring at the same four walls, for one more day.

Her phone rang.

"Cathy, it's me again. I just finished talking with Mr. Whittaker and thought I'd check in."

"What did you find out?"

"Nothing. Absolutely nothing. The man's completely incompetent. I gave him a piece of my mind and left."

"Did you tell him about Melissa's text and Raul's phone call?"

"Of course I did. He made a few notes. I don't know, maybe I'm reading him wrong, but I just didn't get the impression he'll do much about it. So how are you doing?"

"I'm okay."

"Just okay? Is something wrong?"

"Nick—my husband and daughter are missing."

"You're right. That was insensitive."

"It's okay. I appreciate all your help."

"I wish I could do more," Nick said. "You're doing okay, though?"

"All things considered."

"Then I think I'll check on a couple of things before I head back to Antigua," Nick said. "So I'll see you in a while. But remember—"

"I know: don't go anywhere, don't talk to anyone."

Cathy was tired of waiting. She walked over to the window and pulled back the drape. She wondered what Mr. Whittaker thought about Melissa's text. Nick said he thought Mr. Whittaker might be involved somehow, but that didn't make sense. The man was just incompetent. Lazy. Didn't want people telling him what to do. She bet Nick's thrashing made him even less likely to help. Matt always said when Nick wanted something done, he acted like he was a hammer and everyone else was a nail. If they didn't do what he wanted the first time, he pounded a little harder. Matt laughed when he said it, but he still said it.

She hadn't really seen that side of Nick—although he had been pretty over-the-top on the whole "Don't leave, don't talk to anyone, don't answer the phone" thing. But he was just trying to help. Trying to protect. Even if he was a little overbearing. And he had dropped everything to come. A fact he apparently wasn't going to let her forget.

She pushed the sliding door open and stepped out onto the terrace. It was beautiful. How different things would have been if—*Enough of that.* She blinked back her tears and gazed out over the grounds. They really were beautiful.

She wished she could talk to Mr. Whittaker herself. He was the one person she knew in the country who spoke English and had the authority to do something. He must have resources he could pull in. She could tell him about Santiago and maybe he could send some reinforcements to the area. Maybe if she talked to him, as a woman, as a mother, if she appealed to him instead of beating him up. Built his ego a little. It couldn't hurt. She wasn't doing anything now except twiddling her thumbs.

Whoever had taken Melissa wasn't after her. That much had become evident after reading Melissa's text and talking with Raul. All the threats, phone calls, the fruit basket, for heaven's sake, had stopped once Matt was gone. Not a single thing had happened to indicate that someone was after her since that night when Matt had left. It was all in her head. And Nick's head. She could leave the room with or without Nick's permission. Her leaving didn't pose a threat to anyone, and who knew? Maybe she could actually do something to help. Cathy studied the map of Antigua until she located the bus terminal. It was only a few blocks away. She could get to the embassy in an hour or so and easily be back before evening. She put the map and notebook in her purse, unlocked the door, and glanced out. A couple was engaged in conversation at the end of the hall; otherwise, it was empty.

She probably should tell Nick where she was going. It wasn't as though he could stop her; she just didn't want to hear what he would have to say. But if something happened, no one would know where she had gone. She needed to be smart as well as independent.

She wrote a note and left it on the bedside table. Then she cracked the door and peeked into the corridor; the couple was gone.

As she positioned the *Do Not Disturb* sign on her doorknob, someone approached her from behind. She jumped when she heard the footsteps.

"I'm sorry; I didn't mean to scare you," the man said. His eyes scrutinized her. "Enjoying your vacation?"

"No. I mean, yes. Please excuse me." Before he had a chance to respond, she slipped back inside the room, closed the door, and bolted it. She leaned against the door and waited for her heart to stop pounding. *So much for being calm, cool, and confident.* But Nick did say he'd seen someone watching her room.

She pulled out her phone and dialed Nick's number.

"Nick, you said you thought you saw someone watching my room yesterday. By any chance was he about six feet tall and a little stocky, with blond hair?"

"That sounds like him. Why?"

"He's still outside my room."

"Why were you outside your room? You're not going somewhere, are you?"

"No, I was putting the *Do Not Disturb* sign on my door when I saw him," Cathy said. "I thought I'd try to take a nap."

"Seeing him outside your door once might have been a coincidence. But twice, with everything else that's happened—not likely. I'll be there as soon as I can. A nap sounds like a good idea, but whatever you do, just keep the door locked."

Cathy held the phone in her hand for several minutes after she hung up. She double-checked the lock on her door. Nick had seen the man watching her door yesterday. And now he was outside the room again. What did he want with her family? She slumped onto the bed and stared at the door.

Why was he watching her door? Was he waiting for the right moment? To do what? What could he possibly want with her? Nick said he would protect her, but he was in Guatemala City.

I've seen him before, she thought. *Where?* And then she remembered. It was that first night in the meeting room. She'd thought then that he looked familiar.

I can't stay here, she thought. *I can't stay here and wait.*

There had to be another way out of the room. Cathy's eyes shifted to the sliding door. She crossed the room and slid the door open. What if the blond stranger was listening at the door? She walked back to the television and turned it on. She took one last look around the room and then returned to the open door and stepped out onto the patio.

Cathy boosted herself over the short wall and dropped onto the hotel grounds. She looked around. No one. She crossed the street and headed west along Calle Oriente.

There was little traffic on the cobbled streets. Cathy moved quickly, weaving through the people walking along the sidewalk. Finally she reached a large parking lot lined with refurbished American school buses. Most were painted bright colors: blue, red, or green with gold accents and were embellished with a woman's name. Cathy approached a man who was working on one of the buses.

"Por favor, I need to go to Guatemala City," she said.

"*Sí, señora, es Guate.*" He pointed at the sign on a nearby bus which read, *Antigua Dueñas Guate.*

After thanking the man, Cathy boarded the bus and found a seat next to a young mother with a baby cradled in a sling across her chest. The baby gave her a wide toothless grin, and Cathy smiled back. Even though she was scared, it felt good to be out of her room and away from the blond stranger.

Cathy arrived in Guatemala City in about an hour and hailed a taxi to take her to the U.S. Embassy. Tears filled her eyes when she saw the American flag. Surely here she would find help.

* * *

Nick approached the large wooden door. It was framed by stone and centered on the pink stucco wall. Strips of gold-edged purple, blue, and white cloth were twisted together and draped over the entrance. Beside the door, the sign read, *Casa Santo Domingo.* Nick pushed open the massive door and stepped inside. He stopped at the front desk to check for messages before heading down the candlelit corridor toward his room.

Pausing in front of Cathy's room, he read the *Do Not Disturb* sign. Who exactly did she think was going to be knocking on her door? The maid, he supposed, but he couldn't help but wonder if the sign wasn't intended for him. He knew he'd been coming on pretty strong. If he wanted her compliance, he probably needed to back off a little.

Just then the door across the hall opened and a man fitting Cathy's description stepped out. "Hello," Nick said, crossing the hall. He held out his hand and introduced himself. "What brings you to Guatemala?" he asked. "Business or pleasure?"

"I guess that depends on who you're talking to," the man said. "But I have a question. Do you know the woman who is staying in that room?"

Nick nodded. "Why do you ask?"

"Just wondering if she's all right. This morning I met her in the hall. She looked like she was going somewhere until she saw me. When I spoke to her, she turned tail and ran back into her room like a scared rabbit. You'd think she'd seen a ghost."

* * *

Once inside the embassy, Cathy climbed to the second floor and walked down the long hall until she found the door with Curtis Whittaker's name beside it. She opened the door and approached his secretary.

"I'd like to see Curtis Whittaker, please."

The young woman looked up from behind her desk and smiled at Cathy. "I'm sorry, ma'am, but that won't be possible. Mr. Whittaker is not here."

"When did he leave?"

"He's been out of the office all day."

"But that's not possible. My friend was here this morning and spoke with him."

"You must be mistaken. Curtis Whittaker has not been in all day."

CHAPTER 40

MATT HAD LISTENED TO THE movement through the trees for what seemed like an hour. At first he thought it was an animal, but the steady plodding convinced him otherwise. Someone was coming toward them.

Eduardo stopped pacing and stared into the dense forest. He looked back at the other men. "It sounds like we're going to have company."

"There are two sets of footsteps," Santiago said.

Matt nodded. His hands shook as he pressed against the rock and tried to ignore the pain that shot through his leg.

The three men watched and waited. Matt wiped the sweat from his brow with the back of his hand and licked his lips. They tasted salty. In spite of the humidity, his mouth was dry. His heart pounded in his ears as the strange combination of fear and hope threatened to overpower him, and his knees buckled beneath him.

Santiago reached out to steady his friend. "It's going to be okay."

Eduardo glanced over his shoulder at the others. He raised his gun and leveled it at them before turning back toward the dense forest. An animal rustled in the trees. Time stopped as they listened to the crunch of fallen twigs splintering. Santiago squeezed Matt's shoulder, but nothing was said. The footsteps grew louder, closer.

Waiting was almost unbearable.

The footsteps stopped. Then the branches parted and a man stepped into the clearing. Eduardo joined the man; they exchanged a few words and then moved back into the forest.

Matt felt Santiago's grip tighten on his arm. "I have seen his picture on the TV," Santiago whispered. "His name is Adán Ríos. He is a member of La Cofradía."

Before Santiago could say more, Eduardo emerged from the trees and called to Matt. "You will see your daughter, as we agreed, and then we will move on and there will be no more games."

"As soon as we see Melissa," Matt agreed.

"Understand, Mr. Miller, that you and your daughter have served your purpose and are unnecessary to me now."

Santiago broke in, his voice cold and steady. "I will never take you to the jade if you harm this man or his daughter. You can kill me first."

Eduardo shifted his eyes to Santiago. "Such loyalty you have for your friend. But I have seen fear in your eyes. We will see if your loyalty lasts."

Eduardo turned and nodded at the man Santiago had identified as Adán Ríos. Adán stepped back between the trees. He returned a moment later, his hand gripping Melissa's arm, propelling her forward. Matt stifled a gasp when he saw her. Her normally silky red hair was matted and dull, her face sunburned and smudged with dirt. Scratches covered her arms and legs, and her clothes were torn. A rag was drawn tightly across her mouth.

When their eyes met, Matt saw tears flood her eyes. She tried to jerk her arm away from Adán; he tightened his grip.

Fighting every impulse in his body to run to her and rip her away from the man who held her, Matt forced his voice to be calm. "Everything is going to be okay, 'Lissa. We just need to cooperate with these men."

Eduardo stepped to where Melissa stood and flipped his gun around. "I'm going to tell you what I told your daddy. I don't need either of you anymore, so you're what you Americans call *excess baggage*. Do you understand what I'm saying?"

"There's no need to threaten. We're all going to cooperate with you," Matt said.

"I'm sure you will," Eduardo said. He then turned to Adán. "You have delivered the girl, and I trust that you were paid as agreed."

"Are you dismissing me?"

"I have no further need of your assistance."

"It looks to me like you have your hands full," Adán said. "It intrigues me that you don't want me to continue with you. One man with three captives. You are outnumbered. Yet you dismiss me like a schoolboy who has brought you a newspaper." Adán spat on the ground and then raised his eyes again to meet Eduardo's. "No, I think I'll continue on with you. That won't be a problem, will it?"

Eduardo glared at Adán.

"Good. I'm glad we understand each other," Adán said.

Even though it was late in the day, Eduardo insisted they move on. Santiago led the way up the hidden path, stepping over fallen logs and pushing branches aside as he went, supporting Matt as much as he could with his free arm. Every

step was excruciating for Matt and made thinking of anything else almost impossible. But he kept moving, knowing that his life and Melissa's depended on it.

Eduardo walked behind Santiago and Matt, followed by Melissa and Adán. Periodically, Matt glanced over his shoulder to see Melissa. He felt angry and helpless as he watched Adán grasping her arm, pushing her forward, yanking her when she stumbled or hesitated. Yet there was nothing he could do.

They hiked until it was too dark to see and Eduardo directed everyone to stop. Adán found a boulder and sat against it, pulling Melissa down beside him. He laid his gun across his lap, opened his pack, and pulled out a chunk of bread, some fruit, and a bottle of wine. Adán ate in silence and wiped his mouth with the back of his hand. Finally he untied Melissa's hands and offered her a piece of bread. She shuddered and turned away. He shrugged and leaned back against the boulder. She sat still for several moments then reached up and brushed the tangles from her face. Glancing sideways at her captor, she lifted her hand and in a quick motion, yanked the rag from her mouth.

Matt watched all of this, wishing he could go to her and cradle her in his arms. She turned her head to face him and their eyes met. Matt saw her eyes fill with tears.

He pushed himself up, stopping only when he heard the click of a gun and Eduardo's voice saying, *"¡No te muevas!"*

Santiago grasped Matt's arm. Matt closed his eyes. His throat ached, and he felt nauseous. As terrible as not knowing had been, this was almost worse—seeing her but not being able to reach her, to touch her, to comfort her.

An owl hooted somewhere in the woods. And then a bloodcurdling scream sliced through the quiet night. All four men leapt to their feet, their eyes focused on Melissa. She screamed again and again. Matt stared frantically into the blackness, trying to see what she was seeing. And then he made out the shape of a large snake coiled beside a nearby tree trunk. Matt heard the cock of a gun, followed immediately by an explosion.

CHAPTER 41

RAUL COULD HAVE PUSHED ON, but the utter exhaustion in Miguel's eyes told him they needed to stop and rest. Even more than speed, he needed Miguel's mind to be sharp. A wrong turn could cost them hours in the wilderness.

After encouraging the others to do the same, Raul found a shady place to rest and quickly fell asleep. When he woke, the afternoon shadows were filtering through the trees. Raul lay still, listening to rodents burrowing in the brush and birds calling to one another. After a while, the faint sound of voices drifted to him. He pushed up onto one elbow and looked around.

A few feet away, Miguel sat beside Marcos, talking quietly. Raul strained to hear what they were saying, but their voices were too low. When Miguel turned, Raul saw his profile, his rumpled hair and dirt-smudged face. Raul heard Miguel laugh and saw his lips curve into a grin. If things had been different, he might have had a son like Miguel.

He would have liked to be a father.

Raul tugged his boots on, lacing them tightly around his ankles, then stood and brushed himself off. He walked over to where his pack sat on the ground, squatted beside it, and pulled out a bottle of water.

"Hermano Silva!"

Raul looked over and saw Miguel holding a gun. The boy's eyes were wide with excitement. "Look! Marcos is teaching me how to shoot!"

Raul's heart leapt to his throat. All the animosity he had fought as he climbed beside Marcos now sprang to life. "Miguel, put that down and come to me," he said.

Marcos stood. "What's wrong, Raul? The boy is old enough to handle a gun."

Confusion crossed Miguel's face as he looked between the two men. He took a step back toward Marcos. "I want to learn to shoot."

"Put the gun down and come to me."

No one moved. Raul reached for his gun and pointed it at Marcos. "Get out of here."

"Raul, please—you're frightening the boy," Marcos said.

"Get out of here."

Miguel dropped the gun. "Hermano, what are you doing?" His eyes moved between the two men.

"I'm protecting you," Raul said.

"Think about what you're doing, Raul," Marcos said. He repeated, "You're scaring the boy."

"Get out of here."

Miguel took another step back. "Please don't shoot us. I promise I won't touch the gun again."

Raul heard the fear in Miguel's voice, fear and confusion. Then he heard other voices ringing in his ears, pleading, begging, as he saw the army move through the villages. He could see the flames and could smell the smoke as the houses burned. He could see the chaos as people ran from their homes, could hear their screams.

"Please don't hurt us." Miguel's voice reached him through the fog. It hit Raul with a force that nearly doubled him over. He dropped his arm and felt the gun slip from his hand and land on the ground beside him.

No one moved or spoke for several moments. Finally Miguel broke the silence. His voice was almost a whisper. "Why did you do that?"

Raul stared at the ground where his gun had fallen. He didn't move, couldn't move. His feet were lead, his body drained.

"I thought you were a good man," Miguel said.

The boy's words echoed in Raul's head. Pain sliced through his chest. He tried to breathe and felt like he would suffocate.

"He is a good man," Marcos said.

"Then why did he do that?" Miguel asked. "I thought you were friends."

"We were friends, Miguel," Marcos said. "We were very good friends a long time ago, when we were your age. But something happened. I did something—something terrible—and he has never been able to forgive me."

"What did you do?"

Marcos studied the ground. He looked at Raul and then away again. Finally his eyes turned back to Miguel. "I am responsible for the death of someone he loved very much."

Raul wheeled around and escaped into the woods where he would be hidden. He dropped to his knees. Closing his eyes, he gasped for air as wave after wave of pain washed over him—pain for all he had lost so long ago, pain for his weakness.

Raul didn't know how long he had been there when he felt Miguel's hand on his shoulder and heard the boy's voice. "We must go on, hermano. We have to find my father and Elder Miller."

Raul wiped the moisture from his eyes with the back of his hand and sat up. Miguel knelt next to Raul and awkwardly touched his arm. "Is it true? Did he really kill someone you loved?"

"It is true. But you are right. We must find your father. I am sorry for frightening you. What happened, happened a long time ago, and it was between Marcos and me. Can you forgive me?"

Miguel nodded. "And you have to forgive him."

"I thought I had, but some things are too terrible to forgive."

"God will help you forgive him, if you ask Him."

"I have asked. For many years I have asked."

Then Raul was on his feet again, walking toward his pack. Without a word to Marcos, he motioned for Miguel to lead the way.

Raul, Marcos, and Miguel hiked in silence through the remainder of the day and late into the night. When it was too dark to see, they stopped to eat and rest until daybreak. Raul removed his pack and loosened his shoes before settling against a large rock. He stretched his legs and yawned then glanced across to where Marcos sat on the ground. Raul was grateful Marcos respected his need for space. Raul shifted his eyes to watch Miguel puttering around the campsite.

"Miguel," Raul called softly. "You need to rest. Daylight will come, and we will need to be on our way."

Miguel walked over to Raul and sat down next to him. "How do you know Elder Miller?" he asked.

"I don't really. I met his wife and daughter on a tour bus. Hermano Miller wasn't with them. He came after his daughter disappeared."

"You were taking a tour of Guatemala?"

Raul smiled. "No. It's my job. The tour company hired me to protect the tourists. The people pay a lot of money to visit Guatemala, and it's my job to keep them safe."

"Tell me about you and Marcos. He said you were friends once."

"We were friends."

"Please, tell me what happened."

Raul looked over at Marcos; he was asleep.

"Marcos and I grew up together. My father worked in his father's fields. When my father died, his father took me in and treated me like his own son." Raul stopped, and the two sat together in the dark for a time before Raul

continued his story. "When we were just a little older than you, we joined the army together."

"You were in the army?"

"For a short time."

"What happened?"

"It was a long time ago, long before you were born. Guatemala was torn apart in civil war. One regime after another took over. Each one promised better things, but in the end, they were all the same. They told us we were fighting Communism."

"But you weren't?"

Raul shook his head. "It seems the government thought the enemy was the Maya. They went into tiny villages and accused the men of helping the guerrillas."

"Were they?"

Raul stared into the shadows for a long time before he responded. "They found mass graves full of women and children. Women buried with babies in their arms. The villagers were unarmed. Some—those who could—fled to the hills. The rest were slaughtered."

"But you were in the army?"

"When I realized what was happening, I left."

"But Marcos stayed? Is that why you hate him?"

Raul closed his eyes and didn't answer.

"He said it was because of him that someone you loved was killed," Miguel said.

"He spoke the truth."

"What happened?" Miguel asked again.

Raul shook his head. "You must forgive me, but it was a day I have tried for many years to forget."

"Was it a woman you loved?"

Raul nodded, his throat constricting.

Raul turned away, but Miguel persisted. "What did you do after you left the army?"

"I joined the insurgents and tried to fight back. One day, I came face to face with a soldier. I looked into his eyes, and I knew he was scared. He begged me not to kill him. In that moment I saw myself, and I realized that my enemy was just like me."

"Did you kill him?"

"No. I dropped my gun and ran away. I decided then that I would never use a gun again."

"But you have a gun now?"

"A gun I have never fired." Raul exhaled slowly. "I didn't pick up a gun for a long time." He paused. "I was on a bus full of people one day. The bus pulled to a stop, and a man climbed onto the bus and pulled out a gun."

"What happened?"

"I watched and cowered, like everyone else. There was nothing I could do. I realized that my skills—the terrible, horrific skills I had honed in the army and tried so hard since then to forget—those skills could be used to protect."

"And that is what you have been doing since then?"

Raul nodded. "That is what I have tried to do."

"But you said you have never fired your gun."

"And I pray I will never have to. Now, you must go to sleep. Tomorrow will soon come."

CHAPTER 42

CATHY'S HEAD WAS REELING.

"Would you like to see someone else, ma'am?"

The phone in her purse rang. She pulled it out and stared at it then returned it to her purse unanswered. *Nick.*

If Nick's hunch was right, maybe his threats had motivated Curtis Whittaker to action. Or to disappear. But why would Nick lie to her? Did he think she'd freak out if she knew Mr. Whittaker was gone? Could he have talked to someone else in the embassy? No; he'd specifically mentioned Mr. Whittaker. She was sure of it.

"Are you all right, ma'am? Would you like to speak to someone else?" the young woman asked again.

"My friend was here this morning," Cathy said. "I wonder if you might remember him." She described Nick and then asked, "Do you remember seeing him?"

"No. I'm sorry, ma'am, but no one by that description has been in this morning. Is there anything else I can help you with?"

"Would you possibly have a quiet place where I could sit and collect my thoughts for a few minutes?"

"Of course." The receptionist led her back into a small dark room with two overstuffed chairs and a round table. File cabinets lined the walls. "You can stay as long as you'd like." She turned on the light and pulled the door shut behind her.

Cathy sat on one of the chairs. There had to be a logical explanation. There was no reason for Nick to lie to her.

Nick had said he thought Mr. Whittaker was dirty. If that was true, his receptionist could be covering for him.

Cathy closed her eyes. Maybe she could stay here, in this room, in this chair, until the whole thing was over. The phone in her purse began to vibrate again. She pulled it out and stared at Nick's name until the phone stopped

ringing. She had to talk to someone. Scott was there when she and Matt had talked to Mr. Whittaker. He would have connections. She opened her phone and scrolled through her contact list. He wasn't there.

What about Raul? Again, she scrolled through the list. She found his name, pressed the call button, and listened. The phone rang and rang. No answer. Ignoring the growing ache in the pit of her stomach, she scrolled through the list again, more slowly. There had to be someone.

The phone vibrated in Cathy's hand again. She held it, willing it to stop ringing. It had been several hours since she'd left the hotel. Nick must be wondering what was going on. He wouldn't give up.

Why would he lie to me?

Maybe she should just ask him. Tell him what she had learned and give him an opportunity to explain himself.

And then a memory came to her mind. It had been one of those sleepless nights when both she and Matt had woken up at some unearthly hour and started talking.

"I called Santiago today," he'd said.

"What about?"

"The usual."

"And?"

"I don't know. You know how he is. He wants to do whatever I want him to do. But it's not *me*. I don't know if he gets that." They'd lain in the dark for several moments before Matt spoke again. "Did I do the right thing when I agreed to work for Nick?"

"Well, you're bringing home more bacon."

"That's true—but bacon's not the only thing that's important."

"What does Nick want?"

"He wants it all. And he wants it yesterday."

Cathy's mouth went dry.

Get a grip, Cathy, she thought now. *Being greedy doesn't make Nick a kidnapper.* But it did give him a reason.

The man Nick said was watching her room at the hotel. Mr. Whittaker. Raul. He'd tried to convince her not to trust anyone. Was it all a fabrication to make her afraid?

This was insanity. Nick couldn't be responsible for all of this. There had to be another explanation.

Her phone rang again. She pressed the button to silence the ring. The battery was at eighteen percent. She needed to charge her phone, and her phone charger was at the hotel. She should have brought it with her—but why would she have?

Maybe she could buy another one, although she had no idea where she would begin to look for one. And she couldn't be without her phone.

Was there anything else she had to have?

Her passport.

Cathy opened her purse and rummaged through it, finally dumping the contents onto her lap. No phone charger and no passport. She'd been so rattled she hadn't thought to pick them up.

She had to go back to the hotel. She had to face Nick. As long as she acted natural, everything would be okay. If he wanted to hurt her, he'd have done it a long time ago. Certainly there had been plenty of opportunities.

She'd go back to the hotel and get her things and then—

If Nick wasn't at the embassy today, where was he?

He'd left first thing in the morning, right after she'd told him about her text message and her conversation with Raul. He'd said he was going to see Mr. Whittaker. He'd said they needed to have a Plan B. And then she'd suggested Mr. Whittaker might send some reinforcements to help Raul.

"That's a really good idea—but do we know where Raul is?"

"I'm trying to remember what he said. I think it was Salamá. Pretty sure that's right. Any idea where that is?"

If Nick was dirty, she had given him information which could lead him directly to Matt.

But Santiago and Matt weren't at the house in Salamá. And by now, Raul would be long gone as well. Even if Nick went there this morning, he wouldn't have found anyone there.

Except María and her children.

Nick wouldn't hurt María. Or her children.

He wouldn't hurt Melissa. Or Matt.

Cathy had to warn María. She had to get to Salamá.

She would go back to the hotel and act like nothing had happened. Tomorrow she would find a way to get to Salamá.

Cathy left the embassy and retraced her steps to the bus station in Guatemala City. An hour later, she climbed off the bus in Antigua and walked the few blocks to the Casa Santo Domingo, slowing as she reached the hotel. She pushed open the wooden door and peered inside. There was nothing out of the ordinary. She moved through the open-air corridor, past the statuary and the flower baskets, until she reached her room. Her hands shook as she fumbled with the lock, pushed the door open, and slipped into the room. Everything was just as she had left it. She double-checked the chain lock, turned off the TV, and swept the note she had left for Nick into the garbage.

Cathy sat on the edge of the bed, twisting the rings on her finger. They felt loose. She stared at the narrow gold band her husband had placed there so many years ago. *We were so young.*

A light tapping on the door drew her attention. The tapping grew louder, insistent. And then she heard his voice, calling her name through the door. She had to answer it.

"Am I glad to see you," Nick said when Cathy cracked the door open. "I've been trying to get a hold of you for several hours, and I was starting to wonder if something had happened to you. What have you been doing?"

"I accidentally turned my phone off."

"You had it off all afternoon and didn't notice?"

Cathy forced a laugh. "Why is that hard to believe? It's not like I'm making phone calls."

"Are you going to let me come in?"

"Honestly, I'm really tired. I haven't been sleeping much."

"I understand. I won't stay long."

Finally Cathy stepped back so he could enter. "So tell me what you found out in Guatemala City."

Nick pushed the door shut and turned to face her. "As if I wasn't worried enough, the guy in the room across the hall asked me if you were okay."

"Really? Someone asked about me?" Cathy swallowed.

"He said he tried to talk to you, but you ran back into your room like a scared little rabbit. What did he say to you?"

"I don't remember what he said."

"Under the circumstances, I'd think you'd remember every word he said." Nick's words hung in the air. "That's why you called me, isn't it? To ask if he was the man I'd seen loitering around your room."

"Yes, I guess you're right. I forgot about that."

"You forgot? How is that even possible?"

"I don't know what you want me to say, Nick."

Nick's voice softened. "I'm sorry, Cathy. I don't mean to give you the third degree. I've just been really worried about you. When you didn't answer the phone, I started imagining the worst. If you hadn't opened the door just now, I was going to talk to the hotel staff and see if I could get a key. I've been really worried."

"I'm sorry, Nick."

"It's okay. Just, please, be careful." He walked across the room to look out the window. "You asked about Guatemala City. I can tell you one thing; I called Mr. Whittaker's superiors and gave them a piece of my mind. I don't think he'll be on the U.S. government's payroll much longer."

When Cathy didn't answer, Nick continued. "I called the park headquarters in Tikal to see if they could tell me anything. They said they had done everything they could and they're absolutely sure she's not anywhere in the park. As big as it is, I don't know how they could be sure of that, but that's what they said."

Cathy nodded and waited.

"How are you holding up, Cathy?"

"All right. I've been thinking about Mr. Whittaker and how you wondered if he could be involved," Cathy said.

"It wouldn't surprise me. Nothing that man did would surprise me."

"You're sure it was Mr. Whittaker you talked to?"

"Of course. Why are you asking?"

"No reason." Cathy stopped. Her face burned. She turned away from Nick so he wouldn't see it and walked to the door. "I'm awfully tired, Nick. I haven't been sleeping well, and I'd really like to go to bed now, if you'll excuse me."

Nick followed her across the room. He put his hands on her shoulders and turned her to face him. "Cathy, I'm worried about you. I'm sorry I've been so overbearing. You know I'm just trying to take care of you."

Cathy forced herself to meet his eyes and smile. "I really do appreciate what you're doing."

Nick studied her for several seconds before he reached for the door. "Don't turn your phone off again, okay? And don't talk to anyone."

Cathy nodded.

After Nick left, she shut the door and replaced the chain. She sat on the edge of the bed and stared at the corner fireplace in the darkening room. Finally, she slid from the bed and onto her knees. She waited for several minutes as she tried to silence her mind, and then she pleaded for comfort and to know what she should do. She remained on her knees long after her prayer was finished, listening for the still small voice. Finally it came, reminding her of the verses she had recently read in section six of the Doctrine and Covenants. She picked up her scriptures and found the familiar words: "If you desire a further witness, cast your mind upon the night that you cried unto me in your heart, that you might know concerning the truth of these things. Did I not speak peace to your mind concerning the matter? What greater witness can you have than from God?"

Cathy read the words over and over, and as she did, peace distilled on her soul, reminding her of the night she had wept and begged to know, and the quiet assurance that had come into her heart, that everything would be okay. She sat on her bed, basking in the comfort and warmth that enveloped her entire body. All was well. The Lord was in control. She knelt again, thanking Him for allowing her to feel His love and comforting Spirit.

CHAPTER 43

Day 10

AT FIRST DAYLIGHT, RAUL, MARCOS, and Miguel had begun again, fighting their way through the tangled brush as they climbed in elevation. Even Miguel's cheery disposition was dampened as exhaustion took its toll.

Finally, they came to the remnants of a stone road. Miguel glanced at Raul and grinned. "You see? We're almost there," he said. "This is the road in hermana Miller's dream."

"I believe you are right, my young friend," Raul said.

They followed the road as it curved through the mountains.

* * *

Melissa welcomed the daylight. She had been awake most of the night, and when she did sleep her dreams were haunted by visions of the snake. Now she stared at the snake's remains from where she sat and felt the same fear she had felt the night before, even though she knew it could no longer harm her. The snake was at least three feet long and thickly built, with diagonal stripes and diamonds of various shades of brown.

Eduardo picked it up and held it out to Melissa. She flinched.

"Does the snake scare you?" Eduardo said. "You could be telling your daddy goodbye today. Or maybe your daddy would have cut off your leg to try to save your life." He looked at Matt. "What do you think? Would you cut off your daughter's leg while she screamed in pain? Or would you watch her slowly die? A young girl like her—I wonder how long it would have taken for the venom of a fer-de-lance to spread through her body."

"¡*Vámonos!*" Adán's voice was hard, cold.

Eduardo turned toward him. "I am in charge, and you'll do well to remember that."

"Your silly games bore me," Adán said. "You like to play with your prey." He raised his gun and fired it, barely missing Eduardo. "We go when I say we go," he said. "¿Comprendes?"

Eduardo glared at Adán but didn't respond.

Adán turned to the others in the group. "¡Vámonos!" he repeated.

Once again, Santiago led the way through the jungle. Melissa walked behind her father, wincing each time she saw him cringe as he put weight on his foot. For the first time in her life, she wanted to take care of him.

Late in the afternoon, the ground began to level out. They came to what must have once been a stone road. They followed the dry stone pathway as it wound through an old mining area. Eventually they came to a place littered with the remains of an ancient people.

"We're here," Santiago said. Boulders, some as large as buses, extended as far as they could see.

"Where is the jade?" Eduardo said.

Santiago motioned to the area around him. "Maybe it is here in these boulders."

"Maybe?"

"The boulders with jade look the same as all the others. You can't tell by looking at the stone." Santiago walked over to one and tapped it. "We work hard to find the jade you want to rob from us. We hike up the mountain, and then we search for the right pieces and carry them out of here. Once we have them at home, we chisel them until we have the best pieces. It is hard work, but it's what we do to take care of our families."

"That is of no concern to me," Eduardo said. He stared out at the rolling hills covered in gray boulders then brought his eyes back to rest on Matt. "Your friend wanted me to keep you alive. But keeping you alive just complicates things."

"What are you talking about? What friend?"

Eduardo spoke matter-of-factly, as though he were discussing a dinner menu. "He thought that we could all go home after this and nobody would need to get hurt. But it's not that simple." He pulled the gun from his pocket.

"Please," Matt began. "Please don't do this. We have done everything you asked us to do. Please let us go. We will walk away from this place and never look back. I give you my word of honor on that. You can have it all, all the jade. It means nothing. Please, just let us go."

Eduardo laughed. "Of course you say that. You would agree to anything now, wouldn't you? Beg all you want; there is no one who will help you."

"You are wrong," a voice called from behind the tree line. "There is someone."

Eduardo whipped around, his gun raised. "It seems we have company." Slowly Eduardo circled the area, his eyes focused on the brush and trees.

* * *

After instructing Miguel to stay behind, Raul had inched forward to the edge of the clearing. He had watched and waited as the exchange took place and was as surprised as those in the clearing when he heard Marcos's voice—loud, resolute. He looked up at Marcos standing beside him and could see disgust in Marcos's eyes.

Raul glanced back at Miguel. Miguel's eyes were wide with fear. Raul held his finger to his lips before turning back to the scene unfolding through the trees in front of him.

Marcos was right. Adán was gripping Melissa's arm with one hand. Raul watched as Adán used his free hand to pull a gun from his belt and hold it straight in front of him.

"Raul," Adán called. "Are you out there, my old friend? Come where I can see you. I think I found the girl you were looking for."

Raul wiped his forehead. He exchanged a glance with Marcos. Marcos nodded and stepped into the clearing.

Adán stared at Marcos. "What are you doing here?"

"Let her go, Adán," Marcos said. "She is innocent."

"And when did you become the champion of the innocent? When we were in Plan de Sánchez? You were not so worried about the innocent then, were you?" Adán said.

Marcos's mouth twisted. He reached for his gun.

Raul stepped out into the open.

Eduardo turned his gun toward Raul. "This is becoming quite a party. Now, why don't you go back down the mountain before you get hurt, little man."

"Let them go," Raul said.

Suddenly Eduardo turned his gun toward Matt and cocked it. Melissa yanked away from Adán and ran at Eduardo, ramming into his side, clawing at his arm. He shoved her; she lost her balance and sprawled onto the ground.

Then Eduardo again leveled his gun at Matt and fired.

* * *

Miguel watched Raul step into the clearing. He waited, his heart hammering in his chest.

"Let them go," he heard Raul say.

Miguel crept forward, stopped, listened; a gun was cocked. He scrambled to the edge of the woods where he could see through the trees. His eyes darted around the group until he located his father, standing next to Elder Miller. Another man stood in front of them.

He heard a gunshot. As though he was watching a movie in slow motion, Miguel saw his father dive onto Elder Miller, pushing him to the ground. He heard his father gasp and saw him clutch his shoulder.

"¡Papá!" Miguel screamed. He leapt to his feet and hurled himself through the trees, straight toward Santiago. "¡No, Papá, no!"

Raul tried to tackle Miguel, but Miguel wrenched away. Raul grabbed his arm and held him. "Listen to me, Miguel. You've done your part here. Go back where you were, and stay there. That's the best way you can help your papá."

Miguel stared at the pool of blood spreading in a widening circle, staining his father's shirt. He saw his father's face blanch and his mouth contort as he tried to push himself up from the ground.

"Well, look at what we have here," Eduardo said, turning toward Miguel.

"Go, Miguel. Now, while you can. Stay out of this." It was his father's voice, commanding him. Miguel hesitated only a moment before he began backing into the woods, tears streaming down his cheeks.

"Your son has come to rescue you? What an interesting turn of events," Eduardo said. "But I do hate to kill men in front of their children. Children should be protected from such things, don't you think?"

Miguel stopped and clenched his fists. "Today I am not a child," he whispered.

"Go, Miguel. Go now," Santiago said. "I'm telling you, as your father, to go."

Miguel shook his head.

Raul turned to Miguel and spoke softly. "Miguel, think of your mother, and obey your father. You're making things worse by being here."

Miguel turned then and ran into the woods. Once inside the dense growth, he slid onto the ground and wrapped his arms around his knees. Burying his face in his hands, he sobbed. What good was it to bring them here if in the end he couldn't help his father?

He heard Eduardo's voice coming through the trees. "Let's get this over with."

Miguel braced himself for a gunshot. Instead he heard another voice, Raul's voice. "I think you've forgotten something."

There was a pause. Miguel heard footsteps crunching as someone moved closer. Raul's voice came again. "I don't want to use this, but I will if I have to."

Then Miguel heard a gunshot. He jerked with a start and scrambled back to the edge of the forest where he could see through the trees. He had to help his father.

* * *

Melissa lay on the ground where she had landed when Eduardo shoved her. She held still, afraid to move, afraid to do anything that would attract attention. Then, out of the corner of her eye, Melissa saw Adán lift his gun, cock it, and point it toward Raul. She screamed and then screamed again when she heard a gun fire and saw Adán collapse on the ground. Melissa twisted around and saw Marcos with his gun trained on Eduardo.

Eduardo backed toward the forest. Just then Miguel plunged through the trees toward Santiago. Eduardo stepped into the boy's path and caught him by the arm. Yanking Miguel to his chest, he wrapped his arm around him and held him securely. Eduardo pointed his gun at Raul.

"How quickly things change," Eduardo said. "Drop your guns or the boy dies." He pressed the gun into Miguel's side.

"Leave the boy out of this," Raul said.

"I grow weary of your games. Put your guns on the ground and push them over to me."

Melissa watched Raul place his gun on the ground. She saw Marcos hesitate, his eyes on Raul. Eduardo shifted his gun toward Marcos and pulled the trigger. Melissa screamed again as Marcos fell. Holding Miguel with one arm, Eduardo kicked Raul's gun out of the way.

Marcos's gun lay several feet away on the ground. As Eduardo moved toward it, Miguel wrenched free of his grasp and dove onto the gun.

Melissa edged toward where Adán lay lifeless in the dirt, her eyes fixed on the gun lying next to him. She stretched as far as she could, her hand inching toward the gun. Her fingers touched the metal. Closed on the handle. Slowly she drew the gun toward her.

She glanced at Eduardo. He was pointing his gun at Miguel lying facedown in the dirt. "Give me the gun and I'll let you go to your Daddy," Eduardo said. "Otherwise, you can tell him goodbye."

Melissa raised the gun and fired.

CHAPTER 44

No one moved for several seconds, and then Raul crossed to where Eduardo lay limp on the ground. He bent and checked for a pulse then stood again.

"He's dead," he said.

Miguel had gone to his father and was wrapping the gunshot wound with strips of cloth he had torn from his shirt.

Melissa remained frozen to the spot where she was sprawled on the ground. Matt rushed to her side and pried the gun from her fingers. Then he gathered her in his arms and held her close, stroking her hair. He kissed the top of her head. "It's over, 'Lissa. It's all over. Now we can go home."

Raul knelt beside Marcos and pressed his neck. "He has a slight pulse." A circle of blood seeped through Marcos's shirt, spreading rapidly. "He's losing a lot of blood," Raul said. He ripped a strip off his shirt and tied it around Marcos's wound. Squeezing the hand of the man he had both loved and despised, he felt his throat tighten. "Come back to us," he whispered. "Please come back."

For just a moment, Marcos's eyes flickered open.

"Stay with us," Raul said. "We're going to get you help."

Marcos closed his eyes and gasped for breath. Then his eyes opened again. "I'm so sorry," Marcos said. "Please forgive me."

Raul looked into Marcos's eyes and saw the eyes of a little boy, pleading for one more chance. Tears filled his eyes. "Stay with us."

"Please, Raul, please let me die knowing you have forgiven me."

Raul's tears overflowed onto his cheeks. Peace filled his body. He reached out and touched Marcos's face. When he spoke, his voice was barely a whisper, "I forgive you, my old friend."

Marcos smiled and closed his eyes. He took one last ragged breath and was gone.

Raul rocked back on his heels and stared at Marcos. He bowed his head then stood and walked away from the others in the group. He leaned against

a boulder for several moments before his knees gave out and he sank to the ground. Pressing his face against the boulder, he covered his head with his arms and sobbed.

It was dusk, and night was coming quickly. Melissa and Miguel explored the area, looking for a place where they could spend the night. Miguel made a fire to help them stay warm and discourage any animals that might be attracted to their scent, while Melissa searched for food in the packs and presented her findings with a flourish. They ate their rations and relaxed for the first time in days.

After everyone else was settled, Miguel approached Raul with a chunk of bread and some cheese. Raul shook his head without looking up. Miguel knelt beside him and waited. Finally Raul spoke.

"Yesterday, I wanted to take his life," he said. "I told him to leave us."

"You did not know this would happen."

"But I would have wished for this to happen. And yet he saved my life."

Neither spoke for several moments. Then Raul continued. "When I saw him lying there—it was as if he were young again. As if we were both young again, young boys playing together. And I realized in that moment that Marcos was a mere boy when it all happened. He was scared, and he thought he had no choice. He made a terrible mistake—a mistake that has caused me great pain for many, many years. But he was just a boy, and he lived with that regret, just as I have lived with my grief. In the moment he was lying there, I felt peace."

"And you forgave him."

Raul nodded. "With God's help." He looked at the boy seated next to him and rumpled his hair. "You were right, you know. How did you get so wise?"

Miguel grinned. "I listen to my mamá and my papá."

CHAPTER 45

FEAR IS AN INTERESTING WEAPON, he thought. No fingerprints, no evidence, no mess to clean up. With a few carefully constructed suggestions, otherwise capable people could be held captive—paralyzed by their own imaginations.

No one was watching Cathy Miller; no one listened to her conversations. No one but him, her self-appointed protector. Yet, after losing both her daughter and her husband, it had been easy to convince her otherwise. Cathy's dependence on him had been established. She wouldn't be leaving her hotel room again.

* * *

Cathy packed her passport and a few essential items in a shoulder bag. Enough to get by but not enough to create suspicion. She left her makeup case open on the bathroom sink and the majority of her clothes piled in her suitcase, just in case someone came into the room.

It was still early. Cathy turned on the TV as she had done before. Then she went to the patio door and slid it open. As she was about to step outside, she heard a voice. She froze, listened. It was Nick's voice, quiet, muffled, but unmistakable, on the patio just over the wall from where she stood. She stepped back into the room and slid the door shut. She hesitated for only a moment before she walked to the room door.

Cathy unbolted the door and peeked around the door frame. The hall was deserted. Stepping into the dimly lit corridor, Cathy locked her door and hurried down the walkway, past the other rooms. As she reached the end of the passageway, she heard a door close. Without glancing back, she turned down a side corridor and stepped into an empty room.

In the front of the room, a stage was draped in white gauzy curtains. Rows of chairs, also covered in white fabric, faced the alcove. Centered at the front of the stage, tiny white flowers spilled from a wooden box. Light filtered through translucent draperies along the back of the stage.

She slipped onto a chair at the back of the room and listened. Nothing. Wait. Footsteps.

They were getting closer. Then they stopped.

"Like it?" a voice from behind her said. "It's called Our Lady of the Rosary chapel. I think it's rather ethereal, don't you?"

Cathy twisted in her chair to face Nick.

"Hello, Cathy," Nick said. "You're not leaving, are you?"

"I came here to pray," Cathy stammered.

"Think God will hear you better here than in your room?" Nick's eyes drifted to Cathy's shoulder bag. "I'm not sure I believe you."

"I've been cooped up in that room for more than a week, and I'm going a little stir crazy. I thought some fresh air would help."

Nick nodded. He walked to where she was and extended his hand. The ruby glinted on his finger. "Let's go for a walk."

"But I'm not supposed to leave the hotel."

"You're not supposed to leave your room."

Cathy could feel her heart beating in her throat. Ignoring his outstretched hand, she stood and slipped past him and out into the corridor. At the end of the hall, she could see an iron gate. An alcove built into the cracked gray rock wall housed a collection of pottery. He followed closely behind as she walked toward it. She stopped beside the display, feigning interest in the clay bowls. She had to get away from him.

"I didn't know you had an interest in archaeology," Nick said.

"There's a lot you don't know about me."

Nick laughed. "I guess that's true. Why don't you tell me about yourself."

She turned to move away from the display, and Nick stepped in front of her, blocking her path. "I want to go back to my room now," Cathy said.

"I'd be happy to go for a walk with you so you can get some fresh air." He touched her arm. "I've been so worried about keeping you safe I haven't thought about how you must be feeling."

Cathy cringed at his touch but forced herself to stay still. "You don't need to worry about how I'm feeling," she said.

"Of course I do." He moved his hand to her shoulder. His voice was soft, almost soothing, as he massaged her shoulder. "You feel helpless and scared. You want to help, but you don't know what you can do, and you don't know who you can trust. You see the enemy around every corner. Every pair of eyes seems like they're watching you. You wonder what happened to your husband and your daughter, and you wonder if you will ever see them again and what will

happen to you if they don't come back. He raised his hand to touch her cheek. "A woman alone in a Latin American country must feel completely vulnerable."

"Look, I really appreciate everything you're doing to help me, but right now, I'd just like to be alone."

Cathy's words hung in the air for several seconds before Nick spoke. "Do you think that's wise knowing someone is watching your room?"

Cathy swallowed and forced herself to smile. "*You're* watching my room, checking out anyone who looks suspicious. You told me before that nobody would get past you." She paused. "I shouldn't have left my room this morning, but I was going a little nutty. I really appreciate you looking out for me. You don't have to worry about me leaving again."

"I'm glad to hear that."

"Now, if you'd walk me back to my room, I'd like to spend some time alone," she repeated. When Nick didn't answer, Cathy added, "Like you said, I have a lot to think about."

When she was back in her room, Cathy's hands shook as she bolted the door. She sat on the edge of the bed and fumbled with the hem of her shirt. She took a deep breath and blew out the air. She had to get to Salamá.

She knew Nick was watching her room, waiting for her to try to leave again. Occasionally she heard his voice outside the door. It was just a matter of time before he would knock on the door and want her to let him in. She had to get away from the hotel. She stared at the patio door. It was now or never.

Cathy teased the sliding glass door open and listened. Nothing. Only the sounds of traffic on the street. She slipped outside and closed the door. When she didn't hear anything out of the ordinary, she hoisted herself over the wall and crept along the outer wall of the hotel, pausing to listen beneath a window framed by grapevines and ironwork curlicues. Baskets of greenery surrounded the window; a crucifix hung at the top. Only the bars, firmly affixed to the front of the window, were an unsettling reminder that Guatemala was a volatile place.

* * *

Nick decided to check out the lunch buffet before attempting to contact Cathy. Give her some time to think. He loaded his plate with pepián, frijoles, and fried banana and found a quiet corner to eat. The food was good here; he'd give them that.

Nick was getting antsy. If his calculations were correct, they should have reached the jade by now. Only a few more days.

Soon he would be comforting the grieving widow.

Of course, he never signed Matthew Miller's death sentence—never could have. They were friends. But he was a realist, and he recognized that some things were simply unavoidable. Unfortunate, really.

Matt was a good man, better than most. If things had gone the way Nick had originally planned it, Matt would have come off the mountain shaken up but unharmed. He would have collected his wife and daughter at the hotel and returned home. Nick would have lamented with Matt, reassuring him that he had no choice but to reveal the location of the jade; that none of it was his fault and there was absolutely nothing he could have done differently. He even would have tried to find another position for Matt in the company. And when that proved unsuccessful, which of course it would—he couldn't have risked having Matt come across a plump new bank account—he would have written him a brilliant letter of recommendation. After that, they would have exchanged annual Christmas cards.

Matthew Miller could have returned home unemployed instead of in a coffin.

But, in spite of Eduardo's assurances, Nick knew Eduardo Guerrero would not leave witnesses.

And Widow Miller was too attractive to be left alone.

CHAPTER 46

IT WAS MIDDAY NOW; THE sun was high in the sky. The streets of Antigua were busy. Cathy hurried across the street and retraced her steps from the day before, arriving at the bus terminal just as a bus pulled into the station and unloaded.

A rack on top of the bus overflowed with tapestry satchels, bedrolls, pillows, and loosely woven plastic bags filled with cans of food. Passengers climbed the parallel ladders on the back to retrieve their belongings.

The crowd jostled her as she made her way through the crowded terminal to the bus that would take her to Salamá.

* * *

It had been a couple of hours since Nick had left Cathy in her room. He tried to call both her cell phone and room number, but there was no answer. He tapped on her door and, when there was no response, tried to call again. Maybe she'd decided to take a nap.

* * *

It was early evening when the bus pulled into Salamá, a picturesque town surrounded by mountains on all sides. Pine forests mingled with lush meadows of olive and orange trees. Cathy climbed off the bus. It felt good to stop moving. The ride from Guatemala City had been slow; the bus had stopped frequently for people standing alongside the road, as well as at every town.

Cathy pulled her cell phone from her pocket; Nick had tried to call. She shuddered as she remembered being with him, wondering who he was and of what he was capable. It was good to be far away from his ever-present eyes.

Just then she noticed two lanky young men in dark slacks and white shirts. Gratitude and peace filled her heart; once again her prayers were being answered.

She approached the young missionaries. "I wonder if you could help me find someone," Cathy said after introducing herself. "She is a member of the Church and lives somewhere in this city."

"We'd be happy to help," said one of the elders.

"I think the best place for us to start is at the church," said his companion. "Our bishop should be in his office tonight, and I'm pretty sure he has contact information about all the members here."

"That sounds good."

"I hope you're up to walking, 'cause I'm afraid we don't have an extra bike for you," the first elder said with a grin. "And I don't know if you'd feel much like riding one if we did."

Cathy laughed. "Walking sounds great after sitting for hours on a bus."

As they strode down the streets, Cathy quizzed the missionaries about their families, their hometowns, and how long they had been serving. When they finally reached the church, she followed them down the hall to the bishop's office.

The bishop stood to greet them. He was a small man, more than a head shorter than the two missionaries, but he grasped Cathy's hand firmly and looked into her eyes with a steadiness that invited respect. Cathy listened as the missionaries spoke to the bishop. After they finished, the bishop pulled a book off his desk.

"*¿Y el nombre?*"

The missionaries turned to Cathy. "He's asking what her name is."

"Muchas gracias," Cathy said to the bishop. "Her name is María Gonzales. Her husband's name is Santiago, and she lives—well, I'm almost sure she lives in Salamá."

"María Gonzales?" The bishop leaned back in his chair and laughed out loud. Still chuckling, he turned to the missionaries. "I think maybe you can find Sister Gonzales without my help."

The missionaries looked sheepish.

While one elder apologized to the bishop, the other turned to Cathy and muttered, "This is pretty embarrassing, but Sister Gonzales's husband is the ward mission leader. I guess we should have asked you who you were looking for before we came here."

"Then you know her? You know where she lives?"

"We have dinner at her house at least once a week."

Cathy thanked the bishop again, and the three stood to leave.

Once outside, the elders pumped Cathy for information about why she wanted to see Sister Gonzales. Their embarrassment at failing to question

Cathy before they interrupted the bishop seemed to fade quickly as they listened to Cathy's explanation.

When they reached the blue cinderblock house, they tapped on the door, and after a few moments, the door opened a crack.

"*¡Elderes!*" María said. "*¿Quién es ésta mujer?*"

Cathy stepped forward and held out her hand. "I am Cathy Miller. My husband is Matthew Miller."

"Elder Miller. *¿Es su esposo?*" María opened her arms and embraced Cathy, kissing both her cheeks. Then she invited them to come in.

With the missionaries translating, Cathy explained why she was there and listened to María's account of Matt's arrival with a man she didn't recognize. "I do not know for certain, but I think he was a bad man."

"Do you know where they went?" Cathy asked.

"I only know they went to the jade." María wept openly as she explained how two more men had come the following day and how her son had insisted he accompany them to find his father. "I am grateful for his bravery, but I fear for him."

* * *

After unsuccessfully trying to contact Cathy again, Nick approached the desk clerk and asked for access to her room. The clerk looked uncomfortable. "This is not allowed. The privacy of the hotel patrons should not be violated."

"I appreciate your position; I really do. And normally I wouldn't even consider asking this, but it just isn't like her not to answer her phone," Nick said. "She wasn't feeling well when I last talked to her. She has a medical condition." He looked down at the desk. "I could never forgive myself if something happened to her."

The desk clerk led Nick to Cathy's room and unlocked the door.

The room looked exactly the way it had when he'd left Cathy a few hours earlier. The blankets on the bed had been pulled up, a novel lay on the nightstand, and a suitcase stood in the corner of the room. Nick walked around the room and then stepped out onto the patio.

She was gone.

His eyes narrowed as he took in the stone wall enclosing the patio. He had underestimated her.

"Thank you, sir," he said after they exited the room. "Please let me know if she contacts you. I am terribly worried about her."

The clerk nodded, and Nick returned to his room.

Where did Cathy go?

The only person in Guatemala who knew where to look for Matt and Melissa—besides Eduardo, of course—was Santiago Gonzales. And Santiago, according to what Cathy had been told, wasn't at home.

Cathy had said Raul Silva, the man from the tour company who just happened to be the man who'd discovered the bodies, had gone to Santiago's house in Salamá. According to Raul, Matt had been there and had left with Santiago. Cathy might have tried to contact Raul. But if Raul was trailing Matt, she wouldn't be able to reach him.

And then it came to Nick, and when it did, he knew he was right: Santiago Gonzales had gone, leaving his wife alone.

Cathy was headed to Salamá.

CHAPTER 47

Day 11

IT WOULD TAKE NEARLY TWO days to get off the mountain.

First thing in the morning, the group left the jade field. They followed the stone road as far as they could and then hiked through the heavy underbrush, stopping only when hunger, pain, fatigue, or darkness overcame them.

Melissa stayed close to Matt. Sometimes she linked arms with him, shyly at first, hugging his arm, helping him. His heart was full. He'd come close to losing her. All the little things that had annoyed him before seemed insignificant. She was safe, and that's all that mattered. They didn't talk about Eduardo and how he had died. They would have to at some point, of course, but he would wait for Melissa's lead. For now, he was simply enjoying her company. Stripped of everything but each other, they learned how to talk as they climbed down the mountain. She told him about Carlos and how he had sacrificed his life.

"There were so many things he didn't know," she said, "and yet, underneath it all, he was a good guy. He risked everything to keep me safe." She turned her head to hide the tears that welled up in her eyes.

"I'm sorry he's gone," Matt said. "But I'm also grateful to him. If it wasn't for his sacrifice, you might not be here with me right now."

Melissa nodded and wiped her eyes. "I know, but I wanted to help him understand things. And now I'll never be able to do that."

They walked without talking for a few minutes before Matt spoke again. "What Carlos did in luring you away was very wrong."

"But Dad—"

"Hear me out. He must have known it was wrong, and he must have regretted it a great deal."

"He told me he was sorry."

"So maybe he felt that in rescuing you, he was making up for what he'd done wrong. Even to the point of giving his life for you. In a way, it's like he atoned for his mistake." Matt paused for a moment before continuing. "And now he's in a better place. He's in a place where he can learn the answers to all his questions. All those things you wanted to share with him."

"I miss him."

"I know." Neither said anything for a while after that, each lost in their own thoughts. Finally Matt broke the silence. "You know I love you, don't you?"

"I love you too, Dad."

"Did they—hurt you?" Matt asked. "The men who kidnapped you."

"No. I was scared they might, especially one of them. He creeped me out when he looked at me. But Carlos watched out for me. I don't know what would have happened if he hadn't been there." Her voice became wistful. "Dad, do you think there's any way we could find Carlos's family?"

"I don't know, Melissa."

"I wish we could."

Matt nodded. After a pause, he said, "I'm sorry for how I've been about Josh. Maybe when we get back, you can bring him over and I can get to know him better."

"No, Dad, you were right. Josh isn't a good influence on me. He's always trying to get me to do things you and Mom wouldn't approve of. You know—push the limits. And when I tell him that, he just kind of makes fun of it. When I saw how Carlos took care of me, I kept wondering if Josh would have done those things, and I realized I don't think he cares that much about me. And you know what's crazy? I've been going through all this, and I'll bet he's already started dating someone else."

"Does that hurt to think about?"

"A little, I guess."

"You know, when the time is right, you're going to find someone who will love you with his whole heart, who will be willing to sacrifice for you the way Carlos did."

"The way you feel about Mom."

Matt smiled. "Yes, the way I feel about Mom. When she agreed to marry me, I thought I was the luckiest man in the world. And I was right. She was beautiful—she looked a lot like you, you know—smart, talented. And the most amazing thing was that she loved me back."

"I hope Mom's all right."

"I'm sure she is."

"What do you think that man meant when he said your friend wanted him to keep you alive?"

Matt shook his head. He had replayed Eduardo's words over and over in his mind as they hiked, trying but unable to make sense of them.

Your friend wanted me to keep you alive.

Eduardo's implication was unthinkable; there had to be another explanation. That's what he told himself, and he prayed he was right.

* * *

Four-year-old Ana was unusually clingy. It was as though she knew something was terribly wrong. Again and again, Ana looked at her mother, her chocolate eyes full of uncertainty, and asked for her daddy and her brother. María made excuses, excuses that the little girl refused to accept. Finally María gave up and pulled Ana onto her lap. Ana buried her head in her mother's chest. María sang to her and stroked her thick black hair. She held her daughter long after she felt the little body relax and heard her breathing deepen. Leaning her head back against the chair, María closed her eyes and silently prayed. Tonight, her prayers included an expression of gratitude for the woman who dozed on the couch across from her.

María had spent the five days since Santiago left doing what she did every day and trying not to think too much. She knew thinking would paralyze her, and she had to function for Ana, if for nothing else.

It was good to have another woman in the house. In the twenty-four hours since hermana Miller had arrived, they had settled into a companionable routine of child care, meal preparation, and household chores. Although communication was nearly impossible, they felt comforted being together.

A dog barked outside. Holding Ana in her arms, María walked to the window. Except for the dog, all was quiet. At the end of the street, she could see a single parked car. *Strange,* she thought.

Ana stirred. María kissed her forehead and then carried her in to her bed.

CHAPTER 48

A QUIET TAPPING ON THE door woke Cathy. Who would come to the house this late? She opened the door.

Nick stood in the doorframe. "Am I ever glad to see you," he said. "I've been searching everywhere for you."

"How did you find me?" Cathy said.

"When you didn't answer your door or your phone, I asked hotel management to check your room. I was afraid something had happened to you."

"But how did you know I was *here?*"

"I didn't know. I thought about your conversation with Raul and wondered if you might come here. So I came, hoping I'd find you. It was just a hunch—the only place I could think of. And then once I got to Salamá, I just started asking people. Finally ran into a couple of young men who knew Santiago. Crazy thing—they said they brought *you* here yesterday."

"The missionaries."

He ran his fingers through his hair. "I can't begin to tell you how worried I've been."

"I'm sorry I worried you."

"You don't need to apologize. You're okay, and that's what's important. I kept thinking about that guy who was watching your room. I was afraid he'd—" Nick shook his head. "Do you mind if I come in?"

"I don't think that's a good idea," Cathy said.

"I've driven three hours to find you and walked all over this town asking people if they knew Santiago, and now you're not going to let me sit on the couch or have a drink of water?"

"This isn't my house, Nick—"

"And you don't think the owner of the house would offer his employer a drink of water? Come on, Cathy, let's go inside where we can sit down."

When Cathy didn't answer, Nick pushed past her and into the living room. He walked over to the couch, sat down, and leaned back against the cushion. "So what's going on? Why did you leave without telling me what you were doing?"

"I wanted to come here, and I knew you'd try to keep me there."

"Okay, that's fair. I was trying to keep you safe. But that's not all, is it? I want you to be honest with me. Why did you leave?"

Cathy swallowed and forced her voice to be even. "Have you been honest with me?"

"Of course."

"What about Mr. Whittaker?"

"Mr. Whittaker? At the embassy? What about him?"

"You lied to me about going to see Mr. Whittaker."

"What are you talking about?"

"You didn't go to the embassy. The receptionist told me you hadn't been there. Where did you go? Why did you lie to me?"

"The receptionist told you I wasn't there? That's interesting. He's got her lying for him. I told you from the first time I met him that he was dirty, and this proves it. He's hiding something."

A door at the end of the hall opened. *"¿Hermana, te encuentras bien?"* María called. *"Me pareció escucharte hablar con alguien."* María stepped into the living room.

Nick stood and offered his hand. *"Buenas noches,"* he said. *"Me llamo Nicholas Slade. ¿Puede ser que seas la Señora Gonzales? Encantado de conocerte. Vine aquí para ayudarte."*

María nodded and motioned for Nick to sit again on the couch. She hurried into the kitchen, returning momentarily with a glass of water.

"Muchas gracias, señora."

María looked between Nick and Cathy.

"What did you say to her?" Cathy asked, her voice tight.

"I told her I was here to help the two of you, of course," Nick said, and then he turned his attention back to María. As the two conversed, Cathy's stomach churned. Nick's voice was warm, friendly. He could be telling María anything, and there was nothing she could do about it.

After what seemed like forever, Nick yawned and turned to Cathy. "I think it's time to call it a night, don't you? María invited me to sleep on the couch."

CHAPTER 49

Day 12

CATHY LAY AWAKE IN THE dark most of the night. When she finally drifted off to a restless sleep, she dreamt of Nick and woke up in a cold sweat. She could hear María in the kitchen. She lay still and listened until she heard Nick's deep voice.

Cathy stayed in the bedroom as long as she dared, replaying their conversation, before splashing water on her face and smoothing her hair. Finally she emerged from the bedroom and forced herself to smile when she saw Nick sitting on the floor cross-legged, playing with Ana.

He looked up and met her eyes. "Well, good morning. Sleep well?"

María interrupted with a call for breakfast. Nick scooped Ana up in his arms and carried her to the breakfast table. Cathy busied herself at the table, avoiding Nick's eyes as much as possible, but it was unnecessary. Nick's attention was focused on Ana and María. Cathy listened as he teased Ana and made her laugh; occasionally María would laugh as well.

Nick seemed so nice, helpful, likeable. Was it possible he really was just trying to help?

No. He was playing with her head.

* * *

It was late in the evening when they arrived where they'd begun, in the tiny village of Chilasco. Immersed in darkness, the group hunted until they found the car Marcos, Raul, and Miguel had left there several days before. Raul had retrieved the key from Marcos's pack when they were on the mountain; now he removed it from his pocket and unlocked the door.

The group piled into the car. Raul pulled it onto the road and headed for Salamá. They would stop at Santiago's house to let his wife know they were

all right and then get treatment for Santiago and Matt. "You know what I'm looking forward to the most?" Melissa said. "Besides seeing Mom, of course?"

"A shower? Eating real food?" Matt asked.

"Yes! How did you know? Seriously, though, I'm looking forward to just getting back home and being a better person."

"Well, don't change too much, because I happen to like you the way you are."

* * *

Cathy's nerves had been on edge all day. Every time Nick met her eyes, Cathy was filled with revulsion. She hated everything about him. Hated how he played with Ana, chasing her on his hands and knees around the house. Hated how Ana giggled and climbed onto his lap. Hated that Nick talked to María— and she couldn't. He was building María's trust in him, just as he had with Cathy, and Cathy resented that. Her attempts to communicate with María about her suspicions had only brought confusion. Never before had she so badly wished she could speak another language.

So after supper, when he walked out the back door with Ana's small hand tucked in his own, Cathy felt a mixture of panic and relief. She watched through the window as Nick tossed a ball for Ana to catch.

* * *

A knock on the door drew Cathy's attention away from the window. María stepped across the room and cracked the door open. When she saw Raul, she threw the door open and motioned for him to enter.

"¡Hermano! ¡Volviste!" María said.

Cathy simultaneously exclaimed, "Raul, I thought you were—"

"I was, and I am," Raul said, his eyes scanning the room. "Are you all right?"

María's eyes were glued to the door. Her hand moved from her chest to her mouth, and her eyes filled with tears. "¡Mijo!" she cried.

Cathy turned to see Miguel and Santiago step through the door. María flew across the room and threw her arms around them. She clutched them and kissed their cheeks. "¡Estás herido!" María said.

Before Cathy could ask about Matt and Melissa, they walked in the door. All the emotion of the past twelve days overcame her as she reached for her husband and daughter, hugging first one and then the other.

"Por favor trae unas vendas," María said to Miguel. Then she beckoned for Santiago to follow her into the kitchen. Miguel disappeared into another

room, reappearing a moment later with bandages. He joined his parents in the kitchen. Cathy could hear the water running and their voices as they talked softly.

"I was so afraid I would never see either of you again," Cathy whispered.

"So was I, Mom," Melissa said. "I was so scared."

"I told you I'd find her," Matt said, pulling Cathy into a crushing embrace, his voice was husky.

Melissa wiped her eyes. "Way to take all the credit, Dad," she teased. "I mean, you were a hero and all, but I'm pretty sure we wouldn't have made it without Raul."

Matt laughed. "Good to have you back, Melissa! I was starting to wonder if you'd been swapped with a girl who just looks incredibly like my daughter, except a whole lot dirtier!"

"I'm insulted. Are you suggesting I need a shower?" Melissa said.

Cathy laughed and turned to Raul. "How can I ever thank you?"

"It was not only me who helped them, hermana. But I am happy we have returned and that you are well. And now I will leave you to your happy reunion."

"First let me get you something to eat," Cathy said.

"Thank you, but no. There is something else I need to do."

"Can we help you then?"

Raul shook his head. "This is something I must do alone. I will come back."

After Raul left, Cathy hugged Matt and Melissa again. "I'm so grateful you're back," she said. "So grateful this nightmare is over."

"As am I," Nick said.

No one had heard Nick come through the back door, but now they turned to look at him. Ana was perched on his shoulders.

"I came to Guatemala as soon as I heard you were gone, Matt. And I have to tell you—I'm looking at you and I hear your voice, but I still can't believe you're standing here. And Melissa too. But you're okay? You're both okay?"

"Other than a sprained ankle, I've never been better," Matt said, all emotion gone from his voice. He extracted himself from Cathy's grip and took a step toward Nick. Nick lowered Ana from his shoulders and set her on the floor in front of him, her hand in his.

"What a relief! But—what happened? Where were you?"

"Turns out it was all about the jade. A man wanted me to take him to the jade field."

"The jade? Seriously? But why Melissa?"

"As far as I can tell, Melissa was bait. He knew I would do anything for my daughter."

"And after you took him to the jade field, he let you go?" Nick asked.

"He didn't plan to. Of course, he didn't plan on Raul showing up either. But he did say something about keeping us alive, so I think that was the original plan. Kidnapping was okay, but apparently murder was a little outside your comfort zone."

"What are you talking about?"

"It seems the person behind the kidnapping, behind all of it, stood to gain a lot by knowing the location of the jade. I asked myself who would gain from that knowledge. At first, I didn't even consider you—it never crossed my mind that such a good friend could do something like that. But what other explanation was there? I tried to come up with one. All the way down the mountain, I tried to figure out some other explanation for what Eduardo said. My life, my daughter's life, had to be worth more to you than money."

Nick laughed. "Matt, you're not serious."

"You masterminded the whole thing." Matt's voice rose as he spoke. "You hired men to kidnap my daughter and to force Santiago and me to take them to the jade."

Ana began to wail. Nick picked her up. "You're scaring her, Matt. You don't want to scare a little girl, do you?"

When Matt didn't answer, Nick continued. "I left everything the second I heard you were in trouble, put everything on hold to come here and help find you and Melissa. This is how you thank me? You know, I'd be insulted if I didn't know what you've been through. So I'm not going to overreact to your accusations. Whoever is behind this obviously found out I was coming and decided to use that information to deflect attention away from himself."

"Who knew you were coming here?" Cathy asked.

"Anyone who bugged your phone or your room. It's not that hard," Nick said. "The irony is that I warned you to be careful about that, but you wouldn't listen."

"You said the man across the hall was watching me."

"Yes, I did. I saw him hanging around your room on several occasions. I tried to warn you, but did you listen? No."

"He tried to talk to me."

"And doesn't that seem a little odd? You'd think if he was here on vacation he'd be out seeing the sights, not trying to strike up a conversation with some random woman. Except you weren't random, were you? He was watching you. And it wasn't just because you're an attractive woman."

Cathy flushed.

Turning back to Matt, Nick said, "We need to get you and Santiago to a hospital immediately. And I think Melissa should be checked over as well."

"What I need right now is to see you in handcuffs being hauled off to a Guatemalan prison," Matt said.

"Do you have any evidence to back up your accusation? Even in Guatemala, you have to have at least a shred of evidence." Nick paused for a moment before continuing. "You know, if I hadn't been out of town, you would have been on that plane sitting next to Cathy, and none of this would have happened. So I guess in that way, I am responsible. At least you're okay. I don't think I could have forgiven myself if anything worse had happened."

Before Matt could respond, Nick pulled out his wallet, withdrew several large bills, and handed them to Cathy. "Please make sure they see a doctor."

"I don't want your money."

Santiago, María, and Miguel came back into the room.

"Tiene una maravillosa pequeña y ha sido un placer conocerles," Nick said, smiling at María. He tousled Ana's hair and then set her on the ground.

Nick turned back to Matt and Cathy. "I'm going to go now and let you get some rest. I'll talk to the police as soon as I leave here. I don't expect them to do a lot, but at least I can tell them about the man who was stalking Cathy in the hotel. And then I guess I'll head for the States. Probably need me more there than here at this point. I'll see what's happened to the company in our absence."

"And Matt," he said, "take as long as you need before you come back to the office. Spend time as a family. You certainly deserve it after all you've been through. Just give me a call when you're ready." He turned to Cathy. "I can't tell you how relieved I am that this terrible ordeal is over for you and that Melissa and Matt are safe."

When the door was closed behind Nick, Cathy sank onto the couch. "Do you really think he did it?"

"I don't know, Cathy," Matt said. He watched Nick climb into his car and drive away. "All I've got is one comment from a criminal. That's not exactly enough to indict someone." He shook his head. "I don't even know if *I'm* convinced he did it."

"There's something else," Cathy said. "Nick lied to me. He told me he talked to Mr. Whittaker at the embassy, but when I went there myself, the receptionist told me Mr. Whittaker hadn't been in all day. Nick did everything he could to keep me trapped in that hotel room. Day after day, he filled my head with fear that someone was watching me and that I couldn't trust anyone—not even Raul. How ironic. I sat there in the embassy that day and remembered how

you told me Nick wanted to go in and get the jade—all the jade. And I knew I couldn't trust him. That's why I came here. I was trying to get away from Nick. And then he followed me here." Cathy reached for Matt's hand. "I'm so grateful you and Melissa are back and that you're all right. But, Matt, if he did do it, he can't get away with this."

CHAPTER 50

Day 13

RAUL CLIMBED OFF THE BUS at Rabinal and walked along the dusty street, past the mud-brick houses covered with stucco, to the imposing but dingy white cathedral. The plaza was still there, exactly as he remembered it. It had been nearly thirty years since he had been in this town. He'd left the day Sofía was killed and never returned.

He walked on until he came to the cemetery, at the back of which stood a ten-foot-tall monument. He approached the monument. Crude, colorful figures had been painted, depicting the massacre: soldiers wielding machetes and guns leading women and children to the top of the hill, corpses scattered on the ground.

A fifty-foot-long mound stretched behind the monument—a mass gravesite where the recovered bodies had been reburied.

An old man wearing a leather cowboy hat walked up behind Raul while he was studying the monument. He spoke in a low voice. "People do not want us to tell what we saw, but someday, what happened here will be known."

"You were here then?"

"In Río Negro. Like most of the men, I was in the hills, hiding." He met Raul's gaze. "It is something I will always regret—why did we not make the women come with us? But the answer is simple. The women wouldn't leave. They didn't think the children could survive in the wilderness with nothing except what we could find to eat. And none of us thought the army would kill the women and children. They said they were looking for the guerrillas. They thought our women, some of them heavy with child, and our little children were guerrillas?" He shook his head. "It was an excuse. When we came back, they were all gone—my wife, my children, gone."

"What did you do?"

"I hid in the mountains for many months, living on what I could find to eat—grass, roots, raw fish. If I cooked, they would find me. If I farmed, they would find me. And finally they did find me and took me to Pacux." He nodded in the direction of the resettlement village built to house those displaced during the massacres. "They kept all of us there. We did not have a change of clothes or even tortillas to eat."

"Do you still live there?"

"Sí. One hundred twenty-five families live there, maybe more. It is a hard life. The land they gave us—most of it is too rocky to grow anything. Only one farm to grow food for all of us, and only in the wet season. If we had water to irrigate, we could grow food in the dry season, but they do not give us the water pumps they promised." He stared at the horizon. "We survive. For a long time, I was afraid to speak of what happened. Others who told the truth disappeared. But now I am an old man, and I am no longer afraid of what they will do to me. The truth must be told. Those who did these things must be brought to justice. It is not right that they walk the streets here in Rabinal and live in nice houses and we have to see them every day, look at them, and know that they took everything from us. It is not right."

The man removed his hat and held it in front of him. He continued. "Seven families have gone back to Río Negro. But what can they do there? They want to fish, but they have no nets. They cannot grow food because their farms are under the lake—that dreadful lake! All of our people slaughtered so they could build their dam and make electricity. I ask you, is it a better life for them? They live in straw shacks, and every morning they wake up and see that lake—the lake filled with the blood of our families."

"What about Plan de Sánchez? Have people gone back there too?"

"There is a monument in Plan de Sánchez. It is better there, I think. The vice president came and apologized for what they did." He laughed bitterly. "The people put on a play for his entertainment, a play about the massacre. They made him watch it before they would listen to him talk. But why do you ask about Plan de Sánchez? Did you know someone there?"

Raul nodded. "A young woman. Her name was Sofía Alvarez. I was coming to visit her the day she was killed in the massacre."

"And you are sure she was killed?"

"No one survived that day."

The old man nodded. "Those were terrible days. Days none of us will forget. But you do not live around here now?"

"No, I live in Guatemala City. I work for a tour company." Raul smiled ruefully. "I'm afraid I haven't been of much use to this last group, so I had better be

going. They will fly home to the United States tomorrow evening, and I think I should go to the airport to at least tell them goodbye."

"Please, before you go, tell me your name."

CHAPTER 51

FIRST THING IN THE MORNING, María took Santiago and Matt to the small medical clinic in Salamá. Cathy puttered around the kitchen while the others slept. After a while, she peeked in on Melissa, just to remind herself that the ordeal was over. She sat on the edge of the bed and studied her daughter. What had Melissa endured? What scars would she carry home with her? Melissa's eyes fluttered open.

"Hey," Cathy said. "How are you feeling?"

"I was dreaming." Melissa sat up on the bed. "It was so real. I was with Carlos on the river, and we were talking. And then the crocodile started coming and—" Melissa's voice broke.

Cathy put her arm around Melissa and hugged her. "It's over. You're safe now."

"I know, but Carlos *died* protecting me. Why did it have to happen? Carlos was a really good guy underneath, you know? You met him; didn't he seem nice? I know I shouldn't have gone with him, but he was always kind to me. He took care of me and helped me and then—"

"And then he sacrificed his life for you."

Ana began to stir.

Cathy put her finger to her lips and gestured for Melissa to follow her out of the room. They sat together on the couch in the living room. Cathy stroked Melissa's hair while she unloaded the grief and fear and regret she had been carrying inside for nearly two weeks.

They were still talking when Raul returned from Rabinal. "Please, join us. Melissa has been telling me about Carlos," Cathy said.

"I wish there were some way to contact his family," Melissa said. "I keep thinking about his mother and his little brother and sisters. They must be scared and wondering what happened to him when he didn't come home. How will they ever know what happened to him or what he did for me?"

"I understand how you are feeling. I know what it is like to lose someone and never know exactly what happened," Raul said. "Today, for the first time in many, many years, I went to the place where my Sofía was killed, to try to find peace."

"And did you?" Melissa asked.

"Yes, some," Raul said. "I wish I could have seen her one more time. Told her goodbye. I wish I knew where her body rests. I wish I could place flowers on her grave. But there is no grave with her name. It is as if she never existed, except to me."

"I'm so sorry, Raul," Cathy said.

Raul acknowledged her comment with a nod. "We cannot change what happened to Carlos, but we can give his family the answers that I did not receive. We can tell them what happened to him."

Melissa's eyes widened. "What do you mean? How?"

Raul smiled. "Let me tell you about how Heavenly Father loves Carlos." Raul then told them of the day he had been in Santa Elena and of the young boy who'd approached him with a picture. "I did not know then why Heavenly Father told me to find out where the family lives. But I know now. It was to help them, and it was to help you, Melissa."

"So you can take us to them?" Melissa said.

"There is a small airport in Cobán," Raul said. "We would need to find a pilot, but we could fly from there to Flores."

María had returned with Matt and Santiago while they were talking. Now Santiago spoke up. "I know someone who flies. Perhaps he would be able to help."

* * *

Eduardo's phone rang and rang, but there was no answer.

Nick dialed another number. When the voice on the other end of the line picked up, he said, "I need you to check on Eduardo Guerrero. He isn't answering his phone."

"I'll need some time."

"I'll be there in a few hours."

"I'll be out of the office in a few hours. Relax, get a drink, see the sights. Come see me in the morning. I'll know something by then."

"I'll be there in a few hours. If you want to be paid—"

"I don't think you want to push me, Mr. Slade. I'll be out this afternoon. Come in the morning, and we'll talk."

* * *

Santiago's friend was waiting at the landing strip with a small plane.

"Thank you for doing this on such short notice," Raul said.

The Millers bid Santiago and his family goodbye, hugging each one before they climbed onto the plane and settled in for the short flight to Flores. From there, they caught a chicken bus to San Andrés. Directly across the street from the bus stop was the marketplace. They asked a woman selling peppers for directions.

It was a short walk to Carlos's neighborhood. Dogs barked as they neared the haphazard jumble of shacks scattered on the hillside. *He couldn't have lived here,* Melissa thought. *No one should have to live in a place like this.* The shacks were constructed of cornstalks, cardboard, and adobe, with rusted strips of corrugated metal for roofs. Clothes hung from clotheslines strung in every yard.

Raul stopped to speak to a woman hanging her laundry; she nodded and pointed. They continued making their way through the maze of crisscrossed clotheslines, broken toys, and garbage embedded in the dirt until they reached a hovel on the edge of the neighborhood. A banana tree stood in the front yard; two weathered chairs were propped against the side of the house, and chickens and ducks ran freely in the yard. Raul rapped on the side of the house. A boy pulled back the blanket that covered the doorway and stepped outside.

Although Melissa couldn't understand his words, she could see that the boy recognized Raul. He disappeared inside, returning momentarily with his mother. She was thin, her face drawn, her black hair pulled into a bun. As Raul spoke to her, two barefoot little girls came out of the house and stood near their mother, listening. *His sisters.* Tears filled Melissa's eyes as she thought of Carlos there with them. Raul spoke quietly. The mother dabbed at her eyes and nodded. Finally she turned to Melissa.

"*¿Estuvo con mi hijo cuándo se murió?*"

"She's asking if you were with her son when he died," Raul said.

Melissa nodded. "Please tell her that Carlos died because he saved my life."

With Raul translating, they talked and wept until there was no more to say. As they prepared to leave, Carlos's mother came to Melissa and held her hands. She kissed both of Melissa's cheeks and hugged her tightly.

"Gracias," she murmured over and over again as she held Melissa and sobbed. Finally she released Melissa and turned to Raul, Cathy, and Matt, kissing and embracing each one in turn. Then she returned to Melissa, thanked her and kissed her cheeks again, and held her for another long moment.

"He was a good man," Melissa whispered. "You should be proud of him."

As they walked to the bus stop, Raul confided that he planned to return after everything was settled. "I promised her she will see her son again," he said. "Now I want to introduce her to the missionaries."

Melissa turned to her parents. "Do you think I could get a Book of Mormon in Spanish and write my testimony in it? And then maybe Raul could give it to her?" she asked.

"We would be happy to arrange that," Matt said.

CHAPTER 52

IT WAS A SHORT RIDE back to Flores. Raul and the Millers boarded a plane and arrived in Guatemala City early in the evening. In stark contrast to the rural villages where they had been, Guatemala City was an urban whirlpool of traffic and humanity. Bright-red buses sped down the narrow streets. Women selling jewelry, posters, and hats pushed carts on the sidewalk. Melissa watched as boys scrambled out of the back of a truck equipped with a wide hose, grasping and pulling it out of the truck bed to water the grass. Nearby, children slid down a hill on pieces of cardboard.

They hailed a taxi and drove out of the city toward Antigua.

Antigua was charming and peaceful; its cobbled streets dotted with clusters of uniformed school children walking home, backpacks slung over their shoulders. The surrounding hills were lined with pine trees, interspersed with coffee plantations and cornfields. Higher, above the tree line and enveloping the city, stood three volcanic cones.

They passed an open-air laundromat where women and children scrubbed their clothing in cement troughs full of water. Roses, lilacs, and bougainvillea were everywhere. The taxi stopped in front of the Casa Santo Domingo.

"I want to go to the police station," Raul said as they climbed out of the taxi. "I will meet you back here as soon as I am finished. You have my number if you need to reach me before I return."

"Thank you, Raul. And when you get back, we'd like you to join us for dinner," Matt said.

Raul nodded. "Of course. I won't be long." He climbed back into the taxi and drove off.

Cathy and Melissa were gazing at the architecture. "It seems like a lifetime ago we first arrived here," Cathy said.

Matt led the way through the wooden doors into the lobby, stopped, and motioned toward the adjoining courtyard.

"This used to be an old monastery," Matt said to Melissa. "After an earthquake destroyed it, the hotel was rebuilt on the ruins."

Melissa looked around, taking in the broken walls, the fountain, and the moss-covered brick. "This place is incredible," she said.

Cathy smiled. "Wait until you see the room."

They moved through the corridors lined with flower boxes and greenery to their door.

"It's beautiful!" Melissa said as she stepped into the room. She walked over to the patio doors, pushed back the curtain and gazed outside at the grounds. When she spoke again, her voice was wistful. "I wish I could have stayed here."

"I don't see any reason why we can't stay tonight," Matt said. "Our plane doesn't leave until tomorrow afternoon."

"It would be nice to have a little time here to enjoy the ambiance, now that we're all together," Cathy said.

"What's going to happen to Nick?" Melissa asked. "Is he going to get away with everything he did?"

"We'll do everything we can, but first we have to be absolutely sure he's responsible," Matt said. "And the most important thing to me is that you're safe."

* * *

While he waited for Cathy and Melissa to change clothes, Matt wandered around the room. A small white paper in the wastebasket caught his eye. It looked like a business card. He picked it up and glanced at the name on the front, *The General Office of Foreign Trade*, followed by a name and address in Guatemala City. Someone in the Guatemalan government must have recently stayed in the room. He dropped it on the bed and stepped out onto the patio.

The sky was a cloudless blue. Across the grounds, he could see a scarlet macaw on its perch. In spite of everything, he loved Guatemala. The people were gracious and humble. He thought of the family they had met that afternoon, their abject poverty, their desperation, and he felt love for them, the same kind of love he'd felt while he served in Guatemala on his mission. After being there, he couldn't bring himself to hate Carlos—Carlos was a product of his circumstances. And tomorrow Matt would leave, and for the first time since his mission, he wondered if he would ever return.

Matt came back into the room and closed the patio door. As he crossed the room, he saw the business card he had tossed onto the bed. It had flipped over, and on the back, he could see something handwritten. He picked it up and stared at a name and phone number, written in bold, familiar pen strokes. The name made Matt's hair stand on end: *Eduardo Guerrero.*

Matt's mind whirled. He stepped into the hall where he saw Raul waiting and spoke quietly. "I think I may have found the evidence we were looking for."

Raul studied the card. "You are certain it is his handwriting?"

"Absolutely."

"May I keep it? I want to show it to the authorities." When Matt hesitated, Raul added, "You enjoy your family now; I will take care of this. And I will see you at the airport tomorrow."

"We owe you a dinner," Matt said.

Raul smiled and nodded. "When you come back to Guatemala," he said as he walked away.

Cathy and Melissa joined Matt. He told them about the card he had found, and that Raul was on his way to take it to the authorities. While they were talking, the man from across the hall stepped out of his room. A moment later, a woman emerged. They approached the Millers and introduced themselves.

"What brings you to Guatemala?" Matt asked.

"A school," the man said. When the others looked surprised, he added, "We're part of a nonprofit organization working to improve education among the Maya here in the highlands."

"We're helping at an elementary school just outside of town," the woman added. "The children performed for us when we were there today. They sang and danced. You should have seen them! So adorable."

"And I don't suppose you spy on people in your spare time," Cathy said. She laughed at their expressions. "It's a long story."

After their conversation with the couple, music from a marimba band led them to the dining room. The room was dimly lit by votive candles scattered around the room. The Millers settled at a table in the corner. A waiter approached and handed them a menu. Almost instantaneously, low lights came up above their table, enabling them to read their menu; as soon as they ordered, the lights dimmed.

"Now this is the Guatemala trip I imagined," Cathy murmured.

CHAPTER 53

Day 14

NICK STUDIED HIS REFLECTION IN the mirror, splashed aftershave on his cheeks, and finished packing his travel bag. Just a few loose ends to tie up, and then he would be on his way. He would have liked to leave the country the evening before, but his contact in the Office of Foreign Trade had been less than cooperative. By now, the man should have answers. Either way, Nick had booked a flight for later that afternoon.

He checked his phone one more time for messages. Nothing.

Nick still hadn't heard from Eduardo, and that had him concerned.

Ironic, really, that he should be worried. In some ways, things appeared to have played out exactly as he'd orchestrated. But Eduardo Guerrero wasn't known for leaving witnesses—and Matt's comments had been more than a little disconcerting.

Failure wasn't something he had considered.

Nick exited the hotel, hailed a taxi, and asked the driver to take him to the Guatemalan State Building. Prominently displayed in front of the building was the blue-and-white-striped Guatemalan flag. In the center of the flag, the resplendent Quetzel bird perched on a scroll celebrating Central America's independence from Spain, its dark-green plumage curved toward the bottom of the flag. Beneath the scroll on the white center panel of the flag, two rifles and two golden swords were tied together with laurel branches.

Nick entered the building and walked past the security guards and down the corridor to the General Office of Foreign Trade. The outer office was empty, so he proceeded down the narrow hallway until he reached a particular office. He listened at the door before tapping lightly. A voice invited him to come in. Nick twisted the doorknob and opened the door.

The first thing Nick saw when he entered the room was that the man he had come to see was flanked on either side by uniformed police officers. A

third officer stood directly behind his associate, who was seated in his usual place at the desk. The officer standing directly behind his contact spoke.

"Nicholas Slade, I believe. We have been expecting you."

* * *

After spending six days in the hospital tending to Lyle, Vernon was chomping at the bit to go home. He hadn't really wanted to come on this trip in the first place, although, he had to admit, it'd turned out to be a whole lot more of an adventure than he'd planned on when he packed his new traveling pants. That's what Blanche had called them when she bought them. Traveling pants. All he'd ever owned before were jeans. Jeans and a suit for Sunday.

"Sure am glad they found that little girl," he said to nobody in particular.

Scott had stopped by the hospital to check Lyle out and help them get onto the bus headed for the airport.

"Looks like Lyle's going to be okay, so long as he takes it easy," Vernon said, trying to make conversation.

"Sure does."

When they'd called their wives from the hospital, all three had come as fast as they could. They wanted to wring their hands and mop Lyle's brow, but Lyle figured he only needed one of them to do that, and Lila was elected. Blanche and Ella hardly knew what to do with themselves, knowing somebody was in need and they couldn't even make a casserole.

So Gary escorted Blanche and Ella back to the tour, leaving Lila to hold Lyle's hand and Vernon to keep watch, which he was glad to do. He wouldn't admit it to anyone, but he kind of liked feeling needed that way. The women got to cross the Mexican border and see the Tree of Life stone at Izapa, and he got to feel like a man, protecting and all.

Vernon helped Lyle off the bus and into the airport. Had it really only been two weeks since they'd arrived? Seemed like a lot longer than that when he thought about everything that'd happened. Who would've guessed? Two weeks ago, Vernon thought he was coming to Guatemala to learn about Book of Mormon geography—and instead he helped solve a kidnapping case.

"So do you think Joseph came up with that one day over breakfast while he was eating cornflakes with Emma?" Scott asked, breaking into Vernon's thoughts.

Vernon realized too late that Scott had been talking to him. Thinking the question was probably a joke, he chuckled and shook his head. "Probably not."

"You're darn tootin' straight, probably not," Scott said as they walked into the airport and past the security guards. "There's our group."

Vernon and Lila followed Scott as he pushed Lyle's wheelchair toward the group of familiar faces. Vernon accepted a hug from Blanche and then looked around. "I thought the Millers were going to be here."

"Patience, my friend. They're on their way."

A few minutes later, Vernon spotted the trio walking toward him, their arms around each other. He recognized Cathy at once, and Melissa with her striking red hair.

When the group saw them, they broke into cheers. Matt waved and grinned.

Vernon held out his hand. "Vernon Taylor's my name. And you must be—"

"Matthew Miller. Glad to meet you, Vernon. I hear you're a big part of the reason we found Melissa."

"Well, I wouldn't say that."

"I would. From what I understand, your friend here heard one of the kidnappers talking about Melissa. Because of that clue, Raul was able to confront the man, find out where Melissa had been held, and eventually figure out what they were actually after. If it hadn't been for you guys identifying one of the kidnappers and for my wife telling Raul about her dream—well, my guess is neither Melissa nor I would be standing here talking to you right now. So I'd say you had a pretty important role in all of this."

Vernon flushed. "Well, I'm just glad she was found."

"So am I." Matt looked around at the rest of the group. "So you're the people my wife has been telling me about," he said.

"Well now, that all depends on what she's been saying," Vernon said.

Matt laughed. "It's all good, Vernon. It's all good."

"Hey, look, there's Raul," Melissa said.

Raul whispered something to Scott, and Scott nodded and raised his voice. "If I could have your attention one more time, Raul has something he wants to say to all of us."

Everyone quieted and turned to face Raul.

"First, I must apologize for deserting you on the tour. I am sure it was very good, and I would like to have been with you, but something more pressing had my attention."

After everyone laughed, Raul continued. "And I want you to know that just a little while ago, the man who did this terrible thing to the Miller family was apprehended and taken to jail. He will be interrogated and brought to justice."

Spontaneous applause and cheers erupted from the group.

The gate attendant's voice over the loudspeaker interrupted their cheers. "Now boarding at Gate 7, Continental Flight 481 for Houston, Texas."

"That's us," Vernon said. "I'm sorry to say it, but our party has come to an end."

* * *

Raul watched as the last of the tour members gathered their personal belongings and boarded the airplane. Matt, Cathy, and Melissa hung back until the end. Then each one in turn hugged him tightly as they thanked him again and told him goodbye. He waited until they had all boarded and the door had closed before he turned to walk away. That's when he noticed her—the woman standing alone by the wall. It was not unusual to see a woman in the airport, yet something about her made him stop.

She approached him. "Excuse me, señor, are you Raul Silva?"

Raul nodded. "Sí, I am Raul."

"A long time ago, I knew a young man with your name," the woman said.

Raul studied the woman. Her black hair was pulled into a clip; a few gray strands outlined her face. Her face was kind, her eyes dark and luminous. Her eyes—

"Oh, Raul, have I changed so much you do not recognize me?"

Raul took a step back. "It is not possible," he said, his voice barely a whisper. "Sofía was killed in the raid. Everyone in the village was killed."

"It is you." Sofía's eyes filled with tears.

"But how—? How can it be?"

"I escaped, Raul." Sofía reached for Raul's hands. "I escaped and hid and waited for you to come back for me."

Raul clasped her hands. "Are you really Sofía? My Sofía?" He struggled to keep emotion from his voice. "How did you find me?"

"Yesterday morning, you were at the memorial in Rabinal. You spoke to a man there and mentioned my name. He came to me and asked if I knew you. He told me how I could find you. I came this afternoon and have been waiting until I saw a tour group leaving for the United States."

"How do you know the man?"

"We both live in Pacux. It is where they sent us to live."

"Then I will be forever indebted to him. But I cannot believe it is really you. What about Gabriela? I talked to her that day, and she told me what had happened, that you—"

"Gabriela is gone. I do not know what happened to her. But please, let us not speak of that day. It is painful to remember, and today, I only want to rejoice."

Raul gazed at Sofía, the contours of her soft face, her dark eyes, her full lips. "Did you marry?" he finally asked.

"No. I never quit hoping that someday, someday, I would find my Raul. What about you?"

Raul shook his head. "Is it really you? After all these years?"

Sofía laughed. "We have some catching up to do."

Raul drew her into an embrace and whispered against her hair, "Do you have plans? Or would you be willing to have dinner with an old friend?"

CHAPTER 54

As soon as the plane lifted off, Melissa tilted her seat back, curled up against a pillow, and closed her eyes. *She's exhausted,* Matt thought. He reached over and took Cathy's hand.

"You know what's funny? We came on this trip hoping it would shake Melissa up a bit and help her figure out what's really important. This certainly isn't what I planned or hoped for or imagined or would have ever signed up for. But the crazy thing is, I think it worked. I think we have our girl back, in more ways than one."

Cathy smiled. "And I think I have my husband back."

"You're right. And you can never get rid of him."

"In case you haven't noticed, I don't want to get rid of him," Cathy said as she snuggled against Matt and closed her eyes.

"Think you'll ever be willing to come to Guatemala again?"

"I don't know, Matt. Maybe someday, but probably not next week."

"It's a deal. We won't come back next week." He leaned over and kissed her. "I'm never going to take you for granted again," Matt said.

"Can I get that in writing?"

"Sure. Where's a pen?"

AUTHOR'S NOTES

THE IDEA FOR *THE PRICE of Jade* was born one morning as I sat on a balcony overlooking the beautiful Lake Atitlán and brainstormed ideas for plot and characters. When I returned home from that Book of Mormon tour, I began researching Guatemalan history and was amazed to discover both a motive for my villain and a heart-wrenching past for my hero. While *The Price of Jade* is fictional, the following facts provided the framework for the story.

Fact: In late October 1998, Hurricane Mitch struck Central America. It was the deadliest hurricane to hit the Western Hemisphere in more than 200 years. As Mitch tore through Guatemala, a jade field the size of Rhode Island was uncovered high in the Sierra de las Minas. Although the exact location of the jade was not revealed, local jade hunters spent days of hard hiking to reach the grassy hillock, where they used pickaxes to hack open boulders—some the size of buses—of jade. An ancient stone road was also discovered.

Fact: On July 18, 1982, in the Guatemalan village of Plan de Sánchez, more than 250 Achi Maya, mostly women and children, were brutally murdered by members of the Guatemalan Army. The massacre took place during one of the most violent phases of Guatemala's Civil War, under the leadership of defacto President General Efran Ríos Montt. The village was targeted because of suspicions that the inhabitants were harboring guerilla groups. On the day of the attack, points of entry were guarded as men, women, and children were gathered from their homes, murdered, and buried in mass graves. The young women were held separately; a few escaped, but most were raped, beaten, and killed.

In 2004, the Inter-American Court of Human Rights ruled that there was genocide in Guatemala and that the armed forces had violated basic human rights. Twenty-three years after the attack, Vice President Eduardo Stein formally apologized for the actions of the army.

ABOUT THE AUTHOR

LIZ HASTINGS WAS BORN IN Afton, Wyoming. She began writing in the fourth grade, when she wrote plays for her friends to practice and perform during recess. She attended Brigham Young University, where she majored in English. She currently lives in Springville, Utah, and is the mother of seven nearly perfect children who have given her six equally perfect sons- and daughters-in-law and twenty-six grandchildren.

Besides writing, she spends her time teaching kids to read. She loves the mountains, campfires, playing board games, scrapbooking, music, dancing, chocolate, and especially spending time with her family. *The Price of Jade* is her first novel.

D0249631

THE PRICE OF JADE